T0278636

THE WORST
PERFECT
MOMENT

SHIVAUN PLOZZA

HOLIDAY HOUSE · NEW YORK

Copyright © 2024 by Shivaun Plozza

All Rights Reserved
HOLIDAY HOUSE is registered in the U.S. Patent and Trademark Office.

Printed and bound in March 2024 at Sheridan Books, Chelsea, MI, USA.

www.holidayhouse.com

First Edition

1 3 5 7 9 10 8 6 4 2

Library of Congress Cataloging-in-Publication Data

Names: Plozza, Shivaun, author.
Title: The worst perfect moment / by Shivaun Plozza.
Description: First edition. | New York : Holiday House, 2024. | Audience:
    Ages 14 and up. | Audience: Grades 10-12. | Summary: Deceased
    sixteen-year-old Tegan is appalled to discover that heaven is a replica
    of the motel where she spent the worst weekend of her life, and her only
    hope is for Zelda, the teen angel responsible for the supposed error, to
    explore Tegan's memories and unearth her true happiest moment.
Identifiers: LCCN 2023038993 | ISBN 9780823456345 (hardcover) | ISBN
    9780823459346 (ebook)
Subjects: CYAC: Future life—Fiction. | Angels—Fiction. | Memory—Fiction.
    Hotels, motels, etc.—Fiction. | Lesbians—Fiction.
Classification: LCC PZ7.1.P626 Wo 2024 | DDC [Fic]—dc23
LC record available at https://lccn.loc.gov/2023038993

ISBN: 978-0-8234-5634-5 (hardcover)

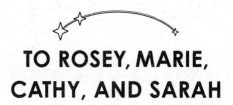

TO ROSEY, MARIE,
CATHY, AND SARAH

ONE

I'm standing in the parking lot of the Marybelle Motor Lodge in Wildwood, New Jersey, and I'm dead.

I don't know how to feel about being dead but I have opinions about the motel.

It's green. A bunch of different greens, like lime and forest and seafoam. The building is horseshoe-shaped, three stories high, so many doors (all painted forest green). In the middle of the horseshoe is a pool, also green—is it supposed to be that color or is it algae? Out front is a flashing sign (neon green) at the top of a pillar (seafoam green). Around the pool there are clusters of fake palm trees (green and brown) and in the lot there is one car (mostly brown).

My opinion is this: I hate it.

Ms. Chiu, my English teacher—that is, my *former* English teacher (I'm dead, remember)—would have asked me to elaborate. *Why do you hate it, Tegan? How does it make you feel? Use quotes, sources, and references, please.*

I liked Ms. Chiu. She wore bird earrings, a different bird for every day of the week, and she had a lisp and a crooked front tooth like a wonky fence picket. But I'm sixteen and I'm dead and

I'm standing in the parking lot of the worst motel in New Jersey so I'm not really in the mood for homework.

How did I even get here? One second I was riding my bike in the Hills, and the next I was here.

Am I a ghost?

I think about that for a second but it's part of the whole I-don't-know-how-to-feel-about-being-dead thing so I stop thinking about it and start looking around instead.

It's gray. Not the motel; that's green, as I said. But everything else is gray: the sidewalk, the sky, every other building. Gray like the little cup of water you dip your paintbrush in that always turns into a muddy, murky sludge. It's windy too. The wind howls through the lot, making the station wagon rock and the palm trees sway. Somewhere, a loose shutter bangs against a wall.

But I don't feel cold.

Last time I stood here—not here exactly; I was closer to the pool and facing away from the motel—but last time I was standing hereabouts, I was cold. I remember how the wind crept beneath my layers of clothes and under my skin, how it seeped into my bones until it was all I could feel.

But not now.

Ms. Chiu, I feel nothing.

No, that's a lie. I feel an irrational hatred for the motel and I guess I feel confused and, like, unsettled. But I don't feel cold, so that's something.

Feelings are *ugh,* though. You let yourself think about how the color green fills you with incandescent rage, and before you know it you're in a tailspin about being dead and I do *not* want to do that. So I focus on the car.

It's my dad's station wagon. One of the doors is a peachy-cream color but the rest of the car is brown. The left taillight is cracked. The windows are dark except for the reflection of the motel's neon sign. A corded rope dangles from the roof rack and down the back window like a little tail—it's even frayed at the end. That's why we called this car the Cow. Big, lumbering, brown, and with a tail.

Dad, can I borrow the Cow?

Don't park out front in the Cow, it's embarrassing.

Your mom's gone to get groceries in her car so take the Cow instead.

See? Feelings: *ugh.* Look at how they creep up on you.

Ms. Chiu, I feel…something. An ache in my chest. A tightness. I hate it. I hate it as much as I hate this motel.

I really should suck it up and start thinking about how come I'm dead and standing in the parking lot of the Marybelle Motor Lodge, shouldn't I? The one place on Earth I swore I'd never come back to.

I should but I won't.

I walk toward the car. It shudders in the wind; the neon sign's reflection is splashed across the two passenger-side windows. I cup my hands around my eyes and peer through the glass.

Empty takeout containers litter the floor, Dad's sunglasses poke out of a cup holder in the center console, a Naruto bobble-head sits on the dash, and a four-leaf clover air freshener dangles from the rearview mirror. But there's no Dad. And no Quinn.

I pull back and catch my reflection in the window.

I don't look like a zombie so that's cool. I'm not see-through, either, so I guess I'm not a ghost. I don't even look like I got hit by a car while riding my bike, which I did. I don't have tire marks or weeping blood or bits of my insides on the outside. I'm just me—cropped brown hair, thick brows, ears that are a little pointy—like a woodland fairy, my dad always said.

So I'm dead, alone, not a zombie, not a ghost, and I'm in New Jersey.

I can work with that.

Behind me are the road (gray), an auto shop (browny-gray), and an office (gray). There are cars parked in the street (black, white, and gray), but I don't see any people. The office windows catch the sun's glare and shine like mirrors. It gives me a headache just looking at them so I turn back to the motel. I guess I should go inside?

I step through a strip of overgrown grass and onto the square of concrete outside the front office. There are double glass doors and windows, but I can't see inside because of the glare and all the posters advertising stuff like room rates, breakfast deals, and a mini-golf course behind the motel. The mini-golf ad is one hell of a poster: it shows a family holding golf clubs, surrounded by clowns and giant mushrooms and a windmill. They're laughing while their heads explode. I remember Dad pointing to that poster, saying, "See? You kids are going to have fun."

You and me got a different idea of fun, Dad.

When I push through the doors and step inside, I can tell from the loud hum that the clunky split-system heater behind the front desk is on, just like last time. The little ribbon flappy things wriggle and wave as hot air pumps out. But I don't feel a change in temperature.

Strange.

The room is small. There's a display with pamphlets on my right, a bad drawing of the water park hanging on the wall beneath the heater, and a long wood-paneled counter in the middle of the room. The walls are lime green.

A bell sits on the counter, like a doorbell stuck to the laminate with duct tape. I move to ring it but then I freeze.

Behind the counter is a desk, and sitting at the desk is a person.

Their head is bent, face hidden behind a computer, one of those chunky old beige ones, and all I can see is their shiny black hair parted in the middle with lots of frizzy flyaways. They're humming. The song is familiar, but I can't quite place it. It's like déjà vu or something.

I clear my throat.

The head doesn't move.

A note stuck next to the bell with yellowing, peeling tape says: *Please ring for attention!*

I press the bell. It rings like an electronic doorbell, loud and piercing in the small space.

After a pause, the head rises. It belongs to a girl. My age, shoulder-length hair, large brown eyes, lips twisted in thought, a pointed chin. Cute. Very cute.

Her eyes narrow and look me up and down. I look me up and down too.

It's only now that I realize I'm not wearing my clothes from the whole bike-car-splat thing. Instead, I'm in the clothes I was wearing the day we came here. The clothes I threw on at 3 a.m., half asleep and panicking. The Mickey Mouse T-shirt I'd slept in, an oversized black-and-white plaid flannel button-down, black jeans, and the Cons I should have tossed out forever ago because the rubber sole is half peeled away.

"You're Tegan Masters," says the girl in a drawl, deep and husky. She has a smattering of freckles across her nose, which is scrunched up as she looks at me.

I shift nervously from foot to foot. "I am."

"You're checking in." It's not a question. She taps a pen against her lips, one of those four-color clicky pens (purple, red, black, and green).

"I am?"

She nods. "Room eighty-four. The Wi-Fi password is 'there is no Wi-Fi' but there *is* mini-golf and pay-per-view and a pool shaped like a rainbow."

She tilts her head to one side, a crease between her brows. I get the feeling I'm not living up to expectations.

There's a tightening in my chest again. Ms. Chiu, I feel… afraid.

I hug myself like I'm cold, but I'm not. I'm just dead and very confused. "Sorry, where am I?"

The girl leans back in her squeaky office chair and smiles, not a toothy smile, just a curve of her lips into something wry. It doesn't make me relax. Pretty much the opposite, actually.

"Forgive me," she says. "I should have said that first, huh?" She holds out her arms, a mini Christ the Redeemer behind the front desk of a two-star motel. "Welcome," she says, "to heaven."

Welcome to heaven…

I hold up a finger: *Please hold while I freak out.*

"Is there any way this is a dream?" I finally ask. My voice is unnaturally high. It's not something a stranger would pick up on but to me it's as jarring as sirens in a quiet suburban street. Which, incidentally, was the last sound I heard before…*before.* They were distant. Too distant. But I remember them. I'll never forget them.

Mystery girl behind the desk shakes her head, shiny black bob swinging. "Nope."

I take a deep breath. (Do I really? I'm dead so…) "What about a coma?"

I'm not really doubting I'm dead but there's dead and then there's *being-welcomed-to-a-heaven-that-looks-like-a-bad-motel-in-New-Jersey* dead.

"Comas aren't my department," she says with a shrug.

I blink. "They're—what?"

She stands and oh okay yes this might be heaven because mystery girl has wings.

Ms. Chiu, I feel *terrified.*

They're bundled close to her body but there's no denying those are wings. Fluffy and pearlescent and a tiny bit translucent, way smaller than the monstrous wings on the archangels I remember from the eight months and six days I spent in Catholic school.

Wings.

On an angel.

Who looks sixteen years old.

Who is standing behind the front desk of the Marybelle Motor Lodge welcoming me to heaven.

The angel in question opens her mouth to speak but I waggle my still-raised finger and pause a second longer, trying not to throw up. I need a minute to think about this. I take a big maybe-breath.

Because I'm dead.

Dead.

Ms. Chiu, I am having feelings about being dead.

The first thing I feel is a surprising amount of determination to just accept it. I've seen *Ghost Hunters*. I know how angry spirits are created and I don't love the idea of getting stuck as a vengeful ghost haunting a T-intersection in Pittsburgh.

So it's not the being dead thing I'm freaking out about. It's the other stuff. The icky stuff like *I'm only sixteen* and *Why me?* and *Who's going to look after Dad and Quinn now?*

I also have a lot of feelings about why heaven looks like the Marybelle Motor Lodge in Wildwood, New Jersey. When I was staying at the real Marybelle it wasn't so great for me. In fact, it was the worst. So this can't be heaven. Or if it is, it must only be a tiny part of it. A place to be like, *Hey, remember how crappy life was sometimes? Well, you don't have to worry about that anymore! Only good times in heaven, baby!*

Under normal circumstances, I'd ask Clem for answers—she's my best friend and she's smart and she knows everything. But she's not here. None of my friends are here. I'm alone.

Almost alone.

The angel is tapping her foot impatiently, so I lower my finger. My complicated feelings about being dead will have to wait. I can't seem to look at them head-on without getting queasy. They're too new. They're so new they still have tire marks on them. For now, I will lock them away and pretend they don't exist. Feelings. *Ugh.*

"I'm Zelda," says the girl. The *angel.*

Zelda? "Like the—"

"No. This is your personalized heaven designed by yours truly. Here, in heaven, we work tirelessly to ensure your eternal rest is the happiest possible." Her voice drones on with the robotic twang of someone reciting from memory. "We understand that being dead can at first be disorienting and that you may find yourself in a state of denial. Should you experience temporary nonacceptance, we offer five free counseling sessions. If you require further information about this or any other service we provide, please ask your friendly personal angel aka me aka Zelda." She hasn't smiled once since the whole "welcome to heaven" thing. And even that smile was kind of sarcastic.

Zelda steps out from behind the desk and she is not what I thought an angel would look like. Not that I ever gave it much thought, to be honest. I had, like, two ideas in my head: naked chubby baby with a bow and arrow, and scary buff dude with long blond hair and a toga and giant wings.

But she looks like me. Like an ordinary girl. She's wearing a faded black sweatshirt tucked into mom jeans, bright red socks, and Doc Martens, the cute Mary Jane ones. She's short too.

"Questions?" she says.

"A thousand."

She nods and crooks a finger. "Follow me, Tegan Masters." She disappears out the front door of the office before I can even ask just one question.

I hurry after her because I don't want to lose sight of the only person I know in this place. Luckily she's waiting for me, standing in the middle of the overgrown garden bed between the walkway and the pool.

"As you can see, every detail has been re-created to the highest standard." She points at the neon sign, the weeds, the algae-green water sloshing gently against the edges of the pool. "It will be exactly as you remember it."

I follow the path of her outstretched arm. It *is* exactly as I remember it, she's right about that: the leaves, the dead insects floating in the pool water, and oh look even the same waterlogged tampon bobbing along the surface. What she's wrong about is that I would care how well this motel has or has not been replicated. I just want to get to *actual* heaven, the part I'll enjoy.

I open my mouth to say exactly that but she spins on her heel and marches away before I can get a word out. I follow but there's a creeping sense of dread in my stomach. Like my feelings, I ignore it.

"Your room is there." She flings an arm back toward the far side of the horseshoe building. "We'll double back in a bit."

I glance over my shoulder. I can't pinpoint the exact door but I remember that our room last time was on the second floor, somewhere in the middle. The number hung crooked and the wood was splintered near the bottom after Dad kicked the door on our second day.

As I chase Zelda down an uncovered path between the office block and the motel rooms, all I can think is: *Wings.* I can't help staring.

I guess that's rude, huh? Like if a person has something different about them and you keep staring at it, that's bad, right?

Quinn has a birthmark on her face. Aunt Lily called it a port-wine stain but I never liked that expression. A stain is something you want to get rid of, but Quinn's birthmark is beautiful. I mean, Quinn's not Quinn without the bloom of deep red that cups her right cheek. The shape of it looks like a cat curled up asleep. Quinn always wanted a cat so sometimes she'd smile at herself in the mirror and run her fingers softly along her cheekbone and purr. But I used to catch Mom's eyes flicking over Quinn's face with a frown, her fingers twitching like she was aching to grab a sponge and just scrub it off.

I hated her for that.

I hated her for a lot of things.

Anyway, I figure staring at Zelda's wings is like that and I feel bad, but then birthmarks are normal and wings kind of aren't.

They are beautiful, though.

"Ta-da!" says Zelda. She halts at the end of the walkway, waving her hands at the mini-golf course. "Nine wacky holes, each wackier than the last. You'll never get bored playing the Marybelle Motor Lodge Mini-Golf Course, which is lucky because you're here for eternity."

I stare at her, trying to work out if she's joking. It's hard to tell. I think she might be one of those people who says serious things and funny things in the same voice.

She stares back at me, eyes glittering like it's a challenge or something.

I quickly turn away and look at the golf course. It's the same as I remember. The broken windmill, the dinosaur without a head, the torn flags that ripple in the wind, the lurid green of the fake grass, the suffocating sense of despair.

I turn back and she's still looking at me, expectant. The wind whips her hair into a mess. "Did you see the windmill?" She points to the fifth hole, where the windmill—missing two propellers—rotates slowly, creaking like old bones.

I get the feeling she wants me to take a proper look around and appreciate her work.

Fine.

I explore the golf course.

I toe the fake grass and jiggle the flagpoles until the dirty rainwater clogging up the holes splashes up over the edges. Eventually I end up by the giant psychedelic mushroom.

There's a shoe on the ground.

A sneaker. It would have been white once but it's gray now, a dirty unwashed gray. It's resting on its side, clumps of mud and grass—real grass—wedged in the treads.

I stare at the shoe and try as hard as I can to ignore the ache in my chest.

"We got every detail right," says Zelda.

I jump. Apparently, angels have super sneaking-up-on-you skills. Zelda's eyes flicker to the shoe and then back to me.

"I can see that," I mutter.

She folds her arms, eyes narrowing as she watches me carefully. I think maybe she's looking for something. I think maybe she doesn't find it because she huffs and turns away.

"Come on," she snaps. "I'll show you to your room."

I take one last look at the shoe, then suck in a deep maybe-breath and turn around. I follow the trail of her voice as it dances on the wind.

"...and lukewarm pizza from the place down the road, extra mushrooms and pineapple. You don't even have to order—the same takeout you had when you were at the real Marybelle will appear in your room at mealtimes. And you can drink as much room-temperature soda as you want from the vending machine in the rec room. Which reminds me: Don't forget the foosball table. I've hidden the little soccer balls in the same place they were hiding last time, which you never did find, did you? But like I said, you're here for an eternity so fingers crossed you locate them eventually."

We're back by the pool when I find my voice and beg her to stop. She turns to look at me with a detached sort of curiosity, like I'm a rare butterfly she's about to chloroform and jab a needle through.

"Okay, but where's the heaven part?" I ask.

She tilts her head, confused.

I try to stay calm. I want to stay calm. If this is heaven, why do I feel like I'm about to explode? "You know, the part with all the good stuff? Cool dead people I want to meet and nice food and every manga I'll ever want to read and my favorite TV shows on a loop and harp music. Elvis." I throw my arms up. "Where is *heaven*?"

"This is heaven," she says.

"No. This is the Marybelle Motor Lodge. It's the worst motel in New Jersey. It's where I had the worst weekend of my life."

She frowns. "No, it isn't."

I point at the tampon that bobs at the edge of the pool. "Yes, it is."

"No, I agree that this is the Marybelle Motor Lodge," she says. "I re-created it myself. I did an excellent and detailed job." It's her turn to point at the tampon. "What I am disagreeing with is you saying that this is where you had the worst weekend of your life."

I laugh. I have to. It's either laugh or cry or scream or all three at once. My hands curl into fists and it's so strange to feel the pinch of my nails against the soft skin of my palms. Because if I'm dead, I shouldn't feel it. Because if this is heaven, how can I feel pain? Because if this is *heaven*, why does it look like the goddamn Marybelle Motor Lodge?

"Listen." Zelda crosses her arms. "Heaven is an exact replica of your happiest memory on Earth. We analyze your entire existence, run some seriously complex mathematical equations, and determine the moment you reached peak happiness. Then we reconstruct it in painstaking detail so you can bask in that memory for eternity."

I take a second to process her words. I take several seconds.

"No," I say.

"Yes," says Zelda. "I'll show you." She waggles her fingers, and *pop!* I stumble back because suddenly there's a giant, floating image in the middle of the air. It's like I'm looking at a movie screen, but there's no screen, just pixels hanging in midair. In the image, I see the inside of our motel room. Me and Quinn are cuddled up in the bed, shivering because the heater is broken.

This is my memory. Playing on a floating movie screen.

Why are you and Daddy fighting? asks Quinn. Her voice. Oh God. I bite down hard on my lip, trying to distract myself from the ache in my heart. "Turn it off," I tell Zelda. She doesn't. On-screen, the door creaks open. Dad shucks off his coat. *Too late for a repairman…tomorrow…how about we build a blanket fort?* I can't listen to him, I can't.

"Stop this. Please." I turn to Zelda. She smiles blandly at the screen as Dad, me, and Quinn huddle inside the blanket fort, eating cold pizza and watching TV like our world isn't falling apart at the seams. Dad sings John Denver. *Leaving on a jet plane.* I can't look. I don't want to look. *I'm scared,* whispers the other me, crying. *Me too,* says Dad. *But we're a team. Whatever happens, we're going to stick together. I'm here. I'm not leaving you. You're my whole world.*

"Turn it off!"

Zelda waggles her fingers and the magic movie pixels vanish. She grins, proud. "See? Happiest moment."

"Are you kidding me?" I shout. I feel like I've been hit by a car all over again. I choke back a desperate, disbelieving laugh. "You think that was my happiest memory?"

Zelda blinks. "Yes."

"I was crying."

"Yes, you were."

I shake my head. "With respect? You suck."

She huffs. "With respect? You're being an asshole."

Did an angel *swear* at me? "Me? I'm the asshole?"

"I don't even need to run any mathematical equations to determine that yes, *you* are being the Queen of Assholia right now."

I take several moments to keep myself from exploding. "Okay," I say. I am calm. I am serene. I am cool as a cucumber. "If I'm going to accept that *that* was my happiest memory—it was not—and that I would enjoy spending eternity in the worst motel in New Jersey—I would not—then where are Dad and Quinn? If this is a replica of that weekend, why aren't they here?"

Zelda waves an impatient hand. "We don't do that. We don't want people fixating on made-up versions of their loved ones so we just stick to locations. It helps people move on."

"Move on to what? This is heaven. You said I was stuck here for eternity."

She clicks her tongue. "Sorry. Can't say. Spoilers."

I breathe through my frustration and contemplate circling back to my dream-or-maybe-coma theory. Because this can't be heaven. This is…

"*Oh.*" Relief rushes through me. I laugh. "I see what's gone wrong. This is a mistake. This"—I wave my hand around at everything—"is my *worst* memory. There's been a glitch. You looked at the numbers upside down or something."

Zelda doesn't laugh with me. "There is no glitch," she says through clenched teeth. "I ran the numbers myself. I'm good at my job."

I back up a step. I don't want to anger an angel. I'm pretty sure they get kind of vengeful and, like, smite you if you annoy them. Then again, I don't want to be stuck in the Marybelle forever for the sake of playing nice.

"I'm sure you're brilliant at your job," I say, "but maybe the angel computer thingy you used to run the numbers was broken."

She rolls her eyes and pulls a pamphlet out of her back pocket. "You need this." She thrusts it into my hands. "Just follow me, okay? I still have to show you to your room. It's my job. I'm good at my job." She marches away.

What the hell? I look at the pamphlet she shoved at me. It has a picture of me on it. Like, this exact me right now—same clothes, same haircut, same holes in my shoes. The me in the picture is backing away, shaking her head, hands up, palms out, eyes wide. A voice bubble spilling out of her mouth says, "Me? Dead? No way!" At the bottom in block letters it reads, HAVING TROUBLE ACCEPTING YOUR DEATH? TALK TO ONE OF OUR FRIENDLY COUNSELORS TODAY!

I screw the pamphlet into a ball and pitch it into the pool.

✧ ✧ ✧

The room is a green hole of depression.

Two double beds (one that sinks in the middle, green blankets, wrinkled), itty-bitty bathroom (green tiles, green basin, green toilet), kitchenette (no forks), TV (not green), wardrobe (also not green), heating unit on the wall (cream, broken), two standing lamps (one that buzzes and one that doesn't, both green), patterned wallpaper (palm fronds, so much green), a set of drawers (the top drawer sticks when you open it, green), and frayed carpet (guess what color).

It would be familiar even if I hadn't just seen it on Angel TV.

Speaking of angels…

Zelda left. "If you need anything, ring the bell in the office or dial nine for room service," she said, then *poof!*—like a magic trick—she vanished.

Now I'm truly alone.

I open a window but the stench of damp and sweat and sour milk doesn't fade at all. I take a maybe-breath and look around. Everything really is the same as the first time. Even my suitcase is in the middle of the room, right where I dumped it and refused to move it all weekend.

The night we came here, Dad burst into my bedroom at 3 a.m. and shook me awake. His smile was manic. "Pack your things,

Teegs. We're going on vacation." Half asleep, fumbling, confused, scared, I grabbed the first things I saw and stuffed them into my suitcase: mismatched socks, not enough undies, too many pairs of jeans, a sweater I didn't even like. No coat. No phone charger.

In the car Quinn cried and I asked Dad what the hell was going on—who decides to go on vacation at 3 a.m. on a Friday? Sure, Monday was a holiday, but today we were both missing school. And what about Mom? She was due back from Dallas on Saturday. What would happen if she came home and we weren't there? But Dad gripped the steering wheel and didn't answer. He just drove and drove and drove.

So leaving the suitcase in the middle of the room was payback. I felt triumphant every time Dad stubbed his toe on the corner and cursed. That first night, Quinn told me to move it out of the way and when I didn't she sat in it. I told her to sleep in there for all I cared. At least then I wouldn't have to share a bed with her. She just wiggled her butt and told me all my things had butt germs now. Dad told her to quit spreading butt germs and go to sleep.

And Zelda thinks eating soggy pizza in a crappy blanket fort made it my happiest memory?

I make my way to the far bed and sit on the edge. It squeaks exactly how I remember.

Maybe this is hell.

I mean, I wasn't exactly perfect when I was alive: I once stole a pack of Reese's Peanut Butter Cups. I argued with Dad a whole lot this past year. I cheated at Monopoly last Thanksgiving. Yeah. Maybe this is hell.

I bounce up and down just to make the bed squeak because

the silence is loud but the thoughts in my head are louder. *I'm only sixteen. Why me? Who's going to look after Dad and Quinn? Who's going to share their pudding cup with Clem? Does Mom know?*

Does she care?

I grab the remote and turn on the TV.

Last time, me and Quinn watched a cartoon all weekend. *Snorks.* I'd never seen it before because it was old but there was a marathon and we were bored and I kind of liked those weird snorkel-headed critters after a while. The theme song got stuck in my head.

The cartoon plays on the TV now and it hits me: This is the song Zelda was humming in the office. I knew I remembered it.

I try switching to a different channel but no matter how many times I click it's always the same show. Because me and Quinn only watched one channel when we were here and Zelda is a perfectionist who got every detail right.

An eternity, and I can only watch *Snorks.*

I laugh.

I cry.

I scream.

I turn the sound up loud, so loud it hurts, so loud it's not a sound anymore but a physical sensation. I keep mashing my thumb against the volume button even when it can't go any higher. I press down hard and hold it and don't let go, even when my thumb aches. There's a ball of anxiety building up in me, the size of a planet. I must be so much bigger on the inside for it to fit in there.

My eardrums throb and I shouldn't be able to think anymore but I do: *Why me?*

I pitch the remote across the room. When it hits the carpet, the case breaks apart and the batteries pop out, rolling until they hit the tiles in the bathroom. I flop back on the bed, sinking toward the middle when it dips under my weight.

Ms. Chiu, I want to go home.

(THE SHOES THEY LEFT BEHIND)

Tegan had never seen the ocean. She was fifteen and she had never been farther east than Harrisburg. But now, she could smell it. In the parking lot of the Marybelle Motor Lodge, six blocks from the shore, the ocean was thick in the air and Tegan breathed it down deep. She could taste it. The salt left a tang on her lips that she slowly licked clean and swallowed. The ocean was inside her now.

If only she could see it.

"It's cold."

The voice came from behind her. Tegan glanced over her shoulder at her little sister, crouched by the pool, toy monkey in one hand, the other hand dangling in the water. It was October, too cold for swimming. The pool should have been emptied already. But nothing in the motel had been cleaned or cared for in a long time. Quinn yanked her hand out of the water and shivered. "Why is it so cold?"

"Where's your jacket?" Tegan moved toward her. They'd only been here an hour; how long did it take to freeze to death, she wondered.

Quinn shrugged. "What's that?" She pointed at the water, at

a small white something bobbing along the surface. Tegan saw leaves and dead insects and a candy wrapper, then realized that Quinn was pointing at a tampon. It didn't look used but it was bloated with pool water, the little string swaying behind it like a tail.

"Don't swim in there," said Tegan. She tugged on Quinn's collar.

"Because it's cold?"

"Because that's a tampon and that's a dead wasp and, yeah, because it's cold."

"I'm bored," said Quinn.

Me too, thought Tegan. They shouldn't even be outside in this weather, but the room had been too small, too green, too thick with silence. She glanced up at the door. Was her father still sitting on the edge of his bed? Still hunched over his phone, staring at the blank screen? He'd hardly moved since their arrival. Hours and hours of driving and then...nothing.

Why are we here? she wanted to scream.

But she said nothing.

"Trash Monkey is bored too," said Quinn. She shoved the toy in Tegan's face. "He wants to play mini-golf."

The sky was a heavy kind of gray. It felt too close, like Tegan might brush her head against it if she stepped up on her tippy-toes.

Tegan followed Quinn to the mini-golf course. Nine holes. Lurid green fake grass. A broken windmill. A red-and-white mushroom straight out of *Alice in Wonderland*.

"Look! A princess left her shoe behind!" cried Quinn.

Tegan wove through the course and found Quinn pointing at a mud-stained sneaker, lying on its side in the middle of the green.

"Cinderella lives in that mushroom and she left her shoe behind," said Quinn. She was good at making up stories. She crouched and poked the shoe. "The princess was in a rush. It was the middle of the night but the king said they had to leave so she packed as fast as she could and she left her favorite shoe behind and that made her sad." Quinn looked up, squinting. "Do you think Mom's sad we left her behind?"

"Mom's in Dallas. You know that. Helping Aunt Lily move. She'll be back tomorrow."

"Will we be back tomorrow?"

"Yes," Tegan said, but it felt like a lie.

Tegan frowned at the sneaker. Her father said you could tell a lot about a person by the shoes they wore, so maybe you could also tell a lot about a person by the shoes they left behind. This one was old and full of holes like the Cons Tegan refused to give up.

Quinn dipped Trash Monkey's paw into the shoe's opening. "It doesn't fit," she whispered. "You're not the princess."

Shivering, Tegan pulled out her phone: two percent battery.

She wanted to message Clem, who always had answers. Maybe Clem would know why they'd driven six hours in the middle of the night, why her father had pulled into the first motel he saw in Wildwood, why he'd crawled straight into bed and hadn't moved since, why he wouldn't tell her what was happening.

But Clem was hiking with Lou all weekend; she'd left Thursday and wouldn't be back until Tuesday. Tegan's last two messages to her best friend were still unanswered.

Her thumb hovered over the screen.

She could message her mom. Maybe. Would she be angry? Would she come rescue them? Tegan flicked to their chat; the last message was three weeks old:

Mom, you're supposed to pick us up. Where are you?

One percent battery.

"There you are."

She startled, turning to find her father at the gate, vibrating with worry. "I didn't know where you were," he said.

Frowning, Tegan slid her phone into her back pocket. "We didn't go far."

"You have to tell me," he said. "You have to tell me if you leave." His worry was a physical thing—it was bigger than her. She shrank from it.

"I found a shoe," said Quinn. "You can try it on to see if it fits."

Her father smiled. "Come back to the room," he said. "I ordered pizza."

"Pizza!" shouted Quinn. She bounced to her feet and kicked the sneaker into the base of the mushroom, then skipped away, hair swinging, Trash Monkey swinging too.

But Tegan couldn't make her feet move. *Why are we here? Why won't you tell me what's happening? What are you afraid of?*

"Come on." Her father gestured for her to follow. "The pizza will be here any minute."

In the distance, Quinn chanted: "Pizza, pizza, pizza!"

Tegan sucked in a deep breath, filling her lungs with ocean. "Okay," she said. She swallowed down her questions, licking them from her lips like sea salt.

THREE

I wake up dead in a motel room.

I'm lying on my side in the middle of the bed, legs curled up, hands tucked between my thighs. I struggle to open my eyes—they're glued shut with crust, which is gross but also proof this is definitely not heaven, right?

I sit up; my back pinches from the crappy mattress. The room is dark and still. The time on the alarm clock says 3:07 a.m. but I remember it was broken all weekend and only ever said 3:07 a.m. so I don't know what time it really is and my phone is a useless lump on the bedside table, probably because it was dead for most of my time at the Marybelle. Anyway, who knows if you even get reception in heaven.

I draw back the blankets, my legs bare, knees knobby. I still can't feel the cold, just the feathery touch of air against my skin. How come I can feel pain and get eye crusts but I can't feel the cold? Maybe it's a one-off heavenly bonus: you're dead but please enjoy never feeling cold again.

I stand up and rummage through my suitcase for a change of clothes.

Here's a question: Who does the laundry in heaven? Do my

clothes magically clean themselves overnight (dream scenario to be honest) or do I run out of undies in four days' time and have to hand-wash them in the sink? I'm tempted to dial nine and ask Zelda. I don't.

I take a shower in the world's tiniest bathroom, standing under the lukewarm spray for a long time, counting the cracks in the tiles.

Forty-three.

Do I even need to shower in the afterlife?

I get dressed and stand in the middle of the room staring into space because I'm not sure what I'm supposed to do next. It's a choice between mini-golf, *Snorks,* sleep, swimming in tampon-infested water, crying, or eating.

I choose eating.

Outside, the sky is early-morning gray with embers of light peeking through the clouds. The air smells of salt, car fumes, and the open trash can at the bottom of the stairs.

I pass by the pool, water rippling in the wind, dead leaves and dead wasp and bloated tampon all happily doing their thing.

Here's another question: How long before I assign human attributes to the tampon and start thinking of her as my best friend because I'm so starved for company? Tammy the tampon.

Hey, Tammy, what you doing today? Going for a swim? That's cool. Me? Nah, too cold for a swim. Think I'll watch Snorks *for the bazillionth time. Because I'll never get sick of watching the same cartoon over and over again, right? Catch you later, babe!*

Ms. Chiu, I have already lost my mind.

The breakfast area is on the ground floor behind the front office. I remember it from last time: it's got a buffet setup, the kind with lukewarm food sweating in silver dome thingies, a toaster oven that takes four attempts to work, and home fries that are soggy on the outside, undercooked in the middle.

The door is open a crack. I push it all the way in with the tip of my shoe. It creaks menacingly, straight out of a horror film.

The room is big, square, and unoccupied. The tables are round (and green), each with a small vase of fake flowers on top and four seats tucked underneath (surprise! The seats are green!). The buffet table lurks in the far corner.

It's the same.

Of course it's the same.

I choose a table close to the window. Through the stiff gauze curtain I spy the pool, and if I duck my head I can sort of see the door to my room. I sit; the plastic chair is too hard and my butt hurts.

Sitting there, staring out the window, the smell of eggs and bacon and grease in the air, I get another jolt of déjà vu, the big kind that rattles your whole body. Aunt Lily would say, *Oop! Someone just walked over your grave, honey.*

Ms. Chiu, please don't let them walk over my grave.

"You know it's not table service, right?"

I start so hard I bash my elbow against the table. "What the hell?"

"Wrong place, sugar," says Zelda. She's standing next to my table even though a second ago she wasn't. "This is heaven." She's wearing the same outfit as yesterday. It still looks cute. I still hate her. "There is no table service in heaven."

"I know there's no table service." I rub my elbow. "I'm just… I don't know. I'm just catching my breath."

She blinks at me in slo-mo, slow enough that I know it's not a regular blink but a judgmental blink. "You're dead."

"I know I don't *need* to breathe but—"

She grins. "Nah, I'm just messing with you. We actually program you to think you still need all that human junk. Eating. Pooping. Breathing. The whole shebang. It helps you adjust to being dead if you continue to think and feel and poop like a human."

Well, Zelda, you screwed up because I can't feel the cold.

"Whatever. I'm going to eat now." I stand up. I hate her. I hate an angel.

She salutes me. "I made sure the mushrooms are extra slimy. Just how they were in your memory."

I walk away, grinding my teeth.

The food is located on one long trestle table covered in a tablecloth (white plus a million food stains). I grab a plate and walk up and down the table, opening the lid of each silvery dome thingy hoping for a surprise. But it's the same as before, right down to the grayish liquid gloop pooling around the scrambled eggs.

Zelda, whomst I hate, is good at her job.

I fill my plate with eggs, bacon, home fries, and corn bread but skip the mushrooms. I don't want any of it but I feel like I'm committed to eating and if I back out now I'll be giving in and Zelda will win. So I pile my plate high and turn around.

She's not there.

Oh.

Okay.

That's good.

I walk back to my table and dump my plate so I can go back for juice. It's the gross stuff clogged up with pulp but again, I am committed.

The orange juice spills over the side of the plastic tumbler as

I set it down roughly and take my seat. The tablecloth is already soiled with rings of coffee and juice so I don't feel bad about another stain.

I bite into my first forkful of eggs—they're rubbery, salty, sweaty, and very, very gross. Lukewarm too; I half expected the temperature to be nonexistent, like the cold air my body happily ignores. But the eggs are as grossly tepid as I remember.

"I did good, right?"

I almost choke.

Zelda angel-zaps into the chair opposite me, dumping a plate overflowing with mushrooms on the table. "Exactly like you remember it, huh?"

I roll my eyes. "Yeah. Every awful detail. Because—and I don't know if I've mentioned this?—the Marybelle is actually *not* my happiest memory. It's my worst. Did I bring that up already? I'm not sure. Maybe I'm glitching because you didn't program me right."

Zelda snorts. "I programmed you fine. Any malfunction you experience is one hundred percent user error."

I grip my fork tightly. "Look around, Zelda. How is this heaven?"

"Well, it's not *my* idea of heaven but—"

"It's nobody's idea of heaven. You saw the video. There were tears. Soggy pizza. My dad sang John Denver. It was a sucky end to a sucky weekend. And now I'm stuck here? This can't be all there is to the afterlife."

"Of course there's more. There's you-know-where." She glances meaningfully at the floor. "All the way down, down, down. But you have to be superduper evil to end up there. Are you evil, Tegan?"

I shake my head.

"Then you have nothing to worry about." She stabs a mushroom and brings it up to her mouth but freezes halfway there. "Except for the *other* place," she says, and shudders. The mushroom wobbles on the end of her fork.

"The other place?"

"You don't want to know." She shoves the mushroom in her mouth. I watch her chew, watch her eyes bulge. "Oh my God, these are disgusting." She smiles. Big. Huge. Blinding. Her lips peel back to show gums and a gap between her front teeth. Cute. I hate it. She keeps smiling as she stabs four mushrooms at once and shoves them all in. "So gross."

I take an unnecessary breath and glare at the egg juice making my corn bread soggy.

I'm losing the game. I don't know what the rules are or even what game we're playing but I know I'm losing.

Zelda jabs her fork at me and speaks with her mouth full. "Tell me about cat cafés."

"Cat cafés?"

She nods. "You know, cafés but there are cats and you drink coffee and play with the cats." She stabs four more mushrooms and giggles to herself as she eats them. "So gross," she mutters.

I seriously do not understand her. She's a puzzle with no answer. Enigmatic, like the *Mona Lisa* but with eyebrows. And wings.

"I've never been to one." I shrug. "I'm not really into cats."

She pauses midchew, glaring at me. Honestly, she looks ready to smite me. "You don't like cats?"

"I don't hate them. I'm just not super into them."

She continues to stare at me with smite in her heart.

I shift in my chair. "Dad's allergic. So."

Zelda raises her brows but doesn't say anything. She goes back to eating. We both do. We eat in silence. It's very awkward.

"Why aren't you eating the mushrooms?" she asks eventually.

In truth, I'm not eating anything, I'm just shifting food around on my plate to give my hands something to do. "I hate mushrooms."

"No, you don't."

"Yes, I do."

"No, you don't. The pizza you guys ordered *twice* had extra mushrooms."

I sigh. "Quinn loves mushrooms. I'd pick them off my slice and pile them on hers. And she hates pineapple so she'd pick it off her slice and pile it on mine."

Zelda blinks at me. Not a judgmental blink, a confused one. "Why didn't you just get two pizzas? One mushroom and one pineapple?"

"Because there's only three of us. Makes no sense."

"It makes perfect sense!" Her wings do this kind of angry twitching thing, like a cat flicking its tail. "Look, you get two small pizzas, one with extra mushrooms and one with extra pineapple."

"Yeah, but Dad likes *both* mushrooms and pineapple on his pizza, so then what?"

She squints at me until I grin and look down at my plate. I may not understand the rules of this game but I think I just won a point. I feel smug until I remember I'm dead and stuck in the Marybelle and everything sucks.

Zelda sits back heavily and picks at the mushrooms on her plate, flipping them over one by one. She pouts.

I ignore her and eat my rubbery eggs and burned bacon and soggy home fries. It's awful. She keeps sighing loudly but I ignore her.

"Why don't you like mushrooms?" She's still pouting.

"I hate the texture. It's like eating a toad."

"They *are* truly awful," she agrees, and reaches for the ketchup. She squeezes it all over the remaining mushrooms—legit drowns them—and dives in. "This is even worse," she says with a grin. "This is disgusting."

I watch her devour the entire plate of mushrooms and ketchup. I feel queasy and also annoyed because I think I just watched her win the war.

"Anyhoo, I have to get back to work." She stands, dusting her hands.

"What *is* your job?"

She waggles a finger. "Sorry. Spoilers."

I hate her. "I hate you."

She sighs, slapping another flyer on the table. This time it has a picture of me weeping over a plate of mushrooms in this exact room. FEELING DOWN ABOUT BEING DEAD? it reads. TALK TO ONE OF OUR FRIENDLY COUNSELORS TODAY! JUST DIAL "HAPPY"!

"Give this place a chance," says Zelda. Her voice is uncharacteristically soft. "If you're determined to be unhappy, then—" Her face twists like she swallowed a lemon, and her whole body shudders. "Just don't go looking for trouble, okay? You might find it."

"What's that supposed to—"

"Ring the bell or dial nine for assistance!" she says, then promptly vanishes.

I push my half-finished plate away and stare at the ring of spilled orange juice (who does the dishes in heaven?). It's suddenly quiet. And boring. It's like I'm in detention and I can hear the clock ticking but the hands aren't moving so I'm stuck writing lines forever.

I don't care what Zelda says, there's been a mistake. How can I be happy here?

I get up and leave. But when I close the door behind me all I can do is stand there like the new girl at school. Friendless, scared, no idea how things work.

I should have asked Zelda how my dad and Quinn are. And my friends: Clem, Lou, and Paul. Maybe Zelda will let me look in on them, just a peek, just to check if they're okay.

Do they miss me?

My feet take me to the parking lot, fast, like I'm trying to outrun my thoughts. I rest a hand on the Cow's hood. It doesn't feel cold or warm. I try opening the passenger-side door but it's locked.

I walk toward the street, remembering that the ocean is six blocks away. Maybe I can finally see it. Maybe I can build a sandcastle and live there instead. But when I hit the sidewalk, I suddenly can't move. There's nothing in front of me but my feet won't pick up, won't go any farther. I reach out and my hand hits an invisible wall.

I can't leave the Marybelle.

My heaven has a limit.

I want to cry but I laugh instead. I don't know why. It just bubbles out.

The smell of salt on the air is stronger than ever, but there's no way to see the ocean from the motel. It may only be six blocks to the boardwalk, but no matter where you stand you can't spot even the tiniest strip of blue. Believe me, I tried.

Suddenly I want to kick the car or put my fist through a window or something, just anything destructive. I want to break *something*.

But then I see the cat.

It sits half camouflaged in the overgrown grass on the far side of the parking lot. An orange cat, an ugly one. Definitely a stray. It's watching me, unblinking.

When I was here the first time we named him Trash Cat the Elder. Quinn screamed in delight when she saw him. She took off running right at him and of course the cat flipped out and bolted. All weekend she kept trying to coax him closer, stealing sausages from the breakfast spread to feed him. It never worked. The cat hated humans.

I turn toward him now and hold out my hand. I wasn't lying to Zelda: I'm not super fond of cats. But I need this. I need a friend. I need to not be alone.

I rub my fingers together like I'm offering food. "Here, kitty."

The cat blinks slowly.

I step toward him and the cat bolts. Because of course I get to spend an eternity being cold-shouldered by a human-hating cat.

Wow. That's a blow I didn't know I could feel. It twists my insides more than I would have guessed. More than the *Snorks* theme song did.

Ms. Chiu, I am alone.

FOUR

The front office is empty. I lean over the counter to snoop, but Zelda's desk is mostly bare. Just the prehistoric computer, the clicky pen, a pad of cat-shaped sticky notes (hot pink), and an empty coffee cup that reads: CUTER THAN CUPID. One of the sticky notes has been scribbled on, ripped off the pad, and stuck to the middle of the desk: *Mushrooms???*

I lean back and frown at the bell inviting me to *Please ring for attention!*

When I gave in and called to book a counseling appointment, the prerecorded voice on the phone told me to go to the motel reception and sit in the waiting room. But there is no waiting room; there's nowhere to sit other than the floor or Zelda's chair behind the desk.

My shoulders are halfway up to my ears, and it's probably because I'm expecting Zelda to *poof!* out of thin air any second and start mocking me. But it's also because I'm about to see a counselor and I haven't seen one of those since school made me go last October. Which was total bullshit. I mean, I did kind of lose my temper and flip a desk in the middle of class, but that wasn't my fault. It was two weeks after we got back from the

Marybelle, I'd just failed a big test, and the anger in me was a monster I couldn't control.

The school-appointed counselor sucked. His breath reeked of coffee and he'd say things like, *If you see the positive in the world, the world will see the positive in you,* in this ASMR-soft voice, his hands steepled and his mouth quirked in a don't-worry-sweetheart-you'll-understand-when-you're-an-adult smirk. I just wanted to shout at him, "I *am* trying to be positive—if I wasn't, I'd have keyed your car the first time we met, my dude."

I did not walk away with the best impression of counseling.

So I'm tense.

I'm dead and I'm tense and I'm looking for a waiting room that doesn't exist.

I glance at the bell again, but then I remember breakfast and the war and the mushrooms so I shove my hands in my pockets to avoid temptation. I'll figure it out on my own.

There's a door behind the desk with a brass nameplate that reads MANAGER and another door between the shelves of pamphlets to my right that doesn't say anything. Maybe it's a storeroom.

Both doors are green.

I figure I probably shouldn't go exploring behind a room marked MANAGER. That's like walking into the principal's office without knocking. So I try the blank door. It's not locked but the handle is stiff when I wiggle it. I dig my shoulder in and shove, stumbling as the door flies open.

It's not a storeroom.

It's a waiting room.

There are three couches (creamy brown) pushed up against the walls, a coffee table scattered with magazines, six doors (not green!), and one large poster of the ocean that reads: *It's a good day to be happy!*

Somehow I don't think this room was part of the motel's original design.

I step inside, letting the door swing shut behind me. It's silent except for my footsteps as I pad toward one of the couches. The room doesn't look real. It's like a TV set. I trip on the carpet (swirly brown) and expect a studio audience to laugh at me as I stumble.

I perch on the edge of the couch; it's the super-squishy kind and I just know if I sit back too far it will eat me up. I cup my knees with both hands to stop my legs from jiggling. And I wait.

Nothing happens.

Nothing happens for a long time.

I'm about to reach for a magazine when the door directly in front of me clicks open. I expect someone to stick their head around and invite me through, but nope, not a thing.

The door and me have a stare-off until I give in and stand up.

Ms. Chiu, I am more anxious than a long-tailed cat in a rocking chair factory.

I take a deep maybe-breath and march across the room.

When I push the door, it opens with a high, groaning *rrrrrk* (thanks, creepy door, for being extra creepy).

Behind the creepy door is a creepy office. There's a desk (space gray), two chairs (space gray), four walls (space gray!), and that's it. This room also feels like a TV set, an interrogation room in a bad cop drama.

I walk into the middle of the room. The light buzzes overhead, flickering. What kind of counseling takes place in a room like this?

"Welcome."

I spin around and if I wasn't dead I'd pee my pants. Because there's someone standing in the doorframe, and it's not Zelda.

Ms. Chiu, am I seeing things?

The woman in the doorframe smiles—familiar crooked front tooth and crinkly eyes—and then closes the door with a gentle click. Her long skirt swishes as she moves toward me. She's wearing a turtleneck and oversized layers in fall colors, like she always used to.

It's Ms. Chiu. My English teacher.

"Ms. Chiu?"

She walks past me—*swish-swoosh, swish-swoosh*—headed for the far side of the desk. She smells of roses, just like I remember.

"Sit." She motions to the chair across from her as she settles into her seat.

Her earrings are doves. Thursday. She always used to wear the dove earrings on Thursdays.

"You're…" I collapse into the chair. My mouth is dry, tongue like a dying fish as I try to wrap it around the words. "You're dead too?"

She laughs, the little doves dancing. "Oh, I'm not dead. I've always been here."

I nod like that makes sense. It does not make sense. It makes even less sense than ketchup on mushrooms.

Ms. Chiu crosses her legs and suddenly the stark TV set office turns into something more familiar: a shoebox-sized cubicle fitted with a desk covered in coffee cups, books, pens, and piles of essays. The stack next to me is from my AP Lit class, and I feel momentarily smug when I see that my academic nemesis, Naomi Long, only got a B+ on *Paradise Lost*. You suck, Naomi.

I turn to Ms. Chiu, my mouth hanging open. Where do I start?

"You were an angel?" I ask. "The whole time I knew you?"

She laughs again. "Ah. I see the problem. I'm not Ms. Chiu. I'm…well, today I'm a Counselor. And as a Counselor, I take on the form of the person you trust most, to make talking easier for you."

"Like a shapeshifter?"

"If you like."

"And this room?"

She nods. The white doves jiggle. "It changes to correspond with my appearance. So that the whole experience is less…jarring." She clasps her hands, fingers hooking together, and rests them in her lap. It's such a Ms. Chiu action that I wonder if I'm being lied to. I wouldn't put it past Ms. Chiu to have been an angel this whole time. She was awesome.

She smiles. "But we're not here to talk about me. I understand you're having trouble adjusting to your death."

"Trouble adjusting?" I splutter. "Are you serious?"

"Quite often, yes."

I shake my head. "I'm not the problem here, okay? Zelda got my heaven wrong. In fact, it's actually pretty traumatic for me to hang out back there. Which, just so you know, means you're leaving yourself open to a major lawsuit. If it's possible to sue heaven. Actually, now that I say it out loud, I'm guessing it probably isn't. But at the very least I'm going to leave you guys the worst review ever. No stars."

She doesn't laugh like Ms. Chiu—the real Ms. Chiu—would have. She just stares at me with a knowing smile, like she thinks she can see through me. And I mean, maybe she can. Literally.

Maybe she can see past all the skin and blood and bone, all the way down deep to the things that hurt.

But so long as it's up to me, those things will never see the light of day. I didn't let Mr. What's-his-face back at school crack me open and rummage through just because I lost my cool and flipped a desk. And I won't let fake Ms. Chiu do it either. I've got a hold on all that now. It's locked away in a storage unit in my brain called "Feelings I Don't Want to Feel." It can't hurt me anymore.

"If you actually want to help," I say, "you should show me how things are back on Earth. If you've got the power to shape-shift, you can magic up a portal, right? I want to see Dad and Quinn. Quinn gets scared at night and sleeps in my room, so if I'm not there—"

Ms. Chiu holds up a hand to stop me. "I'm sorry," she says, and at least she looks like she means it. "Unfortunately, that's not something I can do."

Can't or won't?

I swallow my disappointment. But what else did I expect? Things really haven't been going my way since I died. Maybe I should flip this desk and see what happens.

"Let's backtrack a moment," she says. "What do you mean, Zelda got your heaven wrong?"

"Have you *seen* my heaven?"

"Were you expecting clouds and harps?"

"I wasn't expecting a mistake, that's for sure."

She tilts her head. "Mistake?"

I laugh bitterly. "Zelda's cute but she picked the absolute worst memory for my heaven. It's torture for you guys to make me live in *that* motel for eternity."

Ms. Chiu frowns.

I've always trusted Ms. Chiu. Maybe because I cried my eyes out the first time I met her and she never pitied me for it. It was ages ago but I still remember it. The faded red hatchback. The heat blasting so loud it almost drowned out the radio. Me in the front seat, hoping she couldn't see my tears even though of course I knew she could. She never said, *If you see the positive in the world, the world will see the positive in you.* She never promised me everything was going to be all right. No. She said, "It sucks, doesn't it?" And it did suck.

"Are you sure it's a mistake?" she asks me now.

"Positive."

I flip through the stack of essays until I spy my name halfway down. I tug it free so I can make out the grade: *A-*.

Suck it, Naomi.

At least there was one class I never bombed.

"Do you know how your heaven was made, Tegan?" asks Ms. Chiu.

I snort. "I've only been dead twenty-four hours and Zelda hasn't exactly been forthcoming with answers." I pause and frown. "I mean, she did say *something* about rooting around in my memories and doing complex mathematical equations. But it was pretty vague."

Ms. Chiu smiles. "The thing about memories," she says, "is that they're messy. Think about your kitchen. In the first drawer you had the silverware. And it was divided neatly: knives with knives, forks with forks, spoons with spoons. If you wanted a teaspoon and you opened the drawer, you knew exactly where to find it."

"So long as Dad hadn't cleaned up last." He used to just shove things in anywhere. It made Mom so mad.

Ms. Chiu chuckles. "Right. But the fourth drawer down…"

The fourth drawer down was junk. "Random crap," Dad called it. String, batteries, pens, miscellaneous kitchen utensils with undetermined purpose, pennies, magnets, glue, tape, candles, rubber bands, all shoved in together.

"Humans think their memories are like the first drawer. Categorized, ordered, easy to retrieve," says Ms. Chiu.

"But they're not," I say because I can guess where she's headed with this. She smiles at me and it's an arrow to my heart because it's her my-student-is-on-the-cusp-of-discovering-something-and-I'm-pleased-as-punch-about-it smile. I used to work so hard for that smile. "They're like the fourth drawer down," I say. "A mess. A bunch of mixed-up junk you have to rummage through."

Her smile widens. "And that's precisely what Zelda does. She rummages through the junk drawer searching for patterns, untying knots, turning chaos into order—knives with knives, forks with forks, spoons with spoons—until finally she can reach in and pluck out that one moment of pure, perfect happiness."

I roll my eyes. "Yeah, but she screwed up. She may have thought she was reaching for a spoon but I'm telling you she pulled out a knife. A really sharp one."

"Do you think that's likely?"

"Obviously. The Marybelle sucks."

"Why?"

I clench my jaw.

Ms. Chiu sighs. "What do you think makes a memory 'happy,' Tegan?"

"Not being trapped in a gross motel with slimy mushrooms and a tampon-infested pool."

"That's not an answer," she says. "I asked you what makes

a memory happy and you told me what *doesn't* make a memory happy. You told me what the absence of happiness feels like. What does it feel like to *be* happy, Tegan?"

I push the stack of essays away roughly because I don't know the answer. And I don't want to disappoint Ms. Chiu, not even a fake Ms. Chiu, by not knowing. I'm allergic to disappointment—it makes me want to scratch at the inside of my head until my brain bleeds. "I don't care," I grit out. "Just fix this. Please."

"I can't—"

"But it's not fair. This can't be it. There's got to be a feedback survey I can fill in. A customer service line I can call. A manager I can—" An image flashes through my mind: a door behind the counter in the office with a sign that reads MANAGER.

I sit up straight.

Oh.

Oh.

"Tegan, why don't you—"

"No, listen. I've got it." I lean forward, excited for the first time in forever. "If this was McDonald's and my burger came out with pickles when I'd asked for no pickles I'd be like, *Hello, ma'am, may I please procure a new burger without pickles?* Now, say if Zelda was like, *Stuff you, eat the pickles,* and I was like, *Maybe I'm allergic,* and she was like, *I don't care, eat the pickles. And have some slimy mushrooms while you're at it.* That would suck, right?"

Ms. Chiu blinks at me. "Pickles?"

"The point is I'd ask to speak to her manager. That's how I'd get the burger I deserve. Zelda's got a boss, right?"

"Yes, but—"

"Perfect." I nod, decisive. I have a plan. I may not be able to sue heaven but I sure can complain about it.

Ms. Chiu holds my gaze like a plea. "Tegan. Memories are messy, remember? Zelda can see the patterns, the order, the truth. But you can't, not so easily, not without effort. For you, the Marybelle is tangled up in all kinds of unpleasantness. Everything that happened before and after, feeling like you couldn't talk to Clem about it, the phone calls that went unanswered, your father's reluctance to face it head-on, your mother's—"

"Don't talk about her," I snap. That one stays buried, Ms. Chiu.

But Ms. Chiu squeezes my hand. "You have to try. You have to try to untangle the mess. If you can't, if you refuse to even look at it to try, how will you see the happiness underneath?"

I frown at her hand, her slender fingers, chipped apricot nail polish, a little smudge of ink on the tip of her ring finger. Green ink. It reminds me of Mom, of the patches of rough, red skin on her hands from washing them all the time at work—she was a nurse. I used to wonder what it would feel like if she ever cupped my cheeks or rubbed my arm, what those rough patches would feel like against my skin. But Mom didn't like to touch other people if she could help it. Which was okay. Some people are like that and it's okay. But I could never help wishing I was an exception.

Ms. Chiu's hands are smooth.

"Everything will be all right, Tegan," she says softly. "We can untangle your pain together and you *will* find happiness. I promise."

Promise?

Ms. Chiu, you are not Ms. Chiu.

I stand abruptly. Her hand falls into her lap.

"I'm dead," I say. "What does *happiness* matter when I'm dead?"

She looks up at me with pity. "Tegan—" she starts to say, but suddenly she's not there and the office is a TV set again.

"Thank you for your attendance," says a disembodied, pre-recorded voice. It's the same voice from the phone. "Your time is up. Call 'Happy' to schedule your next appointment. You have... *four*...remaining appointments. Have a great day!"

I pinch my lips tight, holding back a primal scream of frustration. At least I know what to do next.

# FIVE

At reception, I press my finger to the bell and wait for Zelda to look up. When she does I smile sweetly. "Hello. I'd like to speak to your manager, please."

Back when I wasn't dead, I worked retail, which, honestly, felt a lot like being dead. I worked in Dad's shoe shop, Sole Mate ("Your local friendly shoeniverse!"), and there was a lot to hate about that but the thing I hated most was the customers. I don't understand what makes someone look at a kid working her ass off for minimum wage and decide it's okay to be a jerk to her. And then be all *I'd like to speak to your manager, young lady* when you politely point out *Hey, you're being a real dickcheese right now, dude.*

Anyway, all of that is to say I hate myself a little for being the dickcheese in this scenario.

Zelda narrows her eyes at me, leaning back in her office chair, nibbling on the end of her clicky pen. "I'm sorry, come again?"

I grip the edge of the counter tightly. "Hello. I would like to speak to your manager. Please."

"I don't have a manager."

I point at the door behind her marked MANAGER.

She shrugs. "Except for her."

How does one tiny angel cause so much frustration? "Seriously?"

I glare meaningfully at her. She glares meaningfully back.

I take a maybe-breath. "I would like to—"

"Why?" She rocks forward in her chair, flexing her wings like she's cracking her knuckles.

I am determined not to let this deteriorate into a full-blown argument. I don't know if angels get paid or, if so, how far above minimum wage they earn, but I know Zelda is just doing her job and me being unhappy about it doesn't mean I get to be a jerk. I force a smile. "It's nothing personal. You have done an excellent job re-creating my memory of this motel."

She preens.

"But," I say, and her eyes narrow so thin they're like daggers, "it's the wrong memory."

She throws back her head and groans. "Not this again! Didn't you see the Counselor?"

"Yes. We had a productive conversation about kitchen drawers and pickles. And now I would like to speak with your manager. Please."

Zelda gives me a desperate look. "Don't do this, Tegan. You don't know what you're getting yourself into."

"I know what I'm getting myself *out* of." I wave a hand at the office. "This place. I'm getting myself out of this hellhole."

Zelda stands, leaning over the counter until she's so close I notice flecks of gold in her wide brown eyes. She takes a deep breath. "The thing about denial—"

"This isn't denial."

"—is that it's *very* convincing—"

"But it's not denial."

"—kind of like a lyrebird. Do you know what a lyrebird is? It's a bird that—"

"I don't care what a lyrebird is."

"—can mimic sounds. Like chain saws, car alarms, crying babies. Denial mimics reasonable thought, makes you convinced you're thinking reasonably, when in fact you're—"

"I am being reasonable."

"—very much not."

Zelda grimaces. I refuse to look away and we go through another round of intense glaring. It's finally interrupted by the shrill sound of a phone ringing. Both of us jolt. Zelda's eyes grow wide as she looks down at the counter, where a phone has suddenly appeared.

It's an old beige plastic-looking thing with chunky buttons and a long spiral cord. It keeps ringing. Cautiously, Zelda picks up the receiver and holds it to her ear. "Hello?"

The voice on the other end is muffled. I can't make out what's being said, but whatever it is, it makes Zelda go pale and shrink in on herself.

"Okay. Yes. I will. Of course. No, I— Yes. Right away." She replaces the receiver with a gentle click. Immediately, the phone vanishes.

She huffs out a breath, looking up at me with her mouth drawn into an unimpressed line. "The manager will see you now," she says. Before I can ask *Um, what the hell?* she whips around, almost taking my head off with her wings. "Damn all-seeing, all-knowing busybodies," she mutters.

She yanks out a key from her pocket. It's an ordinary-looking silver door key attached to a keychain in the shape of a calico cat. "Follow me."

She opens the door marked MANAGER and on the other side is a corridor so long I can't see the end. Hundreds of doors lead off on both sides. Every single one is space gray; every single one is closed.

Zelda marches down the corridor, not once checking over her shoulder to see if I'm following. No matter how fast I jog, she always remains several steps ahead.

"Where are we going?" I ask.

Zelda doesn't answer and I don't think it's because she can't hear me. Fine. Whatever. See if I care.

Mom was the worst about giving the silent treatment. She'd be silent in the loudest way so you'd know she wasn't speaking to you. It always freaked Dad out. He'd start narrating every thought in his head, anything to fill the awkward quiet until Mom would cave and shout at him to shut the hell up. But I always fought silence with silence.

So we walk and we don't talk. It's another battle, and this time, I'm going to win. I've had practice.

None of the doors are marked, no little brass plaques or anything. After we've walked the length of a marathon Zelda stops and pulls out another key from her pocket—this one attached to a keychain with a black-and-white kitten—and unlocks a random door on the left.

I stand on tiptoe to glimpse the room beyond her. It's another waiting room: fluffy carpet and no windows and two metal chairs facing each other in the middle of the room. Zelda walks in and I follow. Once I'm inside I notice that on the far side of the room there's a door with a sign—MANAGER, HAPPINESS DIVISION—and next to the door there's a desk where a middle-aged white woman sits knitting a scarf (black, white, and gray). Her blond hair is pulled into a French twist and she wears head-to-toe beige. She looks up.

"You?" she says. She says it in a looking-down-her-nose kind of way even though she's looking up at us.

"Me?" I point to my chest.

Zelda sags into one of the chairs. "She means me. And, yes, hello, Carol. It's me. Again."

Carol *tsks* at Zelda but she doesn't stop knitting, not even for a second. Her desk is bare except for three balls of yarn. "I'll let Barb know you're here," she says, but she doesn't pick up a phone; she just keeps knitting. *"Again."*

Zelda scowls. "Sit," she says to me, and glares until I obey.

"Are we—"

"No talking."

I grit my teeth and sit. I have no idea what's going on and I'm pretty sure neither Carol nor Zelda will tell me if I ask.

So I wait.

And wait and wait and wait.

Here's a question: Will I get older? Or will I be sixteen forever? Will I never change? What if I get bored of my haircut? What if I decide I actually do want braces? Will I never grow taller?

When Mrs. Nowak from next door died of a heart attack, Dad put on his I-know-everything voice and said hair and fingernails keep growing after you die. We were in the Cow on the way to her funeral and Quinn was baby-babbling in her car seat and Mom was driving. Then Mom put on her I'm-so-sick-of-you voice and said that was a load of baloney. "It's because your skin shrinks so it looks like your nails and hair grow," she said, "but really they don't grow at all."

I look down at my hands, nails clipped short.

"Who does the laundry in heaven?" I blurt. Carol's knitting needles are a steady *click clack click* in the background, like a ticking clock. "Am I going to run out of clothes or will—?"

"It's the same deal as your food," says Zelda. She sounds bored. Bored and annoyed. "Everything resets after four days."

I frown. "So it's *Groundhog Day.*" I'll wear the same four outfits and eat the same pizza and buffet breakfast and bad Chinese and bland burritos for eternity.

I'll never need a new pair of shoes.

There's a swampy feeling in my chest. "Well, that sucks."

"Lots of things suck," mutters Zelda. She picks at a loose thread on her jeans.

A new voice interrupts us: "Zelda?"

Zelda and I whip our heads around at the same time. A woman stands in the open doorway next to Carol's desk. Tall, broad, Black, close-cropped silver hair, wings, emerald-green pantsuit. She smiles.

"Barb," says Zelda, drawing out the sound.

"You'd better come inside," says Barb. The Manager. Her smile is warm and she's got kind eyes.

Zelda stands and I follow her lead. Carol tuts as we pass, so Zelda gives her the stink eye. Carol smells like Mrs. Nowak—mothballs and ham and lavender. I give her the stink eye too.

In the office Barb waves at two seats next to each other. It's another boring, nothing room: monochromatic tile floor (off-white), bare walls (pale gray), desk (gray), and still no windows.

Barb takes a seat on the other side of the desk.

"Condolences," she says to me.

I shrug and take a seat. "It's okay." It's not. But it has to be or else I'll have *feelings* about it.

Zelda is slow to sit down, like she's counting the exits first. Except there are no exits, not even the door we came through because that's suddenly gone. Which, yeah, okay, that's pretty creepy. But Barb's smile is still nice.

"What seems to be the problem?" she asks when Zelda finally takes a seat. Barb's eyes skitter over Zelda as she says the word "problem."

Zelda scoffs. "There is no problem," she says.

Barb's eyes shift back to me, questioning.

"There's a small problem," I say.

Zelda throws back her head and groans.

Ignoring Zelda's theatrics, Barb smiles and makes a palms-up gesture at me, which I take to mean I should explain.

I shift and my seat squeaks. "Zelda has done a super job re-creating the Marybelle Motor Lodge. Everything is…depressingly accurate. Which is the problem."

Barb frowns.

"Heaven is supposed to be my happiest memory," I continue, "but the Marybelle is actually my worst? I think the numbers got muddled up. Maybe? So I was hoping for a recount."

I haven't felt the cold—not once—the whole time I've been dead but that doesn't stop me from shivering at the icy glare Zelda shoots my way.

"I. Didn't. Make. A. Mistake," Zelda says. She leans over the desk, transforming her icy glare into a charming smile aimed at Barb. "I'm so sorry about this, Barb. Tegan has a teensy-weensy problem with denial. You know the drill. But it's nothing a Counselor can't fix."

I can't match Zelda's glare but I try. "I told you. It's not denial."

"Shut up, you walnut," hisses Zelda. "I'm saving your butt."

Barb holds up her hand for quiet. She glares at Zelda until she collapses back in her chair, arms folded. Barb turns to me.

"Are you certain?" she asks.

I feel Zelda staring at me, willing me to change my mind.

I lift my chin. "Yes," I say. "I'm certain there's been a mistake."

Zelda groans. Barb doesn't take her eyes off me.

I burn under the weight of Barb's gaze for a long time. I wonder again if angels have the power to see through me because that's what it feels like. X-ray vision.

"Let me check your file." Barb finally looks away. She extends her left hand, reaching for the middle of the desk, the *empty* desk. Her fingers wiggle and a creamy manila folder suddenly appears. She pulls it toward her, opens it, and lifts up a single piece of paper.

It's blank.

Barb stares at the blank page intently, her lips moving as though she's reading. I wait for her to say something but after several minutes of silence it's clear I'm going to have to keep squirming while she reads a blank sheet of paper for who knows how much longer.

I lean toward Zelda. "Is that my file?" I whisper.

She rolls her eyes. "No. It's Gandhi's. Whose do you think?"

"Yeah, but what kind of file? Is it like a Santa list? Everything I ever did wrong? Because I did once steal—"

"Let her read, turd waffle. You're the one who wanted to make a complaint." She cuts me a dark look. "Now you have to live with the consequences."

Consequences? Here's a thought: What if Barb sides with

Zelda? Like, what if she looks at that blank sheet of paper and decides Zelda didn't make a mistake, I'm just a bratty teenager with a chip on my shoulder?

"Hey, Zelda? If Barb doesn't find a mistake, what happens to me?"

"You get kicked out," she says without missing a beat. She whistles as she drops her finger slowly from high to low. "All the way to hell." She turns and grins at me, flashing her gums. "I'll make sure to tell Lucifer you're a big fan of mushrooms."

"Ignore her," says Barb. She doesn't even look up from reading. "She's yanking your chain."

Zelda mimes yanking a chain. "Toot-toot," she says, and laughs.

"I hate you."

Zelda taps a finger against her chin in mock thought. "Do you think eternity will be long enough for you to develop a sense of humor?"

"Do you think eternity will be long enough for you to learn how to be funny?"

She pokes out her tongue.

I poke out my tongue right back.

"Enough," says Barb.

We both turn to face the front. Barb eyes us carefully. "Are you finished squabbling?"

Honestly? No.

Zelda shrugs. "She started it."

"I did not. All I did was die, which wasn't even my fault. You're the one who got my heaven wrong."

"I didn't make a mistake," she argues through clenched teeth.

"Then why am I miserable?"

"Because you're dead and in denial!"

"Perhaps," says Barb. "Perhaps not."

Zelda whips her head around so fast it's a wonder she doesn't snap her neck. "Excuse you? Come again?"

Barb waves her hand at the blank paper. "Something doesn't add up here, Zelda."

Yes! Ha! I win!

Zelda laughs. "Now you're yanking *my* chain, Barb. It's denial. She needs to see the Counselor, and if that doesn't work, we send her to you-know-where. Open-and-shut case. You know this can happen with the fast-tracked souls. Maybe you should haul Admissions in here and ask them why they sent me a soul who obviously wasn't ready for heaven."

Fast-tracked? Admissions?

Barb takes a deep breath, fixing a smile to her face. "Ordinarily I'd agree with you, Zelda. But from my cursory glance at Tegan's file, and considering your *colorful* history, I'm going to need to have Upper Management take a closer look at this."

Zelda gulps. Her golden skin turns deathly pale. "Upper Management?"

Upper Management? What does any of this mean?

"It doesn't need to go that far." Zelda scoots to the edge of her seat, imploring Barb with wide eyes. "*Please.* I didn't even make a mistake. I swear. I'm good at my—I mean, I'm *trying*. You know I'm trying."

Barb closes my file. It vanishes with a tiny *pop!* "I'm sorry," she says stiffly, not looking at Zelda. "The complaint is already on record. Upper Management will be notified."

"I didn't make a mistake," whispers Zelda.

Barb smiles warmly at me as she stands. Strangely, it's no

longer reassuring. "Unfortunately I can't resolve your concerns today, Tegan. But rest assured, I'll let you know the minute Upper Management has reached a decision. It won't take long." She gestures behind us. When I turn, the door has reappeared. "We'll get to the bottom of this, don't you worry."

Except no one said how long I have to wait, or what happens if they don't find a mistake, or why Zelda hates me so much. So I think I will worry, thanks.

I shoot Barb a wobbly smile as I follow Zelda through the door.

It spits us out directly into the Marybelle's front office, bypassing the waiting room. Zelda marches behind the desk and plonks herself into the chair. She glares at the cat-shaped sticky note that says *Mushrooms???*

I shift my weight, unsure of what to do with myself. I really didn't want to get Zelda in trouble but...

"I'm sorry," I say.

Zelda closes her eyes, chest rising and falling as she takes deep breaths. When she opens her eyes again, all the life and fire has vanished. "It doesn't matter," she says. "Because I didn't make a mistake. Upper Management will rule in my favor, you'll accept that you're dead, and I'll..." Her voice trails away and she smiles wryly to herself. "I'll be stuck doing this lousy job," she mutters.

"I'm sorry!" I march forward. "But you can't expect me to stay here forever when I hate it. It's torture. And you should be morally opposed to torture. I'm sure it's in your code of conduct. 'Thou shalt not doom dead girls to live in their worst memory for eternity even if it means admitting thou madeth a mistaketh.' What did you expect me to do?"

Zelda doesn't look at me. Her head tips forward, hair hiding her face. All I can see is a sliver of her profile, a tiny piece of nose and chin. Worry wraps around me but I don't understand it. I don't understand my feelings right now and I hate that. I hate uncertainty. I hate feeling lost.

Finally, she tips her head back. Her face is carefully blank. "I don't expect anything from you," she says in a small, emotion-less voice. "I don't expect anything from anyone." Before I can respond, she vanishes.

SIX

And so I wait.

Being dead involves a lot more waiting than you'd think.

I spend the rest of the day in my room with the curtains drawn, watching *Snorks*. I fall asleep at 3:07 a.m. and wake up at 3:07 a.m.

I trudge down to breakfast, anxious about seeing Zelda again. The look on her face when I last saw her sticks with me. Why did she look so…lost? Worry niggles at me like I'm wearing the wrong-sized shoes and my toes are squished against the tip with every step I take.

But when I sit down at the same table as last time, Zelda doesn't *poof!* into the seat opposite to shovel mushrooms in her mouth and sass me. I do kind of feel like I'm being watched, though. A tingling sensation dances up and down my spine. But when I look around, there's no one there.

"Zelda?"

No answer.

Ms. Chiu, am I imagining things now?

Zelda also doesn't magically appear next to me when I sprawl out on a pool lounge after breakfast and read the tattered black Bible that was shoved in a drawer in my room. I read the first page of Genesis, then I flip through for a bit—the print is just so tiny. Leviticus and half of Joshua have been ripped out. I should ask Zelda what happens in those bits. She'll probably tell me it was when giant space bees took over Bethlehem and baby Jesus drove them out by turning wine into honey and I'll believe her and she'll go tell her angel buddies how gullible I am and they'll all laugh at me.

Or she just won't talk to me at all.

I read another page of Genesis, give up and chat with Tammy, then I fall asleep.

Zelda doesn't come that day. Or the next day or the day after that.

A week goes by. Every day I sit on the end of my bed and picture a blanket fort. I think about soggy pizza, John Denver, and a broken heater.

I don't think about Mom.

On the eighth day of no Zelda, Trash Cat the Elder creeps to the edge of the parking lot, where he sits and ignores me. I'm three pages into Genesis, the bit where they list how long people lived for and it's like, "Bob lived for eight hundred and thirty-seven years and his daughter, Nancy, lived for nine hundred and fifty-six years and had thirty-seven babies," and suddenly there's a scratchy ball of feelings wedged in the center of my chest because "Tegan lived for sixteen measly years." It makes it hard to breathe. I know I don't *have* to breathe but I feel all hot and jagged so I put the Bible aside. I grab a bunch of pamphlets from the office instead, lie back on the pool lounge, and read them out loud to Trash Cat the Elder so we can play *Would You Rather?*

"Would you rather touch a baby shark at the aquarium or ride the roller coaster at Morey's? Flick your tail once for shark or twice for Morey's."

The cat stares at me, blinks, then looks away again. Whatever. Be a snob, I don't care. I toss the pamphlets onto the concrete, lean back, and sulk. I stare at the sky above me, thick clouds floating by in a pattern destined to repeat itself every four days. It's not even much of a pattern. Just gray, gray, gray, and gray.

I miss blue skies.

I miss the sun.

I miss so many things.

My neck grows stiff and the tingling sensation ripples down my spine again. I sit up and look around. Trash Cat the Elder has vanished and there's no one else I can see. But I *feel* it. Someone is watching me.

I shiver and stand up, dusting down my jeans. I keep looking around. The creepy feeling won't leave.

"Whoever you are, you can stop spying on me like a pervert," I call out. Only the wind answers.

What kind of creep spies on a dead girl in heaven? I stomp away, angry, unsettled, and more than a little afraid.

That night I can't sleep. It's not just feeling like I'm being watched. It's everything. In the silence, my head gets loud. All the thoughts I'm trying to bury shout at me.

I keep thinking about Quinn. And Dad. And Clem. Sometimes she'd send me a message before bed:

You're my favorite x Sleep tight zzzz.

I pull out my phone but the screen stays black no matter how many times I press the power button. I tuck it under my pillow and stare at the foot of the bed.

Soggy pizza and John Denver and a broken heater. Mom.

I throw back the covers, get dressed, and hurry down to the parking lot, as far as I can go. For the first time in days, I don't feel like I'm being watched. I don't tingle and I don't shiver and when I search the shadows I see nothing.

I'm alone. So incredibly alone.

I listen for the ocean.

I strain until I hear waves crashing on the shore. A distant, gentle *whoosh*. It could be the wind, it could be the blood rushing in my ears, it could be my brain playing tricks. I don't care. I convince myself it's real because I need it to be.

I can hear the ocean.

It's beautiful. It hurts so much. I brush away tears and bite the inside of my cheek to stop more from coming. There's no use crying. Not over spilled milk and not over waves on a beach that I can never reach. Tears are pointless.

Ms. Chiu, how much longer do I have to wait?

On the twelfth day I stomp into the office, press my finger against the bell, and leave it there. The bell rings. And rings. And rings. Zelda doesn't appear. I count to one hundred, holding down the bell. She doesn't come. Two hundred. Three hundred. Damn her. I stomp behind the desk, pick up the phone, and dial nine. It rings out so I dial again. It rings out. I do it again. And again. Eventually I slam down the phone, sit, put my head between my knees, and scream.

I decide that screaming is my new favorite hobby. Ten out of ten would recommend for a good time.

When I straighten up, the blood rushes to my head and for a second I think I see a figure outside the window, standing in the bushes, holding a clipboard. Can you die of fright when you're already dead?

It's a boy. A white boy my age in scrappy black clothes, greasy brown hair hanging in his eyes. Scowling. Hunched. Thin. But between one blink and the next he's gone and I can't decide if I imagined him. I race to the window and peer out. There's nothing. No one.

Ms. Chiu, am I losing my mind?

I push open the office door and hurry over to the bushes. There's a lingering smell in the air. It's like books, like the smell of a new book. I look down and in the mud are two perfectly formed footprints.

I die a second death.

My dead heart races as I look around. I don't see anyone but the creepy tingly feeling is turned up to one thousand volts. My whole body fizzles with it.

"I'll report you!" I shout. "No perverts allowed in heaven!"

My voice is so loud it echoes and my throat hurts after so many days of near silence. I suck down panicked maybe-breaths and dart my eyes in all directions.

No one.

I'm alone.

I kick the mud until I've scrubbed away the footprints. If I make them vanish, it will be as if this never happened. I'm pretty good at convincing myself of things like that. Mr. What's-his-face the school counselor said it was an unhealthy coping mechanism. It all comes out in the end, he said. One big angry explosion.

He had a clipboard too.

I hurry back to my room, lock the door, and fling myself onto the bed. Sleeping is my favorite hobby now. If I sleep until Barb calls me into her office nothing bad can happen, right? I'll sleep and wake up and Barb will tell me there was a mistake and, "We're *so* sorry, Tegan, we feel terrible, Tegan, we really suck, Tegan. Please accept a new heaven, guaranteed to be creepy-pervert-clipboard-boy-free, and would you like me to open a portal so you can check on your friends and family whenever you like?"

I wake up at 3:07 a.m.

It's dark out.

I turn over and go straight back to sleep. I don't dream.

When I wake up next it's 3:07 a.m. and pale gray light peeks through the closed blinds.

I sit up and decide that hating Zelda is my new favorite hobby. Where *is* she?

For breakfast I eat mushrooms slathered in ketchup and I choke back every mouthful. It's the single worst experience of my life and that's saying something. Zelda doesn't appear. Neither does a creepy boy with a clipboard.

Maybe I am losing my mind.

I head up to the rec room and play a one-sided game of foosball. I use a small piece of sausage for the ball because no matter how hard I look I can't find the real soccer balls. To be honest, the whole experience is both gross and slightly more entertaining than I imagined it would be. Eight out of ten.

When I'm done I go outside and offer the sausage to Trash Cat the Elder. Despite the hunger in his eyes, he's too skittish to come out from under the car. So I leave the sausage on the ground and decide it's time to give mini-golf a go. Maybe that will also turn out to be both gross and slightly more entertaining than I imagined it would be. Maybe I just need to keep busy so there's no time to imagine creepy stuff.

Cloud cover hangs low over the golf course and everything feels so depressingly gray.

God I miss blue.

I march over to the kiosk. It's a small wooden booth (green) with a counter that's chest-high and there's a big sign that shows the family from the poster, still grinning as their heads explode. The roller door covering the ticket window (green and white stripes) is locked shut.

The clubs and golf balls for rent are inside the kiosk. I can't play without them.

I walk all the way around the booth. There's a door on one side, but when I try the handle it's locked.

I take a deep maybe-breath and close my eyes.

The thing is, I'm not an aggressive person by nature. Except for that time I flipped out at school. And that time I threw a bunch of Mom's stuff in the fire pit in our backyard and burned it. Other than that I'm pretty chill. So it's mostly out of character when I open my eyes, march over to the mushroom, grab the discarded sneaker, and pitch it at the kiosk.

It bounces off the roller door with a resounding clang, then hits the ground a couple of feet away and rolls back toward me. The whole experience is deeply cathartic so I immediately do it again.

I end up beating the rusted lock with the heel of the sneaker until it breaks open. I rummage through the junk inside without turning on a light and manage to knock over a bunch of clubs. They scatter everywhere. Ms. Chiu would have something profound to say about the mess I'm making but I don't care. I grab a bright pink golf ball and a club from the pile and head out again.

This will be fun, right? I can imagine the ball is Zelda's head.

The first hole is the easiest, just a small ridge to conquer. When I whack the ball, it rolls partway up the ridge before losing momentum and rolling back toward me, landing right by my feet.

"Wow. I suck."

It takes me twelve shots before I get the ball in the hole. I make a note on my scorecard: *hole in one*.

The second hole has a giant toad in the middle of the green—you've got to roll the ball up his tongue into his open mouth and then he poops the ball out the other end.

I knock the ball: *thwack*. It ricochets off the toad's foot and rolls back toward me.

"This sucks." I kick the golf ball, miss, and stub my toe on the green instead. I hate this shitty game. Zero out of ten, would not recommend.

I try fifteen times before I give up, write *hole in one* on my card, then decide my new favorite hobby is beating the crap out of the giant fiberglass toad with my golf club.

I bring the club down hard on the toad. The impact rattles all the way up my arm and across my shoulders. I do it again. And again.

"Take that, Toadie McToad-face!" I shout, and boy does it feel good. "You suck! You can't even fight back against a dead girl with a golf club? What's wrong with you?"

I catch a flash of white out the corner of my eye and freeze midswing.

I turn.

There is a boy.

There is a boy watching me.

It's creepy clipboard boy. He's next to the dinosaur, not even trying to hide. He's staring right at me, holding his clipboard in one hand and a clicky pen in the other. I blink and he's still there. Blink, blink, blink. Still there.

"Who the hell are you?" I lower the club.

The guy doesn't move, doesn't say a word.

"You're not going to answer?" I should be scared. I am scared. But I'm angry too. Because I'm sick of this. It shouldn't be this hard to be dead. I shouldn't be in the Marybelle, I shouldn't be getting ghosted by Zelda, I shouldn't have to wait this long for an answer from Barb, and I shouldn't be perved on by creepy teen boys with clipboards.

I shouldn't even be dead.

I step toward him, chin jutted high in defiance. "What kind of creep spies on a sixteen-year-old girl, huh?"

He stares at me. Has he even blinked?

"Say something!" I shout. "Say something *or else.*" I waggle the golf club at him. "You saw what I did to the toad." He doesn't twitch, doesn't flinch. "I'll tell Barb and she'll smite you and you'll be a little pile of ash and do you know what I'll do? I'll use that little pile of ash as a tee for my golf ball. I'll putt a hole in one off your remains, asshole. Watch me."

Creepy boy doesn't even blink.

"What is your *deal*?"

Finally, he moves. Without taking his eyes off me, he brings the clicky pen to meet the clipboard and makes a giant cross.

"Hey! What does—?"

He scowls, then—*poof!*—he vanishes.

"What the hell?" I ask the empty air. "That's not—" I scream and stumble back as a woman suddenly *poofs* in front of me.

"That windmill is broken," she says without looking up from her knitting. Carol. The secretary from Barb's office.

"What is wrong with you people?" I hiss. My dead heart beats wildly: *thwack, thwack, thwack* against my rib cage. "You scared me half to death, Carol."

She snorts. "Bit late for that."

Ugh. "What do you even want? Did you know there's a creepy guy spying on me? I'm starting to think you guys don't know how to run eternal paradise. And where's Zelda? She's really bad at her job. I haven't seen her for ages. I've been left on my own and I beat up the toad, which I'm sorry about, actually. I really regret that, to be honest." I turn to the toad. "Sorry, dude. I'm kind of in a bad place right now. Literally and figuratively. Didn't mean to take it out on you." I turn back to Carol. "Are you going to stop knitting?"

She sighs. "You talk too much."

"Excuse me? I don't—"

"The Manager will see you now." She flicks my forehead and the world spins.

SEVEN

When the world stops spinning, I'm in Barb's office, holding my golf club in front of me like I'm in a zombie movie, surrounded by the undead.

Barb sits behind her desk wearing a smile and a pantsuit (red). She waves at me to sit down. There are two chairs opposite her but only one is free.

Zelda sits in the other chair.

"I didn't mean to interrupt," says Barb. She nods at my club.

"It's fine. I was losing anyway." I nervously take a seat. I don't know where Carol disappeared to—it's only me, Barb, and Zelda in the office. I try to catch Zelda's eye but she stares resolutely ahead, arms folded.

It shouldn't sting but it does. She's not my friend and I hate her and she's not even that cute so what do I care if she likes me or not?

"Sorry for keeping you in suspense," says Barb, both hands pressed palm down on the empty desk. "How have you been?"

Bored. Scared. Bored. Angry. Bored.

"Okay," I say. I try leaning the golf club against my knee but it keeps slipping because my legs won't stop jiggling. I grip the rubbery handle until my knuckles bleach white. "A bit lonely." I turn to Zelda, super casual and unbothered. "So, where have you been?"

"I have lots to do," she huffs. She's still not looking at me. "My job is *very* important."

"Is ignoring me part of your important job?" I ask because Zelda's like a scab I can't help picking at even though I know it will leave a scar.

The muscle in her jaw twitches. "If you don't like it, complain to Barb. Oh wait, you already did."

"You're *still* angry about that?"

"Angry?" She finally looks at me, eyes blazing. Angel to demon in 0.001 seconds. "I'm not angry. I'm *furious.*" The gold in her eyes flickers like literal flames. "I'm incandescent with rage. The fury in me could fuel the fires of hell from here until the end of time."

Barb clears her throat.

Zelda's upper lip curls as she swings back around to face the front. "Whatever."

I let out a breath, gripping the handle of my golf club tightly. Okay. So Zelda hates me. Good to know. And good thing I don't care what she thinks of me.

"We'll get straight to business." Barb reaches out and *poof!* a manila folder appears on the desk underneath her hand. I should be more impressed: that was real magic and not some dude in Vegas with a silky leopard-print shirt sawing a woman in half. But somehow it feels like basically the same thing?

Barb opens the folder. Inside are two sheets of paper. She picks them up and lays them side by side in the middle of the desk; both sheets are totally blank. "As you know, I took your concerns to

Upper Management." She speaks slowly, picking over her words before she chooses them. I wonder if she's sifting through the fourth drawer in the kitchen of her mind.

See, Ms. Chiu, I was listening.

"After many lengthy discussions—analyzing the data, reviewing your file, interviewing the appropriate parties—we came to a conclusion." Barb looks at both of us. She pauses. She pauses for a long time. I will demolish this room like a piñata with my golf club if she doesn't get to the damn point. "There *was* a mistake," she says.

Zelda melts in her seat, a disappointed pile of goo. "No, no, no," she whines.

"Yes, yes, *yes!*" I pump my fist. Suck it, Zelda.

"But," says Barb, completely raining on my parade, "we don't know *what* the mistake was."

What?

What?

"I can tell you what it was," I say. "Zelda made the wrong heaven."

"Shut up, butt-face," snaps Zelda.

"You shut up, hell-spawn."

"Speaking of hell," says Barb. She raises a brow, effectively silencing us both. "You'll be aware that in the afterlife there is heaven and there is hell. But there is also the in-between. Have you heard of purgatory, Tegan?"

I mean, sort of. But not enough to write an essay on it. Should I tell her I was only in Catholic school for eight months and six days? I shrug.

"When you die," she explains, fingers steepled like a movie villain, "your soul is evaluated to determine which route it should take in the afterlife. This process is called Admissions. And to reach heaven, there are two possible routes.

"The first is via purgatory. You see, Tegan, a human soul accumulates *a lot* of gunk during its time on Earth: mistakes that need to be atoned for, troubled memories to overcome, regret, hurt, trauma, cruelty, and resentment to scrub away. Sins. So many sins."

She smiles like we're sharing a joke. But I'm not laughing. All I can focus on is *soul, sins,* and *scrub.*

"For most souls, it's vital they're purified of those sins before they enter heaven, so that when they arrive, they will be ready to accept eternal happiness. And purgatory is where this purging of sins takes place." Barb pauses, eyes unfocused as if searching deep inside for the right words. "This process is necessary because happiness is…complicated," she settles on. "And true happiness, the kind you experience here, is pure bliss. It is as bright as the sun. To accept such happiness into your human soul is like squeezing a mountain into a thimble. A cleansed soul will stretch, but a contaminated soul will break."

My legs are shaking so much the golf club jiggles. With a huff, Zelda grabs it and lays it on her lap instead. She cuts me a dirty look but I can't focus on that right now.

"The second route into heaven," continues Barb, "is what we call fast-tracking. This is when a soul is deemed clean enough already to skip purgatory and zip straight into heaven." She slides the two blank sheets closer, running her eyes over them slowly. "Purgatory is a highly involved process, monopolizing the majority of heaven's time and resources. Allowing a certain number of souls to skip it helps us avoid clogging an already overworked system. This is the role of Admissions: they assess your soul and determine whether you need to go to purgatory, or whether you can be fast-tracked directly into heaven." Her gaze settles on the white sheet on the left. "You, Tegan, were fast-tracked."

My mouth goes dry. Beside me, Zelda grips the golf club tightly.

"Admissions often takes a chance on young people," says Barb. "The theory being that they haven't lived long enough to accrue the really deep scars, the really baked-on grime. And that whatever gunk they have accumulated in their short lives can easily be scrubbed clean with a little counseling."

I picture myself hunched in a tiny school office as Mr. What's-his-face asks why I got so angry I flipped a desk, and do I think it has anything to do with why I'd rather sit in silence, counting down the minutes until I can leave, than answer his questions about Mom.

I swallow.

"Unfortunately," says Barb, "some young people have gone through such a disproportionate amount of suffering in the years they were alive that their ability to adjust to heaven with a few counseling sessions is lost." She taps the right sheet with her nail, filed to a sharp point. "Your case, Tegan, is borderline. I can see why Admissions might have reasoned that you could skip purgatory, but it's possible they underestimated the weight of the emotional baggage you're carrying." She gives me a pitying smile. I swallow again, this time tasting bile.

"However," she snaps, and I jump. But she's not looking at me, she's looking at Zelda. "From the moment I read your file, I could see there was a strong possibility that it was Zelda who miscalculated." She frowns deeply. "Her calculations were *very* messy. So many shortcuts, so many gaps."

Zelda ducks her head, cheeks ablaze. "I didn't make a mistake," she mutters.

Barb charges on regardless. "Finding the right heaven for fast-tracked souls is a complex process. In purgatory, every single moment from a person's life is painstakingly analyzed, stripped of any gunk, and then..." She waves her hand around, searching for the right words.

"Filed away neatly in a drawer," I say because this is all starting to sound pretty familiar. Ms. Chiu, are you proud of me? "Like a neat kitchen drawer—knives with knives, forks with forks, and spoons with spoons."

Barb smiles widely. "Exactly," she says. "And by the end of the process, a person's drawers will be *so* well organized and *so* sparkling clean that the angel in charge of creating their heaven will have no trouble selecting the correct memory."

She frowns at the blank page on the left. "But for a soul that has been fast-tracked, determining the correct memory is more like...opening a drawer whose contents were put away in a hurry, so some things are out of order. The angel in charge has to rummage through, take shortcuts, make calculations based on less-thorough data, which explains how an error might be introduced." Her gaze lands on Zelda. "*Especially* if that angel is the kind to be sloppy in her work."

Zelda sucks in a sharp breath but says nothing.

Barb shifts her gaze back to me and sighs. "Ultimately, when we reviewed your case, Upper Management failed to reach a consensus. We could not determine where the fault lies: Are you not coping with heaven because Zelda made you the wrong one, or are you in denial because Admissions should have sent you to purgatory to clean your soul first?"

I can hardly get enough moisture into my mouth to speak. "Is it, I mean, if you can't decide, am I stuck?"

Barb closes the folder and stands. She faces the back wall, hands clasped at the small of her back. It almost looks like she's gazing out a window. "You're not stuck," she says. "A simple review of your intake wasn't sufficient to determine where the error was made. Protocol dictates that in the event of any kind of procedural error, the offending party must be accurately identified and dealt with. Thus, we've decided to conduct an extensive investigation."

My breath stutters. "Investigation?"

In the blink of an eye, a figure zaps into existence next to Barb. I yelp and almost fall off my chair. Then I notice his hunched shoulders, the greasy bangs, his all-black outfit, his bored sneer.

Creepy clipboard guy.

"You!" I cry out at the same time that Zelda snaps, "Him?"

"This is Kelvin," says Barb. "Kelvin has recently been promoted to Head of Compliance. He makes sure things run smoothly in heaven. Say hello, Kelvin."

Kelvin doesn't say a thing. His expression doesn't change, either. He just scowls at me, making a note on his ever-present clipboard.

"He got promoted?" gasps Zelda. "Why?"

"Because he demonstrated loyalty, diligence, and aptitude," says Barb. "Because his record is *clean*."

Kelvin smirks.

Zelda looks away with a grimace.

"Over the next thirty days," says Barb, taking her seat again, "Zelda will need to demonstrate that she calculated the path to the Marybelle correctly."

"A month?" There's a crack as Zelda snaps my golf club in two. I don't think she means it but the thing splinters like a toothpick. I stare at it in shock. "That's not enough time! It's—"

Barb eyes the broken club coolly, then lifts her gaze to Zelda's face. "Need I remind you what a certain someone achieved in only a week?"

Zelda lowers her head. She frowns at the broken club like she has no idea how it got there.

Barb powers on. "Kelvin will observe the process," she explains. "He'll assess Tegan's reaction. If you show Tegan how you came to choose the Maybelle and win her honest, heartfelt approval, we'll know you were correct all along. But if your calculations don't add up, if Tegan is not convinced, we'll know you made a mistake." She smiles. "And mistakes, of course, have consequences."

Zelda gulps, but none of this sounds bad to me. Because there's no chance in heaven *or* hell Zelda will convince me. So I'm guaranteed to win.

"During the same thirty days," says Barb, turning her gaze on me, "you will also be investigated, Tegan."

Crap.

"Kelvin will observe you from a discreet distance to ascertain the following: Can you face your fears, your past, your sins, your worries with clarity and objectivity? Or are you unable to accept Zelda's calculations because your emotional baggage holds you back? Are you simply not ready to accept eternal happiness at the Marybelle? If so, we'll know Admissions was at fault." She leans back, a pleased smile on her face. "And you'll be sent to purgatory."

Honestly, it's a miracle I don't flip the desk. "How is that fair?" I say. "If Emo McCreepoid decides I'm not well-adjusted enough to appreciate the Marybelle, I get booted out of heaven?"

"His name is Kelvin," says Barb. "And it would only be a quick trip to purgatory. To really scrub your soul raw of all those icky human flaws preventing you from accepting the light."

I sit back and try to picture what that means, what it would feel like to have someone root through my soul carving out the bits that aren't pure enough.

What if every part of me is stained? What am I left with then?

The fear clearly shows on my face because Barb smiles in reassurance. "Don't worry. It's extremely painful but it doesn't take long. Only one or two thousand years slowly peeling back the layers of your soul, forcing you to confront trauma after trauma after trauma." She glances at my file. "Maybe five thousand years."

I choke on my own spit. "*Thousand?*"

"I told you not to complain," mutters Zelda.

My nails dig into my thighs and I am once again reminded that in heaven, it's still possible to feel pain.

"Listen, Tegan." Barb heaves a sigh. "You're not being punished—*you* didn't make a mistake. If Zelda is proven to be at fault, you'll get the heaven you deserve. And if Admissions is proven to be at fault, you will simply take the path through purgatory that you should have taken all along. And if that's the case, well, it will certainly help with some of your more…*interesting* behavior."

Kelvin flicks his hand and suddenly there's a giant, floating image in the middle of the room, just like the trick Zelda pulled back at the Marybelle. This time the image shows me in the motel office with my head between my knees, screaming. He flicks his hand and now it shows me shoving mushrooms into my mouth, gagging and crying. Another flick and I'm threatening Kelvin with a golf club. Another and I'm talking to Tammy the tampon. He flicks his hand a final time and the image crumbles to dust. Barb and Kelvin stare at me, impassive.

I open my mouth but no words come out.

I try to imagine purgatory. All I can think of is the dentist: white walls, a sharp stench of disinfectant, a masked figure who jabs and scrapes and pulls while I panic because I can't breathe and I can't swallow.

For one or two thousand years. Maybe five.

"If your soul is ready for heaven, you have nothing to worry about," says Barb. "And if not…" She smiles. "Well, a thousand years will pass in the blink of an eye. Sound good?"

I glance at Kelvin. His pen hovers over the clipboard. Somehow I think screaming *No that does not sound good that sounds like actual hell* will earn a big fat X on Kelvin's clipboard.

I smile weakly. "Super," I say.

Kelvin frowns and scribbles something down.

"Excellent." Barb claps her hands. "I just need to hash out some details with Zelda. Nothing you need to concern yourself with. Just logistics. And of course the consequences. Should *she* be the one who fails."

Zelda's throat works as she swallows. Honestly, though, what kind of punishment could be worse than purgatory? She'll probably just have to take a remedial class in Angel 101 or something. Unfair.

"Perhaps you'd like to return to your…" Barb nods at the broken golf club in Zelda's lap.

No, I would not like to return to playing the world's worst

game at the world's worst motel but if I say that out loud will that be a mark against me?

Kelvin stares, unblinking. I bet he has posters of half-naked girls all over his bedroom. I hate him.

I turn to Zelda. Her head hangs low and her lips are pinched tight. I force a smile, gently prying the two broken shards of golf club from her hands.

"I guess I'll see you back—"

Zelda reaches out, lightning fast, and flicks my forehead.

The pain is sharp and I curse. In a blink I'm standing in the middle of the mini-golf course. Alone. Holding a broken golf club.

"I hate you," I say because it feels good to say it out loud. I glance around to see if Kelvin followed me and let out a breath when I don't see him. "I hate all of you. You all suck. Heaven sucks. Being dead sucks."

Ms. Chiu, I would like to start over.

(ALL THE KING'S HORSES)

As light faded from the room, Tegan began to worry. Everything was different in the dark. As if the light had been a veil, keeping reality out of focus. But now the truth was laid bare before her, an endless stretch of night offering nothing to hide behind, nothing to stand between her and the cracks in the walls, the stains, the shadows, the broken clock.

No one had bothered turning on the overhead light; the room was illuminated only by the flickering TV and the orange streetlights outside.

Her dad hadn't moved from his spot on the bed, not for hours. Every time Tegan looked at him, he smiled. A grotesque facsimile of a smile. She hated it. She wanted to go home. She wanted to know why they were here. She wanted to know why she hadn't heard from her mother. It was Friday. Her mother was coming home tomorrow. She was supposed to call and remind them about her flight plans, when to pick her up. But Tegan's father's phone hadn't rung once. And her own phone had run out of battery an hour ago.

Tegan stood and crossed the room with the empty pizza box, leaving it on the bench in the kitchenette. Her father watched her, suddenly tense. Was he afraid she'd run out the door? Would he chase after her and drag her back? Tegan was tempted to try it, just to see what would happen. She wanted him to do *something*.

She met his eye but he looked away, down at the phone in his hands.

"That pizza was gross," she said.

"I liked it," said Quinn. She was already in bed under the covers, Trash Monkey cuddled to her chest. "I like mushrooms."

"You're a mushroom."

"Dad," whined Quinn. "Tell Tegan not to call me a mushroom."

He looked up at them. But he didn't say anything. He just smiled with clouded, unseeing eyes.

Tegan felt too loose. Like the screws meant to keep her together had all been unscrewed. She was going to fall to pieces and all the king's horses and all the king's men wouldn't know how to put her back together again.

"It's too cold," she said. The split-system heater above the bathroom door was pumping air into the room. But she was still shivering. Tegan fiddled with the controls, trying to make the room hotter. "Why doesn't it work?" She looked back at her father. "This place is shit. Let's just go home."

"Don't swear," said her father as he finally pushed himself to his feet.

He vanished into the bathroom, his movements graceless and lumbering like all his screws had been loosened too. The door swung shut, but not quite all the way. Tegan stared at the gap. Inside, the water started running.

"Shit, shit, shit," said Quinn. "You taught me a bad word." She grinned, flashing the teeth she had brushed with Tegan's toothbrush—she'd forgotten her own. She hadn't brought a hairbrush, either.

"Don't swear," snapped Tegan.

Quinn giggled and turned back to the TV. She'd been watching the same thing for hours, a cartoon Tegan had never seen before. Quinn wouldn't let anyone change the channel.

Tegan crawled into bed next to her sister. She wanted to be warm. She wanted to go home. She wanted to charge her phone and call Clem. She didn't care if Clem was busy with Lou. Tegan would call her until she answered.

"What happens if you roll on top of me in the middle of the night?" asked Quinn. She didn't look away from the TV.

"You'll get my butt germs," said Tegan.

"Don't roll on top of me."

"This cartoon sucks."

"I like it."

"Yeah, it's okay."

"Can we play mini-golf tomorrow?"

"Ask Dad."

"Can we swim?"

"No. It's October. No one swims in October, you big weirdo."

"I want to."

"Did you bring a bathing suit?"

"Yes."

"You didn't pack your hairbrush or your toothbrush or a jacket but you brought stuff to swim in?" Tegan ran her hand through Quinn's hair. It was fine and soft.

Quinn looked down at Trash Monkey in her arms. Her lips did the thing they always did—a kind of twisting thing—when she was thinking hard.

"What if Mom gets home and we're not there?" she said. "Won't she be lonely?"

Tegan wanted to say, *Mom doesn't get lonely. She likes it when she's on her own,* but the words were too big to speak. She glanced at the bathroom door, still ajar. "We'll be home soon," she said instead.

Quinn nodded, satisfied, and curled onto her side. She pressed her thumb to her teeth and chewed—a habit she couldn't grow out of. Sometimes she would gnaw the side of her thumb so much the skin would crack and bleed.

Tegan waited for her sister to fall asleep, then sat up, glancing between the bathroom door and her father's phone on the nightstand.

Making a decision, she snapped up the phone. She knew the passcode: Quinn's birthday and her own. She tapped in the numbers and the home screen lit up, a picture of Quinn and their dad cheesing for the camera. Her hands shook as she opened the contacts list and scrolled. Her mother. Tegan needed to call her mother. She'd be out drinking with Aunt Lily, celebrating their last night together, but Tegan needed to hear her voice; she needed answers.

Tegan pressed call and held the phone to her ear. She waited for the call to connect.

A tone rang—too loud in the quiet room—and then a prerecorded voice: "We're sorry, you have reached a number that has been disconnected or is no longer in service." Slowly, Tegan lowered the phone and hung up.

Had her mother forgotten to pay her bill? Tegan stared at the home screen. In the picture, Quinn was missing her front tooth, her eyes scrunched closed. Their father's eyes were wide open, tired and lined. But he smiled anyway, hugging Quinn close, like he was terrified to let her go.

Hands still shaking, Tegan navigated to the call log. Ten outgoing calls to her mother's number yesterday. All unanswered. Just as many to Aunt Lily. All unanswered.

In the bathroom, Tegan heard footsteps—her father moving.

She locked the phone quickly, sliding it back onto the nightstand, where it landed with a clunk. She froze, waiting for her father to walk out of the bathroom, to catch her flushed with guilt. The alarm clock was stuck on 3:07 a.m. so Tegan had to count the passing seconds to the beat of her heart thumping in her chest.

Nothing happened. Her father didn't leave the bathroom.

Her heart still pounding, Tegan slid under the covers and curled around her sleeping sister, scrunching her eyes shut. She wanted to forget. She wanted to go home. She wanted to wake up and discover it had all been a dream. But in the dark there was nothing to hide behind, nothing to stand between her and the cracks in the walls, the stains, the shadows, the broken clock, the words swimming around and around her head: *We're sorry, you have reached a number that has been disconnected or is no longer in service.*

EIGHT

I wake up to the theme song from *Snorks* roaring at full volume. "What the—?"

I roll over and find Zelda next to me, sitting on top of the covers with the TV remote in her hand.

"Yo," she says. "Come with me."

She touches her index finger to my forehead and the world spins.

Suddenly we're standing in the empty hallway of my old middle school. I'm wearing shoes, socks, jeans, and my least-favorite sweater, none of which I was wearing in bed a second ago. Zelda is dressed in a Sherlock Holmes hat, a three-piece tweed suit, and shiny Mary Janes; she's holding a magnifying glass.

"What the hell, Zelda?"

She smirks. "Not hell. But close."

Confused, I look around. I really am standing in an exact replica of my old middle school hallway. Even the smell is the same: stale sweat and cleaning chemicals. I shudder; the thought of her rooting through my memories for the details makes me itchy all over. It's just so *real*. The ripped poster for the spring dance. The crack in the plaster where Paul's cousin broke his hand punching the wall after he bombed a test. The scuff marks on the vinyl tiles—one of them is probably mine from trying to do the moonwalk. The buzzing lights. Clem's locker, with a thousand Sailor Moon stickers on it.

It's so familiar and it's so much like home that surely no amount of scrubbing could ever erase it from my soul.

I wrench my focus back to Zelda. "Is this...is this purgatory?"

She snorts. "No. I stay clear of *that* place. Gives me the creeps."

"Why?"

"Spoilers. But also, did you ever see that old movie with the guy who sticks his hand through another guy's chest and pulls out his still-beating heart with his bare hands?" She holds a straight face for three seconds before bursting into laughter.

I hate her.

"Where have you been?" I ask.

She shrugs. "Around."

"Not around the Marybelle." It's been five days since Barb set up her ridiculous investigation and I haven't seen Zelda once. She left me to freak out on my own. She's the worst personal angel ever.

"Please," she huffs. "Do you know how complicated excursion forms are? The insurance alone is a nightmare. HR really rode my ass on this. And don't get me started on Carol."

"Excursion?" I flick the torn edge of the spring dance poster. "Why did you re-create my school?"

"Not a re-creation, babe. All this?" She swings her arms wide. "It's real. Honestly, I'm flattered you think I could have made it and I'd love to take credit but a certain someone way, way, *way* above my pay grade might get angry at me for that." She winks. She *tries* to wink but she can't so both her eyes squint shut at the same time. I'd poke fun at her except the truth hits me like a car running a stop sign.

Real?

Real?

"Real? This is my middle school? My real middle school on real Earth?"

"Yup."

Ms. Chiu, I am having feelings. Messy, spiky, noisy feelings.

I stare at the spring dance poster. Ms. Chiu, the *real* Ms. Chiu, must be next door at the high school. My legs itch to run to her and say, *Please tell me what I do with all these feelings because they are too big for me and I don't know how to look at them without being crushed under their weight.*

God, I hope this isn't the kind of reaction that will make Kelvin think Admissions got it wrong about me.

"Wait, am I a ghost?"

I look down at my hands. I have a lingering image of them wrapped around the handlebars of my bike—it's the last image I have of them from *before.* They were stiff and white-knuckled from gripping the handlebars tight as I cycled home fast. I wanted to beat Dad so I could start dinner before him. I'm not—I wasn't— a great cook but I didn't want frozen lasagna again and that's pretty much all Dad could do. I was craving fried chicken.

But my hands aren't see-through like a ghost's, they're the same they've always been: small, stubby, thick little fingers.

"Nope," says Zelda. "Not a ghost."

My dead heart pounds. "Am I *alive*?"

She snorts. "No. Again, flattered but no. Angels do not have resurrection capabilities. And if we did, you wouldn't be first on my list." She holds up three fingers, lowering them one by one.

"Grumpy Cat. Betty White. Thomas J. Sennett from the motion picture *My Girl*."

"Then please explain what the hell is happening right now."

Her eyes flick to the poster and back again.

I turn my whole body around to face it. I step up close and press my very real hand to the very real poster, tracing the words underneath my fingertip: *Romeo and Juliet*. That was the theme. I trace the "R" and think, *Hey, I remember that dance: seventh grade.* I was a new transfer kid from Catholic school, but me and Clem became friends so fast—soulmates, she said—that we went as "before and after" Juliets. I was the "after" so I had a knife sticking out of my chest and zombie face paint. And Paul dressed as Queen Mab but Lou wasn't there because she hadn't transferred to our school yet and…

My hand—my small, stubby, thick dead-girl hand—flies to my mouth as the truth hits me hard.

Because this spring dance was four years ago.

Four years.

"Ta-da!" says Zelda. She does a strange little dance—wiggling her butt, flapping her wings, and undulating her arms like a dorky octopus. It's not cute. Not even a little bit.

"This is the past?" I splutter out. This is real *and* this is the past.

She nods.

"We time-traveled? You zapped us into the past?"

"No." She rolls her eyes. "This is happening now. It's always happening. Look, time is complicated. You don't have to understand it."

"Is that because you don't understand it?"

"Shut up, butt-face."

I do shut up but only because I'm freaking out. This is a lot to take in. Because I was dead, and I was okay about being dead (I wasn't okay. I'm not okay), and now I'm... I don't know what I am. I'm dead but I'm standing in my life. Literally, I'm here. Ms. Chiu is here. My friends are here. Dad is at work in his shop twenty miles from here. Quinn is down the road at the elementary school. I could walk out the front door and in fifteen minutes I'd have my arms wrapped around her.

Mom is here.

Oh, Ms. Chiu, I'm going to throw up.

"Cool, huh?" says Zelda. She does her wiggle-dance again. "It's March, a couple months out from the dance. It's Wednesday. And it's raining."

I curl my hands into fists but there's no strength in them. I want to punch the wall, I want to punch right over where the spring dance poster is pinned. I want to scream. I want to run away. I want to find Quinn and squeeze her and tell her I love her and that I'm sorry I left without saying goodbye. I want—I just want. I want so much.

Zelda snaps her fingers. The bell rings and suddenly the air is filled with chairs scraping across classroom floors and voices blabbering and *thump thump thump* as the whole student body moves at once.

"Holy shit." Classroom doors open and people—real, live, people-I-know people—spill out into the hallway and I am swarmed. "Holy shit."

I collapse onto my butt on the gross hallway floor, my head in my hands, and I freak out. Herds of feet shuffle past but no one trips over me or kicks me so that's a silver lining. Zelda clomps over and flops down opposite me with a huff. I peek through my fingers at her.

"You're having a moment," she says.

I nod. I am indeed having a moment.

The counselor I saw—Mr. What's-his-face at school, not fake Ms. Chiu—said if I was ever feeling anxious and overwhelmed I should look around and find something that begins with each letter of the alphabet. It's supposed to focus my mind, calm it.

Air vent.

Basketball shoes.

Coat.

Dirty floor.

Empty can of pop.

Freckles. She has so many freckles.

Ugh, not freckles. Don't look at her freckles. They're not cute. She's not cute. Pick something else. Um…fingers?

I hold my hands up in front of my face, stubby little fingers splayed. "Are you sure I'm not a ghost?"

Her eyes light up. "No, but that'd be cool. If I was a ghost, I'd be an evil one and haunt a cat café. I'd snuggle the cats and mess with people's coffees: 'Who ordered the *flooooaaating* cappuccino?' Purr-fection."

She waggles her eyebrows and grins. I hate her.

"I hate you."

"That's the spirit!"

"But if I'm not a ghost…" I think about Quinn. She's so close. If these hands can touch paper and feel it, then they can wrap around my little sister and never let go.

"No," says Zelda, like she can read my thoughts. Maybe she can. "There are restrictions. You can't leave the parameters of the excursion. HR is very strict on that. And even if we could…" She shrugs. "They can't see us. Or hear us. You could run up and scream in their faces and they wouldn't perceive a thing. We just don't exist for them. I mean, look around you. No one's walking on top of us. Or giving us strange looks like who is that girl having a breakdown and her hot friend with the wings sitting in the middle of our school hallway?"

She's right. All around us people are talking, laughing, and shoving each other playfully but none of them are looking at me and they're definitely not trampling on me. It's like I'm invisible.

Twelve-year-old Naomi Long walks past—fluffy pink sweater, hairband, jeans. She's clutching a folder (green, I hate her) and she doesn't look at me once. I see so many faces I know, four years younger but familiar and real.

Is Clem here?

This is too much to take in. It's a Belly Buster at Denny's; I can't open my mouth wide enough to take a bite and I know when I try all the insides will spill everywhere and it will be gross.

No. I can't freak out like this.

I take a deep breath, scoop up my messy feelings, and lock them away. It's not about denial, it's about survival. And this is how I survive. This is how I prove I'm not too messed up for heaven.

"Why did you bring me here?" I ask.

Zelda gestures at a chunky pink watch hanging loosely around her wrist. The face is blank. "The investigation, of course." She stands up. "You think I've been twiddling my thumbs for the last five days? No, ma'am. I have been *planning*. There's a lot on the line, after all."

I scramble to my feet. "*This* is the investigation? How is

dragging me back to middle school going to change my mind about the Marybelle? Scratch that—I already know the answer. It won't. Nothing can change my mind."

Zelda gives me a hard look. "Kelvin's watching." She steps up close. There's a lot hiding behind her dark, inscrutable eyes and I wish I could unravel it all. "He's watching both of us." She holds my gaze. I want to look away but I can't. There's a constellation of freckles smattered across her nose and before this month is up I might just count them to see exactly how many there are. I'll tell her the number and she'll tell me I'm weird for counting but she'll preen too. And then maybe we'll be friends. Maybe I wouldn't hate that.

"I know he's watching us," I mutter. "But that doesn't mean I'll be convinced."

"Oh, I'll convince you." She sounds so sure of herself. "That's why we're hunting for clues."

"Clues?"

"I have to show you my calculations—how I got from A to B to C, all the way to M for Marybelle. So we're taking a wee saunter down memory lane. Look to the right and you'll see regrets, mistakes, sins, jealousy, and American's Most Embarrassing Moments. Look to the left and you'll see crushes, friendships, laughter, and Feel-Good Family Fun Times. And in the middle of it all are clues, bread crumbs leading us to a two-star motel in Jersey where your one true moment of happiness can be found. It's the path I followed to find your perfect heaven and when we're done you'll see it was the right path." She leans in even closer. "Memory is subjective. But you can get closer to the truth when you're on the outside looking in, when you can see the whole picture. So if you keep your eyes open, there's no telling what you'll learn about yourself." Thirteen. She has thirteen freckles. "Don't you want to know who you are, Tegan Masters?"

I'm not the one with wings but I suddenly feel a whole lot like Icarus.

"Of course I do. I'm not afraid."

Zelda smirks. "Excellent," she says, and points with her magnifying glass, "because look over there."

I look.

Oh crap.

It's Clem. She's tall, basketball team tall, with two long braids that slap at her butt as she walks. She has braces and thick brows and she's beautiful and I miss her.

"Whoa there." Zelda grabs my arm as my knees go weak.

Through the pain-haze of Too Many Feelings at Once, I watch Clem accidentally swing her locker door into the shoulder of a girl standing next to her. The force knocks a stack of books out of the girl's hands and into a scattered pile on the floor. Clem gasps, scrambling to apologize.

No. Oh no no no no no. No.

No.

My poor dead heart flips as I realize the girl next to Clem wearing sweatpants, a yellow sweater, and Cons is me.

She—four-years-younger me—looks down at the spilled books and almost bursts into tears. Because she's had a really shitty day. Her parents have been fighting and she just failed a math quiz and now a librarian is going to yell at her for damaging school property.

"Shoot! I'm so sorry! Let me—" Clem goes slack-jawed at the

book on top of the pile: *Laura Dean Keeps Breaking Up with Me*. Slowly, she grins. "That's my favorite!"

This is the beginning.

This is the beginning of Clem and me.

I take a step forward but Zelda grabs my arm and shakes her head: *No*. How did she know? How did she know I was going to run to that other version of me, grab her shoulders, and scream: *Don't ride your bike home on the twenty-seventh of May in four years' time*?

"We're not here for that," says Zelda. "Besides, she can't hear you and it's a paradox. If you don't die, then who goes to heaven, annoys the crap out of me, complains to my manager, and gets us *formally investigated* by the fun police?"

My head hurts. My head is about to explode.

"It works in the movies," I mutter.

I don't know what I expected from the investigation but it wasn't this. It wasn't time-traveling. It wasn't being a ghost in my own life.

I remember in high school when three boys from the basketball team got drunk on the bleachers and one of them fell and cracked his head open. He was fine; he spent a couple of days in the hospital but he didn't die. The next day, the story spread around school so fast. I stood at my locker before first period and watched the story move from one end of the hall to the other like a baton in a relay race—the story of drunk Steve almost dying, and now he's grounded, and his parents are talking about rehab, and did you know half his head caved in, and Maria said that Sarah said that Nick pushed him on purpose.

Did that happen when I died? Did Clem have to watch *Oh my*

God Tegan Masters got totaled by a Lexus running a stop sign and now she's dead get passed around the school? Did the principal gather everyone in the gym to tell them tearfully, *The rumors are true. Tegan Masters got pancaked on Virginia Avenue,* and did she have a cop give a talk about road safety, and did she offer everyone counseling with Mr. What's-his-face, and did people who didn't even know me cry their eyes out? Did Naomi Long cry? Will I get a whole page in the yearbook?

"It'll make sense," says Zelda. "I promise. You just have to pay attention, okay?"

I swallow over the lump in my throat as twelve-year-old Clem grins, her smile too big for her face. The other me stutters as she tries so hard to impress the girl with the cool stickers and the big smile and the rainbow pin on her sweater. Other me has only been at this school for two weeks but already she knows Clem is The One, the friendship Holy Grail. The one who will make her happy.

Happy.

I slap a hand over my mouth but not quickly enough to cover my bark of laughter. I don't know who's more startled, me or Zelda.

"What?" she says. "What's so funny?"

You know how sometimes you're in bed and it's dark and you spot a creepy shape in the corner of your room and freak out because, is that a *monster*? But then you turn on the light and see it's just the pile of clothes on your desk chair, so you breathe a sigh of relief and remember that monsters aren't real?

That's how I feel now.

"What's *hilarious* is that you made a big mistake," I say. "You can't show me this and expect me to think the Marybelle is better. I may have a few knives and forks out of place, but one thing I know for sure is that Clem made me happy. Way happier than soggy pizza and a blanket fort. And there's no way Kelvin won't see that."

I fold my arms and smirk. Admissions picked me for fast-track because whatever they saw in me wasn't messy enough to worry about. And they were right. I'll prove it. I just have to keep my cool and show Kelvin I've got my emotions under control. Which I can do. I did it all the time when I was alive. Most of the time anyway.

Zelda just looks at her blank wristwatch and nods. "Then I hope you're ready," she says. Before I can respond, she flicks my forehead and the world spins.

NINE

I'm standing in a rainforest. The hot air is syrup-thick and filled with the sound of birds screeching. My head spins.

Clem and twelve-year-old me have vanished. In their place is a waterfall, five tiers of water sloshing into rocky ponds where colorful birds bathe and—there's no other word for it—frolic.

"Is this the Garden of Eden?"

Zelda snorts. "As if you'd be allowed *there*. That's VIP, baby. Strictly need-to-know. This"—she spins a full circle—"is the National Aviary, Pittsburgh. The Tropical Rainforest enclosure, to be precise. Look! That's you!" She points at a sloth hanging upside down from a branch high up in the canopy.

She's right. Not about the sloth but about the location. Behind the lush tropical leaves are brick walls, and the ground under our feet is concrete, and beyond the canopy there's a glass ceiling. All around us, tourists hold up their camera phones. A woman on my left wears a uniform that says NATIONAL AVIARY, PITTS-BURGH. So, okay, I should have realized we weren't in the Garden of Eden. But I'm distracted. And disoriented. And motion-sick from time-traveling/being dead. So excuse my mild confusion.

"That's not me" is all I can think to say, pointing at the sloth.

"Well, it looks like you." Zelda marches away, weaving a loopy path through the crowd and the birds.

I look around. The water, the birdcalls, the heavy air—it stirs a memory in me, a memory hidden too far back in the fourth drawer to retrieve easily.

I catch up to Zelda. "How come we didn't stay at school?"

She points to a bird that looks like an orange Furby. "That's you," she says. "And we saw what we needed to. No loitering." She taps her blank watch and marches on, too fast for my little legs to keep up.

I jog to stay close. "But what did we see?"

She holds up the magnifying glass and her giant honey-golden eye blinks at me. "You tell me, Watson."

Clues. Right. I'm supposed to be objective. And see Zelda's calculations so clearly I can objectively say how much they suck.

We reach the rainforest exit, glass doors beaded with condensation. "I saw myself meeting Clem for the first time," I answer. Clean, objective, and succinct.

Ms. Chiu, are you impressed?

Zelda hums. She's not impressed. With a flick of her hand, the doors open and she slips through.

"Is that wrong?" I ask.

She points at a trash can. "That's you." She rushes through the atrium and toward the next enclosure: Condor Court.

"But that's definitely what I saw," I argue. I saw a lonely girl meet the friend of her dreams. Clementine Andrews. Sailor Moon fan. Basketball superstar. Loud and confident and funny, and she noticed me. She chose *me* to be her best friend. And it made me so, so happy.

Well, most of the time.

"That's right, isn't it?" I ask.

But Zelda only hums as she hurries through the gates into Condor Court.

In front of us is a huge cage full of rocky ledges and dead tree branches and giant birds that look like vultures but apparently are condors (is there a difference?). The birds perch on the rocks and branches, some with their wings extended and some just hunched and creepy-looking, waiting for someone to keel over and die so they can pick the flesh from their bones.

Two girls are pressed against the fence, watching the birds and laughing. They're familiar in a way that could bring me to my knees if I let the full tidal wave of feelings hit me. But I don't. Because feelings are *ugh* and because Kelvin is watching, hidden somewhere, scribbling on his clipboard. Because Admissions did not make a mistake about me.

"That's you!" says Zelda, pointing to what is, for once, actually me. "Eighth-grade science excursion. You got sunburned and it took two weeks for the skin to stop peeling. Clem decided she wanted an African gray parrot and begged her dads for months but they never gave in because African gray parrots live for forty-plus years and cost a buttload of cash. An owl shat on Paul's head and Lou said it was good luck but Paul said it was vandalism. Your science teacher threw up her lunch because she was pregnant but didn't know it yet."

Eighth-grade me links her arm through Clem's and beams at her. They must be thirteen. When they skip away together, they smile and giggle, singing a song I half recognize. Kind of like how I half recognize this memory now. It's not hidden anymore, but it's not clear, either—just flashes, feelings, all out of focus.

And if I'm honest, it's kind of a mess. It makes my head hurt; it makes my heart hurt more.

I take a deep breath.

"My wings are more impressive than yours, you overgrown turkey!" shouts Zelda to a condor flapping its wings. Zelda extends her own pearlescent, fluffy wings and turns to me. "Whose are better?"

"Yours," I mutter, and Zelda preens.

But I'm distracted as Clem and the other me disappear into an observation hut. I stand on my tippy-toes trying to keep them in view but I lose them around a corner.

"Wouldn't this be easier if you just told me what I'm supposed to see?" I ask. Maybe the birds ate Zelda's bread crumbs, the ones we're supposed to follow. That happened in "Hansel and Gretel," didn't it? They left a trail of bread crumbs but the birds ate them.

"Nope." Zelda pats my head with her wing. Like I'm a puppy. "Sucks, don't it?"

"You suck."

"I don't suck. I have the best wings in this entire aviary. You said so yourself. No take-backsies." She tickles the tip of my nose with her wing feathers until I swat her away. She laughs. "Come on. Let's follow."

I sigh and chase after her.

We follow my class through the displays—we follow but I still feel lost. Why here? Why now? I'll never be convinced by the Marybelle but if I can find the clue easily enough, Kelvin will know I'm ready for heaven. We pass the owls and the learning center and the—

"Penguins!" Zelda screeches. She runs to the enclosure, a pool of clear water and rocky caves. "I've never seen real penguins," she says, leaning over the fence. "Look! They waddle." She slaps my arm in disbelief. "They *waddle*!" Zelda presses her arms flat to her sides and waddles in a circle. "Look! I'm a penguin. Waddle, waddle, waddle."

She looks ridiculous in her detective suit. But she looks happy too.

Happy looks good on her.

And it makes me feel…I don't know. Warm. Fuzzy. Like my heart is a balloon seconds from popping.

I quickly look away, searching for Clem and thirteen-year-old me, and spy them sharing one of the pop-up viewing holes where you stick your head in and suddenly you're eye-to-beak with the penguins.

"I want to do that," says Zelda.

"Of course you do."

Zelda tugs me over to one and we squeeze in together.

"What do you see?" she asks.

"Penguins."

Zelda presses her nose to the plexiglass. "They're so cute. Waddle, waddle, waddle." Her entire right side is squished against me and it's a lot. We're breathing the same air, close enough for me to do a recount on those freckles. Yep. Still thirteen. They're like a cluster of suns. Imagine that—a galaxy just made up of suns.

"But that's not what I meant and you know it," she says.

I blink furiously, trying to remember what she asked me.

"Right. Clem and me."

I can do this. I can be objective and find the clue.

I scrunch up my face and think hard. But if I'm honest, it's all too distracting. How am I supposed to see anything clearly and objectively when all I can think about is how much I miss my best friend? I've never been dead before. It's hard to keep a handle on my emotions and deal with the whole being dead thing at the same time. But I'll manage. I always do.

"I guess…I see Clem and me having fun," I say. "I see how happy I am. I see how happy I am in comparison to the weekend at the Marybelle ergo you really suck at this challenge."

"First of all," says Zelda, face squished against the plexiglass, "I do not suck. Second of all, do you think we could smuggle a penguin into the Marybelle? We have water. I could get us fish. Just think about it. And third of all, keep looking. You'll see it."

She grabs my hand and ducks out of the tube, dragging me with her. My classmates have moved on and I can't see Clem anymore. It makes my heart race like I'm a parent in a busy mall who's lost sight of their child. It reminds me that this is all temporary, that any second now Zelda will snap her fingers or click her heels together and we'll be back at the Marybelle.

I don't want to go back.

We weave through a group of elementary schoolers squealing at the penguins.

If I think about this like a jigsaw puzzle, the smart thing to do would be to fill in the edges, the obvious things. But nothing is obvious. Because if these memories are supposed to be clues that point to what made me happy at the Marybelle, then why start with Clem? She wasn't even there.

If she had been, that weekend might have sucked less. Because Clem did make me happy. Before Clem, I was bad at making friends. I had a best friend in elementary school, but she had a best friend and it wasn't me. Sometimes I played with a boy who lived two doors down, creating fantasy worlds full of dragons and princes and wizards in his sandbox. But he moved. At St. Anne's, I was bullied by three girls who said I had buckteeth and gay shoes and that no one was allowed to make friends with me. That's why I changed middle schools. And then I met Clem, and somehow, she liked me, even when I was being myself.

But Clem wasn't at the Marybelle.

We stop at the wetlands. Zelda frowns at a guy selling ice cream sandwiches out of a cart on the side of the path.

"Do you want an ice cream sandwich?" I ask, confused.

She jerks like I've slapped her. "No. Why would I? The rules are very strict. No loitering and no detours."

"But kidnapping penguins is okay?"

"*Pft.* I could fit one under my jacket. Your sweater is big enough to hide three. We could—" She pauses, frowning at the ice cream cart like it grew a mouth and insulted her wings. After a long period of frowning, she turns slowly, scanning our surroundings for…what? I don't know. She turns to the ice cream cart again, then looks at me. "Food is good for triggering memories, isn't it?"

I shrug. I honestly have no idea.

"It is," she says with certainty. "Food is a good memory trigger." She looks up at the sky. "So we should eat ice cream sandwiches to ensure you connect as deeply as possible with this memory!" she shouts. Is she still talking to me? "It's part of my process." She nods and marches over to the cart. "It's scientific," she mutters. "So suck it, Kelvin."

Zelda chooses the coffee on snickerdoodle. "That's a fun word. Snickerdoodle." She waggles her fingers and the sandwich appears in her hand. "Snickerdoodle. *Snickerdoodle.* What are you getting, my little snickerdoodle?"

I point at the chocolate on peanut butter. "That one. And don't call me snickerdoodle."

Zelda waggles her fingers again and the sandwich appears in my hand. "Eat, my little snickerdoodle. Soak yourself in the memory."

I never ate ice cream on this day. But as I lick the corner of the sandwich, I'm reminded of a different day, one when I did eat ice cream. It was two days before I died, and me and Clem were sitting on the swing set in the playground near the river. I told Clem a joke and she laughed so hard she dropped her Fudgsicle. I almost peed my pants laughing at the look on her face. Then Lou joined us and she told a joke that was even funnier and I watched Clem's ice cream melt into the bark chips and I felt sick.

Why do I remember that? Why now? I'm worried my memories are all messed up, like Ms. Chiu said. I think sometimes I'm seeing more than one at the same time. Like a double exposure, one image superimposed on top of the other and then another on top of that and another and another. How am I supposed to find Zelda's bread crumbs when the memories crowd me like that?

I shake my head. None of these memories with Clem matter anyway. None of them change the fact that the Marybelle sucked.

Zelda takes a bite and her whole face lights up. "Amazing," she says, taking another giant bite. With her mouth full, she waves a hand in the vague direction of the wetlands. "So, you're eating ice cream, the memories are flowing, have you figured it out?"

I haven't even taken a bite yet. "I'm trying."

"Are you?" Zelda raises a brow. "Are you really? Or should I do a Tegan and complain to Kelvin that you're not trying hard enough?"

I huff and turn away. "Are you allowed to be this mean to a dead person?"

"I'm not mean. I love humans. They're like big furless cats. Would you like your belly rubbed?"

I look down at the sandwich melting through my fingers. I don't even want it anymore. "Hands off my belly," I mutter.

She snorts. "For real. You're like a cat. Grumpy. Contrary. A little bit evil. Cute."

Cute? What am I supposed to do with *cute*? I do not have the brain capacity to deal with *cute*.

"Did you know cats are plotting murder eighty-seven percent of the time?" she continues, oblivious to how thoroughly *she* is the one murdering *me*. "It's all in the design."

"Just eat your ice cream."

"I can eat and talk at the same time. I'm vastly talented."

"Then eat mine." I shove it at her.

She accepts it gladly. "What was I saying? Wow, peanut butter is gross."

"You were telling me that cats are murderers."

She sighs. "It's a shame you never went to a cat café. We could have taken one of our excursions there. I could have made it work." For a moment there's something genuinely sad in her eyes and it makes me feel squirmy. I don't like it. I don't like any of this.

"My neighbor when I was a kid had a cat and one time I saw it beat up a raccoon," I say. I have no idea why I say this.

"You're a raccoon," she says.

I poke out my tongue.

"Look over there." She nods at the flamingos.

But it's not the flamingos she wants me to see. My class has arrived, half of them leaning over the barriers, trying to get closer to the giant pink birds. I search the crowd for familiar brown hair. Luckily Clem always stands out, a head taller than every-one around her. She was my beacon—I could never get lost with Clem around.

I see her.

She's laughing, bent over double and clutching her stomach. Paul's face is red and he can hardly stand upright. He always laughed with his whole body; sometimes he'd laugh so hard he'd fall out of his chair.

They're laughing at a girl who is parading up and down the path like a model on a catwalk, her head swiveling side to side and her neck so elongated the tendons look like ropes.

Suddenly the girl stops and stretches out her left arm and her left leg, making a weird turkey *gobble-gobble* noise. Then she starts catwalking again. "I saw it on Animal Planet," the girl says. "Flamingo mating dance." She grins and Clem and Paul laugh. I see melted ice cream on bark chips and I feel sick. It's too many memories at once, like dominoes falling so fast they're just a blur.

But I remember. I remember why this day was important.

Because it's eighth grade.

Because it's September.

Because the girl doing the flamingo dance is Lou.

This is the day we met Louisa Lacuerda. This moment, right here.

"Oh my God," wheezes Clem. "I'm going to shit my spleen if you don't stop."

Lou dissolves into giggles and Clem swats her arm. They talk, exchange names, realize they share a PE class, talk about Sailor Moon. Lou screams. "Sailor Mars is my girlfriend!" They laugh and jump up and down with excitement and clasp hands. And all the while thirteen-year-old me stares at their backs.

"Interesting," says Zelda. She shoves the last of my ice cream sandwich into her mouth.

I almost grasp something then—like the black spots that sometimes dance on the edges of your vision but when you turn your head they're gone. Looking at Clem, at Lou and Paul and younger me, I almost see something. Something important hidden in the mess. I feel it—like a half-forgotten dream, like déjà vu—but I can't put the feeling into words.

It vanishes before I can fully grasp it.

I'm not sure I want to.

"Seen enough?" says Zelda. She licks her sticky fingers.

"I've…"

They walk away. Clem bounces as she walks, a ball of energy between Lou and Paul. She throws her head back and laughs at whatever Lou has just said; thirteen-year-old me trails behind them, jogging to keep up.

I remind myself I can do this. I've got it all under control.

"Yeah," I say. "I've seen enough."

Zelda taps my head and the world spins.

TEN

The noise hits me first. A sonic sucker punch to the face: music, laughter, metallic pings and electronic trills and heavy, rhythmic footsteps. Then the lights hit: strobes of purple, pink, green, red. I see neon signs and flashing computer graphics: NEW PLAYER, GAME OVER, PRESS START.

Holy time travel from the afterlife, Batman.

We're at Game Zone, a three-story warehouse packed wall to wall with everything from *Donkey Kong* to *Daytona* to my personal favorite, *Dance Dance Revolution* (I had the highest score seven weeks running, suck it JoshasaurusRex11). It was the coolest place to hang for a hot minute when we were thirteen.

And now I'm back. I'm *in* it. Burrowed all the way in like a tick.

And I have no idea why.

"Welcome to the final stop of our whirlwind first excursion," says Zelda, her gaze ping-ponging from one machine to the next. She reminds me of Trash Cat the Elder, the way he ogles the nub of sausage in my hand with naked hunger. "It's loud."

It is loud. And crowded and stuffy and stinky and *fun;* it's friends, high scores, and hot dogs. It's video game deaths, where you get three lives and if you burn through every one of them you just chuck a couple more tokens in and start over again.

"I don't get it." I turn to Zelda. A bunch of kids run past, skirting around us like we're rocks in a river. "This path, the clues, your bread crumbs, your calculations, whatever you want to call it, it makes no sense. How do you go from Clem, to Lou, to *Game Zone*?"

I thought I had it. I'd almost grasped those black spots dancing in my peripheral vision. But now I'm completely lost again.

She bops me on the nose with her magnifying glass. "You're cute when you're confused. You look like an otter."

I flush with embarrassment. "An otter?"

"Otters are cute."

Cute? Again? I will go insane. "I thought I looked like a sloth."

"It's both. Now focus over there or you'll miss it."

I whip my head around in time to see four familiar figures weave through the crowd, holding hands like a human daisy chain. Clem, Paul, Lou, and me. Strobe lights paint their skin red. They smile and laugh; they are so alive.

"Clementine's fourteenth birthday party," says Zelda.

The memory falls into place, and I scramble to contain the messy feelings threatening to spill out as I look at the four of them.

They're just so alive.

"You ate two hot dogs with bacon, pineapple, and barbecue sauce," Zelda says, like she's narrating a nature documentary, "and you set a new record on *Dance Dance Revolution*. Paul ate four hot dogs with kimchi and cheese and barfed between two *Free Throw Frenzy* machines. Lou got a high score on *Daytona* and Clem got blisters on her feet from new shoes. Before you went home you plucked a mangy-looking plushie out of the claw machine, which you later gave to your sister. It was your idea to call it Trash Monkey."

I watch, transfixed, as fourteen-year-old me makes a beeline for *Dance Dance Revolution*. "Clem?" she calls. But Lou snatches Clem's wrist and hauls them both onto the raised platforms. Fourteen-year-old me watches them dance, the floor tiles flashing beneath their feet. They miss a bunch of steps, too uncoordinated, laughing too hard. "It's my birthday!" Clem yells. "You need to let me win!" They cry laughing when it's over and Clem reaches out to fist-bump fourteen-year-old me, her braces glinting in the pink lights. Other me shouts, "You and me next?" but Lou is already tugging Clem away.

"Do you need a pen and paper to take notes?" asks Zelda.

I swallow down my rising panic. This is…why is she showing me this?

Clem and Lou stumble off the dance floor. Paul slings an arm around Clem's shoulders and whispers in her ear. She laughs. Lou points toward the back of the arcade and says something I can't hear over the noise. She grabs Clem's hand and leads her away. Fourteen-year-old me struggles to keep up with them.

I grip my chest where it hurts. How can a dead heart hurt so much?

Zelda spins the magnifying glass between her palms and I watch it, sort of like I'm being hypnotized, and that feeling I'm trying to grasp, that half-forgotten dream or déjà vu or whatever it is, becomes a little clearer.

I turn to Zelda; she's already looking at me.

"How do you feel about hot dogs?" she asks, and that is…not what I was expecting her to say.

"What does that have to do with—"

She flicks my forehead and suddenly we're upstairs, where there's a giant ball pit and a jungle gym and the claw machines. And a hot dog cart.

"We skipped ahead," explains Zelda, marching toward the food. "And I need you to dig way, way deep into this memory, trigger *all* the emotions. Thus, hot dogs. Are they made with real dogs? Because that feels wrong."

I look around for Clem and the others but I can't see them because it's too dark and too crowded and maybe I don't want to see them. Maybe I'm scared to grasp the truth at my fingertips in case it burns.

"Why aren't mushrooms a topping?" asks Zelda, peering up at the menu board.

She should be skipping around me, poking her tongue out, singing *nah nah ne nah nah*, saying, *Don't you see it, Tegan? Don't you see the clue? It's right in front of you!* But she's ordering a hot dog. "Ooh! Blue cheese, celery, and buffalo wing sauce. Blue cheese smells like vomit." She claps her hands together. "I'll get that one."

Enigma, I think. Layer upon layer of weird and complicated and spiky and confusing and a thousand things I haven't glimpsed yet.

She does an elaborate flick of her fingers and suddenly there's a hot dog with bacon, pineapple, and barbecue sauce in my hand.

She sniffs hers. "It really smells like vomit," she says. She takes a bite, chewing slowly. Her whole face screws up in disgust before she grins and takes another, bigger bite. It's hard to take my eyes off her. "Tastes like vomit too. Amazing."

"Why are you so weird?"

She shrugs. "Spoilers."

"That's not—"

"Time for the final act." She nods at something over my shoulder.

I turn around and my stomach sinks. I haven't even taken a bite of my hot dog and already I feel sick. Because this is it. This is what I didn't want to see.

Clem and fourteen-year-old me are in front of the claw machine, an awkward distance between them.

"Lou's waiting for me downstairs," says Clem, squeezing her phone into her back pocket. "We're going to play *Daytona*. Best of three and whoever loses has to eat three helpings of Monday Mystery Meatballs at school. You want to watch?"

Fourteen-year-old me fiddles with the claw machine controls, trying to hide her disappointment. "But we haven't…" Her voice trails away. How skin-peelingly weird is it to hear your own voice coming out of a whole different body, a younger body, a still-alive body? *Ugh.*

"Haven't what?" prods Clem.

"I haven't seen you much today. We haven't played anything together. You and Lou played *Free Throw*, you played *Dance Dance Revolution*, you played air hockey."

Clem shakes her head. She hates confrontation. "We're all here, all playing games. It's fun. Just join in. No one's stopping you."

The frustration pouring off fourteen-year-old me makes my toes curl. I can see how tightly she's wound; how small she's trying to make herself because she doesn't want to let her feelings spill out into the open in case they stain. (She doesn't know the stains are already there, on the inside, on her soul.) "I was— How can I join in when Lou's always there?"

Clem frowns. "That's not fair. I'm just having fun. It's my birthday and I want to spend it with *all* my friends."

"But you're not doing that. I can't get near you without Lou tugging you away somewhere, just the two of you."

Clem's shoulders rise and fall as she takes a deep breath. "It's not…" She toys with the end of her braid, her nervous fingers seeking a distraction. "You're not being fair. It's my birthday and you're making it about you. I said you could join in but you don't want to because we're not doing what *you* want to do. At least Lou is making sure I have fun."

The words cut. Even now, when I'm just a bystander, they cut. It's an old wound, open again. Fourteen-year-old me doesn't know what to say. She can't hide her hurt.

When the silence stretches on too long, Clem huffs. "Forget it," she says. "You can join in or you can sulk. Your choice."

She doesn't wait for a response. She turns on her heel and walks away.

Fourteen-year-old me watches her, hands curling into fists at her side. Once Clem is gone, she kicks the base of the claw machine once, twice, three times, then starts stabbing the controls, tugging on the joystick hard enough that the machine rocks side to side. The claws grasp at nothing and she curses over and over again until a mangy-looking orange monkey falls down the chute and she yanks it out. She frowns at it for a moment, then tucks it under her arm and marches away.

I watch her leave and feel a tug in my stomach like I need to follow her, like there's an invisible rope tying us together. It hurts to stay where I am.

"Listen, Tegan—" starts Zelda, but I don't want to do this. I won't be able to hold back the soft, broken parts if we do this. Admissions didn't get it wrong, I swear. But that doesn't mean I don't have a few knives out of place. It doesn't mean I won't cut myself if I go digging where I shouldn't.

So I point. "I wanted the cat. See?" Zelda follows my outstretched arm. There's a black-and-white kitten smooshed against the glass in the claw machine. "I was trying to win the cat because Quinn's favorite cartoon was *Tom and Jerry* and it looked like Tom. Or Jerry. Whichever one is the cat. I can't remember which is which. Actually, I don't think I ever knew. Do you know?"

"Tom is the cat."

I look at the kitten plushie now and actually it doesn't look like Tom. Tom was lanky and mean-looking. This cat is round and cute, big eyes and a little pink tongue poking out. Quinn would have loved it.

"Trash Cat Baby," I say. "That's what I would have called it."

Zelda looks at the claw machine, face all scrunched up in confusion. I see her lips move but no sound comes out. *Trash cat baby,* she mouths. Slowly, the wrinkles even out and she smiles. All teeth and gums and a sharp kind of beauty that doubles the size of the lump in my throat.

"I like it," she says. She bounces on her toes. "But we're not here for the cat."

I look at the plushie because it's easier and I don't answer her because keeping silent is easier too. Barbecue sauce drips down my finger.

"You see it, don't you?" she needles.

"You suck."

"Yeah, but Kelvin sucks more so tell me you see it."

I release a shaky breath. "I see it," I admit. It's not floating in the corner of my eye anymore. I see it. Clear and real and right in front of me. Sharp enough to cut. "It was girl meets best friend, best friend meets new girl, girl gets jealous. Happy?"

"Why would that make me happy?"

I shake my head. "I don't know."

"I don't *want* to do this," says Zelda. "I *have* to. It's my job. You made it my job."

She stares me down until I look away. This was so much easier when I was confused. "Fine. I see it. I get it. But it's got nothing to do with the Marybelle." I gesture at the claw machine. There's no more Clem and no more me but I can almost see them there, one memory superimposed onto another. I see it all—Clem at the lockers, at the aviary, Lou doubled over laughing, ice cream, flashing tiles, angry Clem, my heart breaking. "I was jealous." I wipe my face, surprised to find my cheeks damp. "But it's got nothing to do with—"

Between one blink and the next, a figure appears, filling the space in front of the claw machine that fourteen-year-old me left empty. A boy. Black clothes, greasy bangs, clipboard.

I dry my eyes. "Shit."

Kelvin scowls at us both. His gaze skitters over the half-eaten hot dog in Zelda's hand, the crumb of blue cheese on her cheek, my tears, the soft, broken parts of me on show for all the world to see. I swallow, fear making my mouth dry.

"Thought you were supposed to be discreet?" snaps Zelda, hiding the hot dog behind her back. "Thought I wasn't going to have to see your annoying face?"

Kelvin's scowl grows deeper but he still doesn't say anything. Slowly, he brings his hand up to the clipboard and makes a mark on the page. A cross.

I blink and he vanishes.

"Damn you," I mutter. I take a deep breath, trying to loosen the anxiety, the fear, the anger. It doesn't work. "Damn it, Zelda."

"Hey, I hate that guy more than you," she says, pouting. "He's such a suck."

"But I'm the one whose soul he wants to scour."

"Is that so bad?" She waves her hand around. "You want to keep all this? It made you cry."

Do I? Downstairs right now, fourteen-year-old me is calling her dad, begging him to pick her up. He skips a meeting with his accountant to come but she won't tell him why she's crying. Then Clem doesn't talk to her for a week, not until fourteen-year-old me apologizes. Clem will tell her it's okay, that she's not angry anymore. But she is. She's cold, distant. Fourteen-year-old me will spend the next month trying too hard, talking too much, clinging to Clem's side like a leech. It's a shitty memory.

But it's still Clem. I only knew her for four years. If I add up all the time we spent together, it's not enough. And if I start carving out some of that time, every moment that was less than perfect, what am I left with then?

Before Clem, I was invisible. Then she saw me. She *saw* me. She saw my weird, awkward, queer little heart and she asked me to have lunch with her. She became my friend, my best friend. Even the worst moments—the doubt and the worry and the fights. It's all part of her and me. I don't want to lose a second of it.

I jolt as Zelda's blank wristwatch begins to beep.

"Time's up," she says.

Panic rushes through me. I can't leave yet. What if this is it? What if I don't get to see Clem again?

"Wait!" I cry, but Zelda is quicker.

She flicks my forehead hard—too hard. In the blink of an eye, we're back at the Marybelle. My forehead is aching and Tammy is floating and there's no Clem and no Lou or Paul and no Game Zone and no heartbeat in my chest. But there *is* an uneaten hot dog in my hands and there *is* a black-and-white stuffed cat in Zelda's.

"You stole Trash Cat Baby?" I stare at her in disbelief.

She shrugs. "At least it wasn't a penguin," she says.

Poof! She vanishes.

ELEVEN

"You know how you look like that?" I wave my hand up and down at the whole Ms. Chiu-ness of the shapeshifting-immortal-therapy-bot thingy sitting opposite me. "And you make the room turn into all of this?" I wave my arms around the cubicle: the essays, the lipstick-stained coffee cups, the battered copy of *Macbeth*.

Ms. Chiu nods and smiles. Her browny-apricot lipstick matches the stain on the coffee cup and if I made her smile wide enough, I bet I'd see matching smears on her teeth too, because Ms. Chiu always had lipstick on her teeth and that was just another reason to love her.

"Well, can you change it?" I ask.

"Change?"

"I don't want *you* to change," I rush to say. "I like that you look like Ms. Chiu. She was cool. But can you change the location? Can you turn this into the library? Or the Andy Warhol Museum? Or the zoo? Oh! Or Red Robin? I'd die for a burger."

Ms. Chiu laughs.

"These sessions are for you to come to terms with your death," she says, folding her hands in her lap. "It's important you feel safe and happy. So…"

She doesn't wiggle her fingers like Zelda. She doesn't move a muscle. It's more like, one second we're in the office, the next we're sitting opposite each other in Red Robin.

The restaurant is empty but there's a familiar smell of grease and salt in the air and the red vinyl booth is sticky and so are the table and the plastic menu. "Guess what?" I say. "I just came to terms with being dead. Thank you, Red Robin."

Ms. Chiu tilts her head. "Have you?"

"Have I what?" I drag the sticky menu across the table and open it.

"Come to terms with being dead?"

"If I say no will you keep bringing me back here?"

She smiles wide. There it is: lipstick (browny-apricot) smudged on her teeth. "Perhaps," she says.

My heart squeezes so I look away. I scan the menu instead, turning my nose up at the 'Shroom Burger option. Gross. Quinn always got that and every time she bit into it the mushrooms would spill everywhere. "Your burger is pooping mushrooms," I'd say, and Quinn would hit me so I'd say it again and again until she whined at Dad to shut me up. "Don't tell your sister her burger is pooping, Tegan," he'd say, and Quinn and me would laugh because Dad said "poop."

I bet Zelda would order the 'Shroom Burger.

"I'm getting the Banzai Burger," I announce, "because pineapple is the best, and a side of steak fries and a Freckled Lemonade. Please. Thank you."

The second I close the menu, everything I ordered is waiting in front of me. Now that's customer service.

"This is cool." I grab the burger and take a jaw-cracking bite.

It tastes like…*not* lukewarm soggy pizza and *not* sweaty salty bad Chinese and *not* bland burritos, so double thumbs-up.

"Was there something in particular you wanted to talk about today?" asks Ms. Chiu. Sunlight from the window illuminates her parrot earrings. They almost glow. "It's our second session. And I hear a lot has happened since I last saw you."

I shrug. "Are you going to eat too?"

"I don't eat."

"Zelda eats."

"I can eat. But I don't have to. So I don't."

I shovel a fry into my mouth. "But don't you miss it?" Who wouldn't want to eat greasy deep-fried potatoes slathered in salt and spices? That's God-tier food. Food of the angels.

"I've never tried it." She shrugs, elegant and birdlike. "I don't think I can miss what I've never tried."

She watches me eat and I watch her parrot earrings glow in the sunlight and it's kind of nice. Even if it's not real. Even if I'm dead.

"Would you like to talk about the investigation, Tegan?" she asks.

I set my burger down and wipe my hands with a paper napkin. "Sure. We can talk about why Zelda is such a dickcheese."

"A dickcheese?"

I made an angel say "dickcheese." I bet no one in the history of ever has managed to accomplish that. Suck it, humanity.

I toss the used napkin into the center of the table. "On the one hand I'm pretty sure she's using this investigation to torture me so I'll have a meltdown and Kelvin will haul my ass to purgatory and she'll win. But on the other hand she likes penguins. And people who like penguins can't be all bad, right?"

It's confusing because sometimes Zelda makes me forget I'm supposed to hate her. She makes me think, *Hey, you're cool and weird and interesting and I want to unravel all your layers and know you*. Which is sad and annoying. Because she's made it pretty clear what she thinks of me.

"Do you really want to spend our time talking about Zelda?" asks Ms. Chiu. "Or do you want to talk about what happened when you visited your memories? When you saw Clem?"

Ugh.

"It sucked," I say. It's been a couple of days since Zelda unceremoniously dumped me in those memories and the emotional hangover is still kicking my butt.

"And?" says Ms. Chiu.

I snort. *Why did it suck, Tegan? How did it make you feel? Use quotes, sources, and references, please.*

"It sucked for a lot of reasons," I answer, sitting back with a thump. "What you said before: How can I miss something if I've never tried it? Well, I've tried it. I've *lived* it. So I have plenty of things to miss. And I miss Clem."

"Is that the only thing that sucked? Missing Clem?"

Is Red Robin worth this conversation? "I don't understand why you're all so preoccupied with making me talk about things that make me sad. Isn't that, like, for the living?" My eyes flick to the floor. "It's what Mr. What's-his-face, the school counselor, tried to do but I told him what I'll tell you now. Laying my troubles out in the open for you to poke and prod at doesn't help me. It hurts me. And it changes nothing. So what's the point?"

Ms. Chiu runs her finger along the menu, picking at a spot where the plastic is pulling away. There's still a smudge of green ink on that finger, like the first time I saw her. "You've been told about purgatory, Tegan," she says. "You know getting into heaven isn't all smooth sailing. Your soul needs to be prepared. It needs to be tidied so it can be ready to accept pure happiness. Either you clean it yourself—with my help—or purgatory does it for you. At length. Forcefully."

I groan, frustrated. "But I've got all that under control. Why do I need to shine a spotlight on the things that suck? Isn't it better not to stir things up?"

"Do you really have it under control?"

"That's why Admissions picked me for fast-tracking, isn't it? Because my drawer was tidy enough."

"Maybe they got it wrong."

"Or maybe Zelda did. I bet you've seen my so-called happiest memory. Do *you* think Zelda's calculations were right?"

Ms. Chiu shifts her gaze down to her finger, picking away at the plastic. She frowns. "I think it's complicated."

"Did you see me crying in that room?" I press. "Did you hear me tell Dad how scared I was? A blanket fort doesn't fix that. Especially not when we got home and—"

"And what?"

I scoff and pick up my burger. "I don't care about that anyway."

"I think you care a lot."

"I think you're full of shit."

Ms. Chiu smiles and it makes me angry.

"That doesn't have anything to do with Clem anyway," I say, taking another bite.

"Then why do you think Zelda showed you those memories about Clem?"

"Stuffed if I know," I say, mouth half full. "I didn't even tell Clem about the Marybelle, not right away. I was going to, the day after we got back, but she was all giggly with Lou at the lockers that day. They'd just been hiking and wouldn't shut up about it, talking at the same time, telling the same stories over and over, swapping in-jokes. Clem was...*ugh*, this is such a cliché but she was like a sunflower, you know? Sunflowers always turn to face the sun and Lou was the sun." I take another bite and mayo dribbles down my finger. Everything is so messy—my fingers are sticky, there's grease dripping everywhere, and crumbs are scattered all over the table. "So I decided not to say anything to Clem about the Marybelle, because Lou had funny stories and in-jokes and hiking and what did I have? Tears and a shitty blanket fort and more sadness than I knew what to do with."

I blow out a breath. God, I hate being honest. Being honest feels like swallowing a swarm of wasps. Which is exactly why I'm right and Ms. Chiu and Mr. What's-his-face are wrong. Talking about what makes you sad only makes you sadder.

"You think being sad makes you less likable?" asks Ms. Chiu.

"I think I'm awkward," I say. "And shy. And boring. And when I meet people all I can think is: *Don't be too much! Hide your weird! Be a normal, cool person!* That's why I learned to become a shapeshifter, like you. To turn myself into whoever I thought people wanted me to be. At least, I tried to, but apparently I sucked at it because they always worked out who I really was and they didn't like it. They didn't like me."

My stomach twists. I force myself to take another bite but suddenly the burger doesn't taste so good.

"When I first met Clem, I didn't have to do that with her. Because she liked me the way I was. Clem fell in love with friends instantly, though. It was like, *Oh, you like that book? Me too! Let's be best friends forever!*

"Then Lou came along and she was so much cooler than me and Clem *loved* her. And it freaked me out seeing her fall for someone else. I thought it meant she would fall out of love with me. I thought if she loved Lou more than me I'd have to go back to being invisible. And I thought *If I'm competing against someone like Lou I can't be in tears all the time*—that's the antithesis of sunshine. I'd lose for sure. And I couldn't bear that. So I decided to be a shapeshifter again. I hid the ugly bits and the sad bits and I tried so hard to be the sun. I really did."

Until the weekend at the Marybelle. After that, I couldn't sleep and I couldn't focus and I bombed one too many tests and I lost it. I really lost it. Right in the middle of fifth period. They called Dad and they made me go to counseling, which sucked, but the worst part was finally having to tell Clem what was going on. I frown at the mess in front of me as I remember.

"Clem was mad it took me two weeks to tell her about the Marybelle. Or maybe she was hurt. But then she hugged me, let me get her T-shirt all wet with my snotty tears. She hardly let me out of her sight after that. Constant sleepovers, always trying to make me laugh, choosing me over Lou every time."

I look up at Ms. Chiu. "It didn't even feel good," I say. "It felt like a consolation prize. Like she was only spending time with me because she pitied me."

Ms. Chiu smiles. "Her friendship meant a lot to you. It brought you happiness. It's understandable you would—"

I shake my head. "That's not happiness. That's being selfish. I wanted to keep her focused on me and only me forever. Because

I thought if Clem wasn't looking at me, if she was looking at Lou instead, then I'd become invisible again. I'd go back to being a ghost. But what about her? What about what she wanted? I didn't even think about it. That's messed up."

"But you're thinking about it now. That's good."

With a grimace, I drop my half-eaten burger and push it away. I feel sick. "Why is it good?" I ask. Because I seriously think my way is better. Keep everything locked up tight. "Why do I have to confront this stuff?"

"Because you can't accept that something is true until you *know* it to be true," says Ms. Chiu. "Zelda could tell you why she chose the Marybelle, but would you believe her?" She leans forward, parrots dancing. "How will you know unless you really look?"

I did look. But all I saw was *un*happiness.

And that's the problem, isn't it? Zelda's not asking me to look at what made me happy. It's the opposite. She's showing me the things that hurt. Almost like she wants me to fail.

Which, of course she does. If I fail, she wins.

"I am looking," I say. Because I won't let Zelda win. I *am* ready to be happy.

No matter how much I loved Clem, there was always going to be that feeling, that walking-on-ice-and-wondering-when-it-was-going-to-crack feeling of: What happens when she drifts away? For good this time? But that doesn't mean I wasn't happy too.

Because even the things that hurt hurt in a way I don't want to lose. Because feeling sad means I miss my friends, which means I was someone, once, who had friends. And if I'm not someone who cares about Clem and my friends and my family then who am I? Missing them is all I have left. Who am I if heaven takes those feelings away from me?

Ms. Chiu opens her mouth to say more but I push my fries toward her. She looks at them and back up at me.

"How will you know you if you don't try?" I raise my brow in challenge.

With a faint smile, she reaches out. Her fingers are long and delicate, her nails clipped short and painted apricot. She picks up a fry, holds it in front of her face, turning it this way and that, inspecting it like those dudes who look at diamonds with a magnifying glass thingy in one eye. She shrugs, then pops it in her mouth.

"Verdict?" I ask.

"I see the appeal," she says. She takes another fry and plops it in her mouth without inspection. "I think I would miss this," she says. "If it was taken away from me."

I nod and reach for the basket. I'm glad we can agree on one thing.

TWELVE

Feet are gross.

I hate toes that are long and thin like fingers. I hate hairy toes and cracked heels and foot fungus and bunions and sweaty socks and novelty socks. Feet are worse than feelings.

I hated working at Dad's shop. I hated it so much I used to daydream about stabbing myself with a shoehorn fifty times every shift. Honestly, the best thing about being dead is I'll never have to go near a stranger's foot again.

So it's super annoying that Zelda *poof!*ed into the seat opposite me at breakfast this morning after a week of being MIA, flicked my forehead, and now I'm in Dad's shop with a mouthful of egg, watching fifteen-year-old me fit sneakers onto a squirming kid with sweaty *Moana* socks. I turn to Zelda.

"Really?"

She shrugs. "I work in mysterious ways."

"Check her toes," demands the kid's mom. She's got pointy nails (green) and there's something familiar about her but I can't pin down what. It's like when you can't remember a word but it's dancing on the tip of your tongue. She reminds me of something. Something big.

I have a creeping, swamp-monster-rising-out-of-the-mud kind of feeling that bad things are coming my way.

Other me kneels on the itchy carpet and thumbs the empty space at the top of the girl's shoe. Her smile says: *I am looking forward to a shoehorn death.* The little girl's brother dances on a fitting chair wearing a pair of Nikes on his hands, bashing the soles together and chanting "Burrito" over and over. The mother ignores him.

I look around but it's just me working in the shop. I kind of want to know where Dad is, but I also kind of don't. I'm still nursing an emotional hangover from the last memory trip so I'm not sure how my heart will cope with more. Especially seeing Dad.

Did he wake up at 3 a.m. and drive and drive and never stop when he found out I was dead? If he holed up in a motel room, who was there to worry about him? To remind him he couldn't give up?

"How's it hanging?" asks Zelda. "Found those foosballs yet?"

I turn to her. She looks tired, lines around her eyes and mouth. I'd feel sorry for her but she left me alone for nine days.

"I haven't looked," I say. Which is a lie. I absolutely turned the rec room inside out looking. What else am I supposed to do?

Zelda shrugs. "Well, anyway. This is trip número dos," she says, inspecting a loafer she stole from the shelf behind us. "Excited?"

Tired, confused, anxious, and dead—I'm a lot of things but I'm not excited. I *am* still certain she's doing this to sabotage me. My conversation with Ms. Chiu didn't convince me otherwise. "We're basically at the halfway point and you decided to take me to the mall so I could remember how much I hated feet?"

"Nope." Zelda bops the end of my nose with the loafer and

grins at my unimpressed face. "The clue is right there, you just have to know where to look."

"Sounds like hard work."

"No one said this was going to be fun."

"You suck."

"You love me."

I turn away, cheeks on fire. I don't love her. I hate her.

(Except when I forget to hate her.)

"They're perfect," says other Tegan on her knees, smiling up at the mother. "Plenty of room for her to grow into."

"Burrito!"

The little girl squirms in her chair, chin tucked into the collar of her soccer jersey. "I hate them," she whines.

"Burrito. Burrito. Burrito."

The mother closes her eyes in frustration, breathes deeply. She looks like she'd rather be anywhere else. Like she wants to get up and leave them both in the shop, maybe get drunk, maybe eat an entire chocolate cake uninterrupted, maybe pack her bags, disconnect her phone, and move far, far away.

I curl my hands into fists at my side.

"Although…" Zelda chucks the loafer back on the shelf. "This *is* fun. For me. This is fun for me."

I huff. "Why? Because I'm suffering?"

"I mean, yeah. I did a perfect job on your heaven but you snitched, babe. And payback is a bitch. Oooh these are cute." She runs her hand over a pair of maroon creepers. "Your dad has a nice shop."

I swallow over the lump lodged in my throat. My dad does have a nice shop. My dad, who is definitely somewhere nearby. Probably doing inventory in the storeroom. I could run and throw my arms around him and hug him tighter than I've ever hugged him before and at most it would take me ten seconds to reach him.

I can't breathe. I mean I literally can't but also I *can't*.

"Listen," I say, shoving all of that deep, deep down where Kelvin can't see it. "At Paul's thirteenth birthday we camped in the backyard and Clem told a story about this guy who went into surgery for a heart transplant but instead of a new heart they gave him a new kidney."

"Great story," says Zelda.

"Shut up. This is an analogy. You're the doctor and I'm the patient."

"I gave you an unnecessary kidney?"

"Imagine I wake up and I'm like, *Dr. Zelda? Why did you swap out my kidney? My kidneys were fine. I was supposed to get a heart. If I don't get a new heart, I'll die.* And you're like, *Why, yes! That does seem a tad inconvenient, but just look at these beautiful, tiny stitches.* Would I be a snitch if I reported you to the medical police or would that be making a valid complaint?"

"Snitches *do* get stitches," says Zelda.

I have to bite the inside of my cheek to keep from laughing. Because, yes, that was funny. Damn her.

Zelda cracks up at her own joke, snorting loudly and slapping her knee. "I'm a delight," she says. She nudges my arm until biting the inside of my cheek isn't enough and I have to cover my growing smile with a hand over my mouth.

Why do I keep forgetting?

She picks up a chunky black boot at random. "Do you have these in a seven?"

"No." I frown at the mom and her kids. Focus. Find the clue, connect the puzzle pieces, keep your feelings in check, and get the hell out of the Marybelle.

"I know you're lying," says Zelda. "I always know when you're lying."

"How?"

"Spoilers."

"You suck *so* much."

She preens. "But wait. It gets worse!" She points at the shop's front entrance so I turn and look and oh no.

"Oh no."

Turns out the word that was dancing on the tip of my tongue was two words: Evan Kim.

"This is a story in three acts," says Zelda as Evan walks into the shop and fifteen-year-old me melts into a puddle of embarrassed goo. "Act one, curtain opens: Girl meets girl."

I'd seen Evan Kim around school and thought, *Holy lesbian crush, Batman, she's cute,* but I'd never spoken to her. I'd just admired her from afar, enjoying that warm heart-squeezy feeling you get when your crush is a vague, daydreamy kind of thing. But then we joined band at the same time and there was only one dude with a clarinet sitting between us and I discovered she had a cute laugh and a wicked sense of humor and an ex-*girl*friend and my heart squeezed until it burst.

"Why would you do this to me?" I whisper. It's sabotage. It's definitely sabotage. I was revving myself up to deal with seeing Dad, not *this.*

Zelda doesn't answer.

I watch as Evan wanders around the shop while fifteen-year-old me rings up the little girl's shoes, pretending Evan Kim does not exist.

Oh, but she does.

She has shoulder-length black hair, a button nose, a pointed chin. She's smart and funny in a sharp way, maybe too sharp, and she's kind of a nerd and she has this habit of blinking furiously and scrunching up her nose at the same time, and I liked her. I really, really liked her.

Fifteen-year-old me struggles to work the register with trembling hands. I remember that feeling. Like I was naked and written on every inch of my skin were the words: "Hey, Evan Kim, I'm sort of in love with you even though we've never spoken and you don't know I exist!" and Evan could read it. The demon kids and their mom could read it. Astronauts floating in space could read it.

"Hey," says Evan, when the mom and her kids finally leave.

She smiles and fifteen-year-old me dies. I see her soul leave her body.

"Hey," says fifteen-year-old me, a crack in her voice bigger than the San Andreas Fault. She is frozen, freaking out, lovestruck.

I can't watch this. I do not want to watch this.

"I need popcorn," says Zelda.

"Do these come in a six?" Evan plops a pair of white sneakers on the counter. Dad always said it was bad luck to put shoes on tables and I wonder if that applied to counters too. She squints a bit, tilts her head like she recognizes fifteen-year-old me but can't place where from. Maybe my name is on the tip of her tongue too.

Other me picks up one of the sneakers, inspecting the inside. Her hands shake; Evan's eyes flick down, noticing.

Oh, this is a car crash.

"These come in European sizes," says fifteen-year-old me, and shows Evan the inside of the shoe, almost shoving her nose in it. Evan jerks back. "But I can convert the sizes in my head. A six is a thirty-six. I take a seven and a half, which is a thirty-eight. My feet are bigger than yours. But the average shoe size for women in the US is between an eight and a half and a nine so both of us are smaller than average. Which is good when there are sales because our sizes don't sell out as quickly." She frowns at the shoe in her hand, as if wondering why it hasn't shoved itself into her mouth to stop her rambling. "These aren't on sale, though. Sorry."

Zelda laughs. "This is so embarrassing for you."

"Shut. Up."

"So do these come in a six or not?" asks Evan.

Fifteen-year-old me nods, then rushes out back, where she will spend two minutes doing breathing exercises and counting backward from one hundred in an attempt to calm down. It won't work.

"Any observations to make at this point?" asks Zelda.

Yeah. My observation is this: I do not understand Zelda's game plan *at all*. First Clem, now this. At least showing me Dad would have made sense: He was at the Marybelle. The things that happened there—everything leading up to it and everything that happened after—are tied up in him, tied up in so many knots.

I can only figure out what makes the Marybelle my happiest memory if she hands me the right puzzle pieces.

But Dad isn't here. Evan is. And apparently this is a love story.

I shake my head as fifteen-year-old me returns with a shoebox tucked under her arm. She guides the other girl to a fitting chair and kneels in front of her, totally unable to look her in the eye.

Evan takes off her shoes. She's wearing novelty socks: *SpongeBob*.

"Cute socks," says fifteen-year-old me.

Zelda cackles and I want to scream.

Evan wriggles into the sneakers and stands, walking the length of the shop twice before pausing in front of the full-length mirror.

"They look awesome," says the other me, kneeling on the carpet (beige).

"You think?"

"Yeah, but I bet you'd look good in anything."

Oh God.

Evan frowns at fifteen-year-old me via the reflection in the mirror. "Do I know you?"

The other me glances up, pink dusting her cheeks. "We go to the same school. I'm in band."

Evan squints harder, trying to place her. "Sorry," she says.

Other me shrugs. It's no big deal. She's used to being invisible.

Zelda hums. "Interesting."

Before I can react, there's a bump out back, a box falling over maybe, a muffled curse. My head whips around at the sound. The storeroom door is ajar, revealing a strip of orange light and shelves stacked high with shoeboxes. A shadow flickers in and out of view and I hold my breath.

Dad.

Do I want to see him? Do I want to see my dad walk out of that storeroom, a hand running through his thinning hair, dressed in a two-sizes-too-big cardigan, pleated pants, and his favorite Italian leather brogues? Do I want to watch him cross the shop floor with his shoulders curved forward, walking with an invisible weight on his back? I've chased that back through malls and I've piggybacked it and I've wrapped my arms around it and squeezed when I was crying. Do I really think I could see all that—see *him*—and not break down?

"Are you okay?" asks Zelda.

"Yes." I look up at the heavens. "Yes, Kelvin, I'm fine. I'm great. This is awesome."

"You're lying."

"Prove it," I snap.

Her eyes dance across my face, assessing. "You have a tell." She bops my nose. "A big ol' tell."

"I thought you couldn't tell me how you know when I'm lying."

"That was *me* lying. I just like making you angry. You get all huffy and your cheeks go pink. It's cute."

I want to glare at her but my cheeks are pink right now. *You hate her. Don't forget.*

While fifteen-year-old me rings up Evan's sneakers, I stare out the window. Outside the store, in the middle of the mall, there's a circle of fake grass surrounded by a picket fence, and inside the fence are three kiddie rides: a rocket ship, a car, and a unicorn.

When I was little, Dad would let me ride the rocket ship any time I asked. Even when I got too big and struggled to wriggle into the opening, he'd still rifle through his pockets for change and watch me ride it, smiling.

I told him once I should have been born in the future, so that I could stow away on a spaceship just like this one and see the universe. "And leave me at home worrying about you?" he said. "I'd never cope without you, honey."

Stop it. Stop thinking about Dad.

"Let's go." Zelda nods at Evan, a Sole Mate shopping bag swinging from her loose grip as she leaves the shop without looking back.

We follow her; I drag my feet, looking over my shoulder at the storeroom one last time. I can't see him and I know he wouldn't be able to see me, but I still feel like I'm walking away from him again. *I'm sorry, Dad. I didn't mean to leave you.*

I bite my lip. Hard. The pain is a distraction. "Is that it?" I ask, voice carefully blank.

She doesn't answer, too busy looking around the mall with big eyes. There's a steady stream of shoppers passing by us, and Zelda drinks them in like she's been wandering the desert for weeks and she's parched. I do the same, my eyes dropping to their shoes because Dad said you can tell a lot about a person by their shoes. What do those white-and-gray sneakers say about you, guy with a mullet and three shopping bags from Target? What about you, lady with the pink ballet flats and the mom jeans and the rugby top in maroon, yellow, and purple?

My mom always wore running shoes.

But this isn't about Mom.

And it isn't about Dad.

I look over my shoulder again but all I can see is fifteen-year-old me slumped across the counter, head in her hands.

This is about a girl who meets another girl and falls in love.

"I know how this story ends, Zelda," I say. If she thinks I haven't analyzed every interaction Evan and I ever had at least a hundred times over she's sorely mistaken. I've already written the essay on this one and trust me, the conclusion has nothing to do with happiness.

"Maybe how it ends isn't the point," she says.

"Then what *is* the point?"

"That's for you to figure out, babe."

Way up ahead I pick out Evan making a beeline for the mall exit. She disappears through the doors and out of sight.

I huff in frustration. Why does everything have to be so hard? Why am I dead and still struggling with calculations that don't make sense? It's eighth-grade algebra all over again.

I frown at my worn Cons, which look extra ratty against the shiny tile floor. At least Zelda's Mary Janes are— Wait. She's not wearing Mary Janes. Her feet are clad in chunky black boots. *Familiar* chunky black boots.

"Did you steal from my dad?"

I look up and she's blushing furiously. "No. Sort of. He won't know. Hey! Look over there and not at my feet!" Zelda bolts for the unicorn ride and jumps on. "Faster, Sparkles, faster!" she cries, kicking her stolen boots against the unicorn's belly.

And I forget.

I forget to hate her. And I wonder: Would it be so bad if I never remembered?

Because my dad always said you could tell a lot about a person by their shoes, and I think stolen black boots say a lot about Zelda.

THIRTEEN

Before we leave the mall we get burritos from a hole-in-the-wall place next to Foot Locker.

"Memory triggers," Zelda says. She won't look me in the eye.

Zelda waggles her fingers and a Philly Cheesesteak Burrito appears in my hand. A Coke *poof!*s into my other hand, wet with icy droplets sliding down the side. (It still doesn't feel cold, though. Weird.) She waggles her fingers again and a burrito appears in her hand. "Cheese and beans. Extra beans because I've heard they make you fart and I'm eager to test the theory."

A snort escapes my lips. Zelda grins and takes a massive bite. It reminds me of Ms. Chiu, fake Ms. Chiu, tasting a French fry for the first time.

"Verdict?"

Zelda chews thoughtfully. "No farts yet, which is disappointing, but cheese is a revelation."

"The farts don't come until your body has digested the beans. Give it time. And cheese is amazing. We can agree on that."

She hums, chewing. Suddenly she flicks my forehead with her free hand and I stumble as the world spins.

When it stops spinning we're in a hallway in my old high

school. There's a giant banner hanging from the archway in front of us: GO HORNETS! The place stinks of rotting food, sweat, and bleach. But it's home. It makes my heart throb like a stubbed toe.

"So we got our memory triggers." Zelda tears a huge bite out of her burrito and marches up the hallway. "And we got our thinking caps on. Time for act two."

We're headed toward a hum—the hum of hundreds of conversations happening at once, of dishes rattling, of chairs being dragged along tiles.

"What year is this?" I ask.

"We've only skipped ahead a few months," explains Zelda. "It's Thursday. Lunch period just started. You're still fifteen. You just had a science test. You got a B."

I jog-walk up the hallway, chasing her shadow, trying not to spill my burrito. We pass through the atrium, where a giant papier-mâché hornet hangs from the roof. Paul's cousin got suspended when he threw a football and broke one of the wings.

The noise increases. Someone sings the *Powerpuff Girls* theme song at the top of their lungs and someone else shouts at them to *shut the hell up, Todd.* We turn a corner, and ahead of us, through a pair of wide-open double doors, there's a cafeteria teeming with students.

I lower my burrito, stomach twisted with anxiety.

Zelda pauses in the middle of the entrance, licking grease off her fingers. I pull up next to her and scan for my friends. I feel torn: If I *don't* see them, my heart will drop into my stomach and rot in the acid and I'll die all over again. But if I *do* see them, my stomach will launch upward and end up squished next to my heart, which will be beating so fast it will push my stomach through the gaps in my rib cage until it's shredded like cheese. Either would be very painful and very gross.

Focus.

"Why the cafeteria?"

"Be patient," she says. "And watch."

I watch.

I spy Clem in the lunch line, and yep, it still hurts. Grated-cheese stomach syndrome in full effect. I can't see Paul or Lou but there are faces I know well from class and band scattered around. The lunch lady is serving. Rose-May. She always made me smile with her dad jokes and K-drama recaps.

And oh look it's me.

My poor stomach—battered, bruised, and finely grated—now melts as I turn my gaze to the girl standing in front of Clem, holding out her lunch tray as meatballs are spooned onto her plate. She wears jeans, a green sweater, and the same old Cons.

Is it ever going to hurt less?

She—fifteen-year-old me—looks over her shoulder and laughs at whatever Clem has just said.

Zelda nods at me to watch as my younger self and her best friend turn and weave through the crowd, heading for a table.

I notice a couple of things at the same time. One: Paul and Lou are sitting on the other side of the cafeteria. Lou has her hand up, waving us over. Two: Evan Kim is walking toward the center of the cafeteria, looking down at her phone.

It's clear that younger me and Evan are going to cross paths. I feel strange, like my skin is plastic wrap pulled too tight.

Because I remember this and I know it's bad. It's so bad.

Younger me is waving at Paul, trying to make him laugh by

doing the dance we made up, wiggling like a deflating tube man. It's hard to do with a tray of food balanced in one hand.

A dude from the football team leans back in his chair right as other me passes. He's trying to catch someone's attention at the table behind him and he doesn't see the other me. But that me is flesh and blood and real, so no one magically swerves out of her way. Not even Evan, who's too busy typing on her phone to realize she's about to bump into the girl who stares at her in band and who once sold her a pair of shoes.

I remember it felt like it happened in slo-mo at the time. But watching it now, it's over in a second. The guy leans back. Other me is already off-balance because of her weird dance. She swerves out of his way and stumbles into Evan's path. The tray tips. Meatballs and banana milk go flying. They spill all over Evan. Honestly, it's so fast. It's blink and you'd miss it. But no one misses it. A stunned silence fills the room and younger me stares in horror at the meatballs sliding down Evan's shirt. They land with a wet plop on the floor, and oh God this is the worst. This is the absolute worst. The embarrassment burns in me all over again, hot and sour.

Laughter breaks the silence. So much laughter. Then the whispering starts. I watch the story get passed around the cafeteria, like Basketball Steve but worse. *Oh my God did you see it? Tegan Masters tripped no she was pushed no she threw her tray at Evan Kim's head what's her problem?* When other me looks up and sees Evan's face—red cheeks, so close to tears—she runs. She bolts from the cafeteria, right past me. My hand jerks out to grab hold of her but all I touch is air.

Zelda grins at me.

"The story continues," she says, wings fluttering like laughter.

"In act one we had 'girl meets girl.' In act two, we have 'girl throws mystery meat on girl and makes her cry.' What a twist! I did not see that coming."

All I can do is stare.

I vaguely register Clem rushing past—Evan too, but I can't focus. I can't contain my feelings. Which is dangerous. Because feelings are live grenades you have to toss before they explode. But it's too late. I was too slow. And now I'm a pile of ash.

Don't look, Kelvin.

"You going to eat that?" Zelda motions at my half-eaten burrito. I shove it at her and march away.

"We're not going to talk about it?" She chases after me.

I don't know where I'm marching to. Ms. Chiu's office? Quinn? Dad's shop? Five hundred thousand miles away from wherever Zelda is? I can't believe I forgot to hate her. There's a reason I hate her. It's this. It's this right here.

I'm desperately trying to save my butt from purgatory—cupping the soft, broken parts of me in my hands, protecting them like a baby bird—while she's working overtime to open up my wounds under the pretense of showing me some clue. Because apparently she's so bad at her job she can only win by cheating.

"Don't be like that, Tegan," she says, laughter in her voice.

"How should I be? Grateful you reminded me that I was a pathetic loser who was never going to find love? Glad I got run over at sixteen so that I didn't have to die alone and be eaten by cats?"

"Cats eat people?" she gasps. "Well, now I like them even more."

I stop marching and swing around. She stops too, gummy smile wide, a perfect little angel, and I am more convinced than ever she's a demon in disguise.

I zip her mouth shut and throw away the key.

"Um, what?" she says.

I do the mime again. This time, I eat the key.

"Seriously?" she says.

"Seriously. I can't listen to you right now. You make me so mad."

"*I* make *you* mad?"

"I am so mad I could hack up my eviscerated internal organs all over your shoes."

She pouts. "I like these shoes."

"Okay, fine," I snap. "Let's talk about how you can't admit you made a mistake so you'd rather sabotage me and send me to purgatory than fail this ridiculous investigation and get, what, a slap on the wrist?"

"I don't—" She shakes her head. "Listen. Just let me do my job. You think I'm showing you any old random memory for the fun of it?"

"Aren't you? Because there's no way it took you nine whole days to come up with *this*. Me being jealous of Lou plus me sucking at romance doesn't equal the Marybelle. Your math is *wrong*. You're showing me one plus one equals five billion. Don't you get it?"

"*I* get it. You don't."

"You know what? It doesn't matter. Kelvin's going to see it. He's going to see that your calculations suck and the only thing I need is a better heaven."

She snorts. "Or maybe he's going to see how hard I'm working to open your eyes but you keep covering them and pretending you can't see a damn thing."

"I don't do that!"

She flips me off. "How many fingers am I holding up?"

"I hate you."

"See? Right in front of your face and you pretend you can't see it. But I can see. I see right through you."

"Oh yeah? With your superpower angel X-ray vision?"

"You forget," she says coldly, "I've already seen inside you."

My breath catches. I stumble back a step but she follows.

"I've seen every memory you have, Tegan," she continues, "even the ones you think you've hidden." She speaks softly now but her eyes blaze in that familiar way. "You can't hide from me."

"I don't... You're not—" The hairs on the back of my neck rise with that someone-is-watching-me feeling. I turn and—

Shit.

Kelvin stands in the open doorway across the hall from us, greasy bangs tickling his eyelashes, clicky pen gliding across the page. "Subject 3T24B5 continues to demonstrate a pathological reluctance to confront difficult emotions," he reads aloud as he writes. My mouth is suddenly as dry as sandpaper. "Her soul is much dirtier than anticipated."

There's a vise around my lungs, squeezing. Or is it Kelvin's hands?

"Meanwhile," continues Kelvin, smirking, "Angel 4B46_XzA's attempts to present a convincing argument prove sloppy at best."

Zelda grits her teeth. At least for once her anger isn't directed at me. "I'll make you eat that pen, Kelvin."

"When confronted with her shortcomings, Angel 4B46_XzA resorts to threats of violence," he says, scribbling. I liked it better when all he did was scowl. "Unstable? Unfit for duty?"

"Come with me, Snickerdoodle," says Zelda, shoving the last of my burrito into her mouth. She grabs my hand—I'm so numb right now I can hardly feel it. "We're not done yet. Bye, Kelvin. Hope you don't trip over your oversized ego and face-plant in a pile of dog poo."

Kelvin sneers at us as she yanks me into the girls' bathroom.

"That's not good." I shake my head, stumbling as Zelda drags me along. There's a roar in my ears and a storm in my heart. I'm going to lose. "He said 'pathological reluctance.' I'm screwed."

I thought the Marybelle was so obviously the wrong heaven that I couldn't possibly lose. That I could argue all day with Ms. Chiu about which is better—keeping my messy, spiky, noisy feelings locked deep inside versus poring over them with a magnifying glass as they're stripped from my flesh, piece by excruciating piece—and it wouldn't matter because I was sure to win.

But now I'm remembering eighth-grade algebra and how it never made sense to me, no matter which way I looked at it, while Naomi Long always understood it right away. And maybe this is like that. Maybe I don't get it but Barb does and Ms. Chiu does and even though he clearly hates Zelda and wants to rile her up, ultimately Kelvin will understand it too.

Everyone will understand it except me.

"I could end up in purgatory," I say. I hear the words leave my mouth but they don't feel real. "They're going to open me up and scrub me raw until there's nothing left."

Zelda stomps up to me in her stolen boots and zips my lips.

I blink. "What are you—?"

She pulls at the neck of her sweater and drops the key into her bra (do angels wear bras? I don't know, she drops it into whatever is *down there*). "If you let that greasy pen-pusher under your skin I will make you drink the pool water at the Marybelle, so help me God." She gestures for me to look to my right. "Focus."

In a daze, I turn. At the basin, fifteen-year-old me and Clem are washing—*trying* to wash—the mystery meat out of Evan's top. Mostly they're just smearing red sauce deeper into the white fabric.

"Damn it." Fifteen-year-old me is still crying, apologizing between sobs.

Clem holds a hand over her mouth but she's not quick enough—a splutter of laughter escapes.

"Don't laugh," whines fifteen-year-old me. "I ruined her top."

Evan blinks, still in shock. "My grandmother bought me this shirt," she says.

Clem laughs harder, half hunched and wheezing. "I'm sorry. I'm so sorry," she says. "There was just so much meat. It was an avalanche of meat. Just meat flying through the air." She dissolves into giggles.

Suddenly, Evan laughs too. Just a giggle at first, and then she's wheezing like Clem, tears streaming down her flushed cheeks.

Fifteen-year-old me gawks at them, a clump of wet paper towel in her hand, her mouth hanging open. She wants to laugh. She wants to find the funny side. She wants to join in.

The wet towel breaks in half, falling with a dull plop onto her sneakers.

I glance at Zelda. "Why are we—?"

"Find the clue," she says, surprisingly gentle. Is she…is she helping me? "Focus."

I'm trying but…How do you look your messiest, darkest, most tender moments in the eye without breaking down? Is this an impossible task? What do they *do* to you in purgatory to leave you feeling nothing but pure bliss when you see the life you left behind, the people who will grow old without you?

I hug myself. Focus. *Focus.* I can prove Kelvin wrong. I can do this.

Evan wipes the tears out of her eyes. "What am I laughing at? I can't turn up to geography in this. Mr. Kang will pop a nut." Her shirt is so wet in places it's see-through, not to mention stained with thick stripes of red meatball sauce. It's like prom night in *Carrie* on her shirt.

Clem starts laughing again. Fifteen-year-old me throws a clump of wet paper towel at her.

"Stop it. You're not helping."

Clem pokes her tongue out and giggles. "I've got a spare set of clothes in my locker for after basketball practice. I'll grab you my sweater." She winks at Evan as she runs past. Evan smiles, blushing.

The door swings shut behind Clem, leaving Evan and fifteen-year-old me alone. I don't want to look at them; it's so hard to look at them. I turn Kelvin's words over and over in my mind until I can taste their bitterness. *Pathological reluctance.*

Screw you, Kelvin. I can do this. I can be objective. I can find the clue. I don't need my soul purified. I don't need these memories wiped clean, sanitized, scrubbed so raw they become tissue-thin.

I can still win.

"I'm sorry," says the other me. She looks at the remaining mush of paper towel in her hand, her face scrunched. She tosses it in the bin.

"It was an accident," says Evan with a shrug.

They don't say anything for a long while. In the silence I swear I hear the echo of Clem's and Evan's laughter, taunting me. The silence echoes too. A whole lot of painful nothing. Other me glances at herself in the mirror. She's worried about her red puffy eyes. She's worried what Evan thinks of her now. She's worried about wasting this chance to talk to her crush.

"At least it didn't get on your sneakers," she says.

Evan looks down at her feet, the white sneakers somehow unscathed. She smiles. "Yeah. I'd have to buy a new pair. Do you know anyone who could help me with that?"

Fifteen-year old me bites her lip, trying to contain her smile. She thinks it's going okay, all things considered. She thinks, *Hey, maybe this is a really funny meet-cute story. About the girl who threw mystery meat on her crush and they lived happily ever after.* Clem has been telling her to take a chance. "You're gorgeous," she's been saying. "You're funny and smart and cool. Any girl would be stoked to be asked out by you. What have you got to lose?"

"I could make it up to you," blurts fifteen-year-old me.

"You don't have to." Evan's eyes look everywhere but at the other girl.

"I want to," says fifteen-year-old me. She tugs the cuffs of her sweater over her hands, the ends damp now. "The fundraising fair is coming up. I could take you."

"Oh. Um." Evan stares hard at the tiles on the floor. "I wasn't—"

"We're all going," other me rushes to say. Her too-loud, too-desperate voice echoes in the bathroom. "It's going to be fun. I'll pay for your ticket and your rides and your food. To pay you back for—" She gestures at the shirt.

Evan looks up. "You're all going?" she asks. "Clem too?"

My nails bite into the soft skin of my palms. I want to look away; I can't look away. I can't lose.

Fifteen-year-old me nods. "Yeah. Everyone's going to be there. It's going to be fun."

Evan slowly nods. "Okay." A smile softens the sharp corners of her lips. "I'll come."

The bathroom door slams open and I jolt. Fifteen-year-old me jolts too. Clem waves an oversized blue sweater above her head like a flag. "This is way too big even on me but it's all I've got," she says. "Is it okay?"

Evan smiles at her. Warm. Wide. The sharp corners of her lips smooth out completely. "Yeah," she says, reaching out for the sweater. "It's great."

Zelda tugs on my sleeve until I turn around. There's fire in her eyes. It sends a strange jolt of electricity through me. Not fear, something else. I try not to notice it, whatever it is. I have to focus on winning.

Even if that means Zelda loses.

"The plot thickens," she says, and taps my forehead.

FOURTEEN

When the world stops spinning, Zelda is wearing a tux.

A tux.

I gawp at her until she frowns. "What? Why are you looking at me like that?"

The thing is, the very important thing that cannot be overstated, is that Zelda is wearing a tux.

Black. Sleek. Shimmery. Waistcoat with gold buttons, jacket (velvet trim!), cigarette pants, and bow tie. Bow tie! That last one bears repeating: Bow! Tie!

"We need to fit in," she says, blushing.

Fit in? I look down: I'm standing in mud and also wearing a tux: wide-leg pants, white shirt patterned with tiny donuts, pink cummerbund, a velvet bow tie, and a white tux jacket.

We're in a muddy field. A sign over Zelda's shoulder reads: FIVE-DOLLAR ENTRY! DRESS TO THE NINES! There are fairy lights everywhere and people are dressed like it's prom and there's a rainbow of stalls and rides. There's even a Ferris wheel.

The fundraising fair.

Zelda snaps her fingers in front of my face until I focus on her again (Bow! Tie!). "You figured it out yet?"

I shrug because I honestly don't know. But if this is the fund-raising fair, then…

My breath hitches when I see them tossing bills into the donation box at the gates, Evan in rubber boots and a prom dress (sea green) and me in my dad's old pinstripe suit.

The merry-go-round starts up suddenly. The mechanical whir of the painted horses galloping and the tinkling of the music-box song that urges them on drown out any reply I might have. Which is good because I don't have a reply. Just a knotty mess of feelings wedged in my throat that I'd rather eat mud than untangle.

Pathological reluctance…

"This sucks so much," I groan, watching fifteen-year-old me lead Evan into the fair, heading for the haunted house. Evan looks so pretty in her thrift store prom dress and her rubber boots, but she keeps looking around like she's searching for something. Or someone. "Why can't we all just pretend there was never a mistake? You'll do the calculations again and no one will bat an eyelid when the Marybelle isn't my true heaven and I'll live happily ever after and Kelvin will crawl back under his rock and *no one* will touch my soul."

Zelda scoffs. "Heaven doesn't let mistakes slide," she says. "Making judgments and handing down punishments is sort of our thing. Now, come on." She throws me a look over her shoulder as she marches away, hot on the heels of Evan and fifteen-year-old me. "No loitering."

"Fine. But you said the clue wasn't about how this story ends," I say, racing after her. "And this *is* the end."

She shrugs. "It is. And it isn't."

Thanks for clearing that up.

We join the line for the haunted house. "You'll love it," says fifteen-year-old me. She's three people ahead of us in the line, bouncing on her toes. "Me and Clem do this every year. It's scary but fun."

Evan nods. "Did you say Clem was coming later?"

I groan and force my gaze away from them.

There's a tremor in my hand that wasn't there before Kelvin showed up at school. I wasn't exactly taking it easy before—my brain was doing backflips trying to follow Zelda's calculations and find her clues. But now it's like my brain is doing backflips while I stand on a cliff's edge looking down at the rocks below.

At the head of the line, a senior plucks tokens out of hands and waves people to their seats. We slip by him unnoticed, climbing into the cart behind Evan and fifteen-year-old me.

"Scared?" other me asks Evan.

Yes.

I squeeze into the seat beside Zelda. Her wings take up too much room and their silky touch against my skin feels like holding hands. I don't know. It just feels intimate in a way that makes me choke on that knotted ball of feelings still lodged in my throat. Maybe Zelda thinks the same because she tries to wriggle away from me, her cheeks flushed pink and pretty. I've got a front-row seat to her freckles again.

"Don't look at me," she says. "I'm not your clue." She gives up on her wriggling—there's no room. We're pressed up against each other and it's warm and soft and it's making my heart feel like it's made of Pop Rocks. Which is fine. And normal.

"I'm not looking at you." I yank the metal bar down to lock us in place, squeezing us even closer: *Thirteen, thirteen, thirteen freckles.* Okay, so I'm looking, but only because I still don't know if she's trying to sabotage me and there can only be one winner and it has to be me so I need to study her closely and uncover her weak spots. All right?

In front of us the other me is telling Evan she can scoot closer if she gets scared.

I roll my eyes. "I know why we're here." Zelda shifts; her wing tickles my cheek. "I sucked at love."

"Nope."

"I did."

"Well, yeah. But that's not why we're here. And everyone sucks at love." She turns to me; we're squished so tightly together I go cross-eyed trying to look at her. "Are *you* scared?" she asks.

"Of love?"

"No, you silly snickerdoodle. The haunted house."

I laugh. It's a breathless huff. Because nothing is actually funny and I have way too many things to worry about right now and not one of those things is a haunted house. "I'm dead. It'd be ironic if a ghost was afraid of a haunted house."

"You're not a ghost."

"What am I?"

She looks away. "A puzzle to be solved."

The cart jolts forward suddenly as the ride starts. "Whoa," I gasp, gripping the bar tightly.

Lights flash and chains rattle as the cart follows a narrow track into the house. There are skeletons, spiders, and zombies everywhere. I hold my breath, staring at the back of fifteen-year-old me's head until it gets too dark to see.

How am I supposed to see anything clearly in a haunted house?

"That's you." Zelda points at a ghost hanging from the ceiling.

"Shut up."

"Boo!" A mummy jumps out of a coffin and I scream. Zelda laughs. Fifteen-year-old Tegan laughs too, glancing at Evan. She's thinking maybe Evan will want to hold hands and they'll scream and laugh and scoot up close to each other and maybe they'll kiss. But I can see the flash of white light in Evan's lap as she messages her friends; she's not even looking at fifteen-year-old me.

My stomach twists. I don't want to look; I have to look.

The cart rumbles around a corner and Zelda points to a wall dripping with green ooze. "That's you," she says.

I point at a decapitated head dangling on a string. "That's you."

"That *is* me," she says, and I snort.

If I didn't have a tremor in my hand, if I couldn't see the glow of Evan's phone, if I didn't expect Kelvin to jump-scare me around every corner, I could enjoy this. I could pretend I was alive and this was how my date with Evan actually went: making jokes, pressed up close, counting freckles.

Kelvin would hate that: pretending. He'd make a note of it on his clipboard and I'd be one step closer to purgatory.

But what if pretending makes me happy?

"Boink." Zelda flicks the end of my nose. Ouch. "Ride's over, butt-face."

I blink like I'm coming out of a dream. She's right. The cart rattles to a halt outside the haunted house. Fifteen-year-old me helps Evan out, skin on fire where her fingertips press gently against Evan's wrist. I pretend I feel it too, the warmth. But then Zelda climbs out, her wings no longer brushing my arm, and I remember: I can't feel the warmth or the cold. Not anymore.

"Teacup ride!" she shouts.

We follow them to the teacups. (Evan hates it. She says it's a kids' ride. She asks when Clem and the others will get here.)

We follow them to buy cotton candy. (Zelda insists we eat some too. "Memory triggers," she says, but the sugar rush makes my head spin until the only thing I can remember is what Kelvin said.)

We follow them to the carnival games. Fifteen-year-old me tries to win Evan a prize but the games are rigged. (Is that a metaphor? Me throwing a baseball at a pyramid of cans but they're glued down so I'll never win? Is that what Zelda wants me to see? That I was destined to lose no matter what?)

In the hall of mirrors, I watch Evan's bored face stretch like bubble gum. Beside her, fifteen-year-old me is reflected in three mirrors at once. She's trying to catch Evan's eye but no matter how many Evans there are, none of them look back at her.

I frown at my own warped reflection. Five hourglass versions of myself frown back. For a second I glimpse Kelvin and his clipboard behind me. But when I spin around, he's not there.

"Did you know eating four sticks of cotton candy sets your tongue on fire?" asks Zelda. She pokes out her purple-stained tongue in the mirror. "There's a disco inferno in my mouth. I hate it. It's wonderful."

Evan and fifteen-year-old me lean toward each other until their reflections meld into one. Evan giggles and fifteen-year-old me smiles; in the mirror she looks like the Joker. She wonders if this is the turning point; if now they'll start to have fun. She'd built up the date in her head, daydreamed about it a hundred different ways. She imagined herself holding Evan's hand in the haunted house. She imagined winning her a plushie in one of the carnival games, imagined Evan hugging it and whispering a shy "Thanks." She imagined getting stuck at the top of the Ferris wheel and asking Evan for a kiss, imagined Evan saying yes, her lips sweet like cotton candy. She imagines it, even now.

"I don't understand," I say. I picture Kelvin writing that down—"Subject 3T24B5 doesn't understand why this memory is important. Epic fail"—and my heart races. But it's true. I don't understand and I really don't think that's my fault. "This date doesn't have anything to do with happiness." Zelda called this a love story but she's wrong. Love stories have a happy ending.

Or they should.

Mom and Dad didn't have a happy ending.

Does that mean it was never love?

Or is love just the beginning of the end?

Zelda meets my eye in the mirror. "Sometimes the things that matter most creep up on us," she says. "Sometimes we don't see them because they're a part of us—we can't see where they stop and we start. They accumulate deep down in our souls."

I don't look away. I can't.

Thirteen.

"Let's ride the Ferris wheel," suggests fifteen-year-old me loudly, making me jolt. I turn to other me. She is so full of hope—it's reflected ten feet tall in every mirror.

Evan shrugs, eyes on her phone, and there's a knot of dread in my throat. It's like watching a horror movie—the girl who goes to investigate the noise in the basement. You know she's going to die but you still jump out of your skin when the killer attacks.

My feet drag as Zelda and I follow Evan and younger me outside. Clem, Lou, and Paul have arrived, hands full of cotton candy and shoes caked in mud. Paul waves at fifteen-year-old me, trying to grab her attention, but Evan is the one who sees them first. Her face lights up.

"I didn't think you were going to make it!" She races over to the newcomers, clasping Clem's arm and smiling so wide. I stumble to a halt, unwilling to get too close. "We're headed to the Ferris wheel. You can ride with me, Clem."

"Final act," says Zelda, whispering in my ear. "Girl dumps girl for girl's best friend."

I rest a hand over my chest where my heart no longer beats and I wonder how a dead heart can keep breaking.

"I told you I suck at love," I say.

She doesn't take the bait. "Why does this memory hurt?" she asks instead.

I swallow over the lump in my throat. Good question. But trying to find the answer means looking, doesn't it? Really looking. Not just glimpsing the blood but wiping the wound clean to see the cut: how long, how deep, how close to the artery. And I know that's what I need to do to prove that I'm trying, that I'm not falling to pieces. But it's hard. I'm not used to looking.

In the corner of my eye I spy a figure in black on the edge of the crowd, watching. It could be anyone. It could be Kelvin. I don't look at him. I look at fifteen-year-old me.

Why does it hurt?

I really don't know.

We follow them to the Ferris wheel. Evan needles and begs until Clem finally says, "Yeah, okay. I'll share with you." She shoots an apologetic smile at fifteen-year-old me but it doesn't matter, her heart has already broken.

Why does it hurt?

Zelda scoots past the girl running the ride and we board an empty carriage. Fifteen-year-old me is already in the air, sharing with Lou and Paul and trying not to cry.

I buckle us in. Even though she has wings and can fly (I assume?), Zelda grips the bar until her knuckles are white.

"Are you sure you want to do this?" I ask. I'm not sure *I* want to do this. I want to scream: *Does it matter why it hurts? Does it matter what a wound looks like if it's going to kill you anyway?* But Zelda nods stiffly, eyes scrunched shut. "We have to. You need to figure it out." She yelps as the ride starts. The carriage sways as it spins upward and she grabs my hand. "Don't let go."

I look at our joined hands with awe. Hers is bigger, her long, thin fingers the perfect size to link through mine and squeeze. My hand doesn't tremble when she holds it. It feels solid, real, alive.

I can pretend it feels warm.

Suddenly I get that feeling again—something important hidden in the mess, just out of reach. With Zelda's hand in mine, I feel solid enough to reach out and grasp for it.

"I've never held hands," I say.

Zelda opens one eye. "Huh?"

"I never held someone's hand. And it makes me think: What *did* I do? I went on one bad date. I worked in a shoe shop. I played clarinet badly. My best friend had fallen in friend-love with someone else and was probably going to drift away from me sooner rather than later. I spent a shitty weekend in a motel, and then I died."

The thoughts in my head are jumbled. I'm a jigsaw puzzle, five thousand pieces all mixed up and I can't work out how to slot them together in a pattern that makes sense because too many pieces are missing. But I have to try.

"The ocean is some four hundred miles that way." I point with the hand Zelda isn't holding. "But I never even saw it. I never walked on the sand." The carriage stops at the very top. I've got my arm outstretched like maybe if I stretch hard enough I'll touch the ocean. "I never held a girl's hand."

"You are now," says Zelda.

I laugh.

She's right. She said the happiest things aren't the biggest, loudest, or brightest things. They're small and easy to miss because they're so fundamental to everything you are. Like a lonely girl holding hands for the first time.

I look down at our linked hands, and all the things that were so jumbled and confusing are suddenly clear. "So maybe that's why it hurts," I say. "I wanted to be someone who did things. Someone so bright and consequential that a girl like Evan would pick me. She'd look at me and out of all the other girls she'd say, 'Her. I want to hold her hand.' But she didn't pick me, she picked Clem. I wasn't bright enough." I look up, fairy lights reflected like stars in Zelda's eyes. "That's it, isn't it?"

She doesn't say I'm right but she doesn't say I'm wrong, either.

"It sucks," she says, and I nod. It really does suck.

We're silent for the rest of the way down. When the carriage comes to a halt at the bottom, we unlink hands and climb out. I watch fifteen-year-old me vanish into the crowd, but my heart doesn't ache to follow her. I've seen enough.

I turn to face Zelda instead. My hand feels achingly empty without her fingers tangled in mine. "So I figured it out," I say. Kelvin can't say I didn't try. I wanted to look away but I didn't. "But being jealous of Lou plus wanting Evan to pick me still doesn't equal the Marybelle. Two negatives don't make a positive."

Zelda sighs. I feel like I've disappointed her, and it makes me squirm. "You know those optical illusions?" she says. "At first it looks like a vase but then you realize it's also two faces in profile, looking at each other?" She starts walking, gesturing for me to follow. "The thing about you is that you're so determined to focus on the vase you never see the two faces." She stops in front of the ball toss and turns around. "Which one?"

"Huh?"

With the most complicated finger waggle yet—it's like she's finger-painting quadratic equations in the air—the whole stack of cans tumbles down with a gust of air. She turns to me. "Which prize do you want?"

I gape at her like a dead fish until she waves her hand and a large stuffed octopus appears—*poof!*—in my arms.

"His name is Snickerdoodle," she says. "He's yours."

The toy is about half as tall as I am and butt-ugly—pink with purple rings, evil eyes, oddly sexy lips, and only six tentacles. I love him. "You won him? For me?"

She shrugs, trying to act unbothered, but her cheeks are on fire. "It's your own piece of the ocean."

My heart feels like it's on top of the Ferris wheel—jerking in the wind, terrified of plummeting to the ground. I'm speechless.

"Evan Kim wouldn't know a good date if it sat on her head and farted." She lays her hand over mine, slotting our fingers together. And I have to ask myself again: Is she trying to help me? I thought she was sabotaging me—after all, only one of us can win. But this doesn't feel like sabotage. It feels like hope.

"And if it had been me..." she's saying. She takes a giant breath and the words rush out of her at once: "I'd have picked you."

For a second everything around me blurs but we don't zap anywhere. We're still at the fair. I'm still hugging Snickerdoodle. Zelda is still wearing a tux. I think the world just rearranged itself, stretching and bending to fit how big my feelings are right now.

Zelda picked *me.*

There's not a single cohesive thought in my head, just air. "I don't—"

"Zelda," says a voice behind us.

I almost drop Snickerdoodle in the mud.

Behind us stands a familiar blonde with an armful of knitting.

"Carol." Zelda steps in front of me, wings spreading until I'm half shielded from view. "How nice to see you."

Carol keeps knitting, needles *click clack*ing like a ticking clock. "Barb would like a word with you." Her voice is low and cool. "Now."

"But I've got a month," says Zelda. "And Kelvin's keeping an eye on us. Why does Barb need to see me?"

"Kelvin *is* keeping an eye on you." Carol glances off to the side. I follow her gaze until…bingo.

Kelvin. Leaning against the kissing booth. Pen poised over his clipboard. Smirking.

"Two hot dogs," he reads. "Black combat boots, size eight. Two burritos, one Coke. Cotton candy, five servings. Octopus, six tentacles. All unauthorized."

"We didn't—" I start to say, but Zelda interrupts.

"All part of the process," she says, chin lifted high. "I've got nothing to hide."

"Tell that to Barb," says Kelvin.

"Just hurry up," snaps Carol. *Click clack, click clack.* "I haven't got all day."

What if I threw mud in her face, grabbed Zelda's hand, and ran?

"Whatever." Zelda shrugs like it's no big deal. She glances back at me and winks. "It's all good. Nothing to worry about." I know the difference between a real and fake smile, and Zelda's smile right now is the worst counterfeit I've ever seen. "Catch you later, Snickerdoodle," she says.

I gasp in pain as she flicks my forehead. When the world stops spinning, I'm next to the pool at the Marybelle, a stuffed octopus in my arms and mud clinging to my Cons.

Zelda is gone.

(JESUS WEPT)

At breakfast, Tegan's father kept his head bowed over his phone, typing slowly with one finger.

Quinn ran through the room, weaving between the tables, holding Trash Monkey above her head so he could fly. There were four other people in the room, but Tegan's father didn't notice the looks they shot him as his younger daughter ran wild.

Tegan looked down at the eggs she hadn't touched, then back up at her father.

He was unshaven. Perhaps he'd forgotten to pack a razor. There were lines fanning out from the corners of his eyes like little creases in paper.

Tegan's mother was flying home today and still they had not heard from her.

"Can we go see the ocean today?" Tegan asked.

Her father didn't answer. His hand shook as he reached for his coffee. It shook so much the liquid dribbled over the lip of the cup. A black-brown stain seeped into the tablecloth.

"Dad," she said.

He didn't answer.

"Dad." Her voice was loud. Louder than Quinn's giggles. Her dad looked up.

He had schooled his features into a blank page. Tegan watched him closely, hoping to see invisible ink only she could read. But there was nothing.

"Can we go see the ocean today?" She swallowed. "Maybe Mom can join us. When she lands."

He looked at Tegan like he was seeing her for the first time. Like she was unexpected. Like she was a ghost. Tegan gripped the table edge until her knuckles ached, just to prove to herself that she was real.

"We talked about coming here," he said. It wasn't an answer, and Tegan wanted answers. As he looked out the window, Tegan wondered if he was the ghost. Could a person fade away in front of your eyes? "A family vacation," he continued. "But there was never a good time."

Tegan frowned at the eggs. Grayish liquid pooled around their edges, soaking into the corn bread.

The man three tables over from them had a smoker's rasp and an accent. German maybe. Tegan wasn't sure. Somewhere far away. He had probably crossed an ocean to get here.

"We can't miss the Sightseer tram car," he said to the woman sitting across from him. He frowned at Quinn as she ran past.

"We should do that too," said Tegan. "We should ride the tram and see the ocean and do things. We can't stay here. It's green. It sucks. The pool has a tampon in it."

The less her father answered her, the more she wanted to pick at the silence, tear its edges until whatever was hidden underneath spilled out.

He stood. "I need to…" He waggled his phone at her. He didn't meet Tegan's eye.

"Dad."

He walked away, phone pressed to his ear.

Tegan slumped back in her chair, pushing away her plate. The German man was staring at her. She could tell. She swore loudly enough for him to hear.

Through the window she watched her father pacing in the overgrown grass between the pool and the office. He was speaking to someone, a finger in one ear, phone pressed to the other.

It wasn't her mom, Tegan knew.

We're sorry, you have reached a number that has been disconnected or is no longer in service.

Maybe he was talking to Aunt Lily. But she didn't like Tegan's dad. She used to say: *Ask your father to pass me the ketchup, Tegan,* even though Tegan's dad was at the table too. And she'd say, *Who works with feet all day and likes it?* and *I know I've been married four times but no one gets it right the first time, do they, Edie?* and Mom would tell her to shush and Dad would smile and Aunt Lily would suck on her gums in that way that meant she was pleased with herself.

Quinn landed against the table, breathless and giggling. "Are we going to the beach?"

"Yes," said Tegan.

Quinn cheered. She pressed Trash Monkey's paws together so he could clap too.

By the time they met their father in the long grass, he'd hung up the phone and was frowning at it.

"I want to see a mermaid," said Quinn.

"I want to see a shark," said Tegan.

Their father turned to look at them. It was that same look, like he was seeing a ghost.

I'm not a ghost, Tegan wanted to scream, but for once she wasn't sure. Her mother also looked through her as if Tegan was invisible. Maybe she was.

"Let's rest upstairs for a bit first," he said, and walked away without waiting for an answer.

Tegan chased after him. Unease clawed at her. She knew this was wrong. All of this was wrong. But how could she put together the puzzle when her father was withholding so many missing pieces?

"You can rest and me and Quinn will go," she said. He didn't answer and she wondered if the wind was blowing her words away. "Me and Quinn will go," she said, louder. The unstuck sole of her sneaker flapped against the concrete as she walked, a drumbeat. "I'm fifteen. I can take her."

She followed him up the stairs, jogging.

"Dad."

His shoulders were drawn up tight as he continued to walk away from her.

"Dad!"

At the door he stopped to press his forehead to the wood, breathing. Quinn was still at the bottom of the stairs, warning Trash Monkey not to talk to the sharks.

Tegan approached her father, slowly. "You can stay here," she said. "I'll take Quinn and—"

Tegan startled as her father suddenly roared like a wounded animal, kicking the base of the door once, twice, three times. The wood splintered and he dropped his phone. Tegan stepped back until the railing dug into her spine.

165

He stilled, breathing hard, hands curled into fists against the door. Tegan heard Quinn reach the top of the stairs, but she couldn't take her eyes off her father. She was terrified he would vanish if she did.

Slowly, he collected himself, piece by piece. He rolled his shoulders back and pulled the key card out of his front pocket to swipe it against the handle. It beeped, flashing green.

"We should stick together," he said. He opened the door but didn't step inside. "Be a family. We'll go later." He glanced over his shoulder to smile at her. His everything-will-be-all-right smile. But Tegan saw the cracks, she saw the cracks where he had pieced it together in a hurry. He turned away and walked inside.

Tegan sucked down breaths, none of them deep enough to quash the panic inside her.

"Are we not going to the beach?" asked Quinn. She hugged Trash Monkey tight to her chest. Her eyes were wide.

"Later," said Tegan. She cupped the back of her sister's head, fingers gliding through her fine, silky hair. She forced a smile. "Mermaids like to sleep in. If we go later, we're more likely to see one."

Quinn's face lit up. "Really?"

"Really."

Appeased, she raced inside. Trash Monkey danced in her grip as she ran.

After steadying herself, Tegan followed.

Her father wasn't inside the main room, but the bathroom door was ajar, water running. Through the crack she saw her father hunched over the vanity.

She thought about asking him what was wrong. She thought about yelling at him for scaring her, or asking who had been on the phone. But then she saw his reflection in the mirror.

A teacher at St. Anne's once asked Tegan's class: *Can you guess what is the most beautiful sentence ever written?* The class had guessed: *God bless America, I love you, I forgive you, can I be your friend, this puppy is for you.* Eventually the teacher wrote the answer she was looking for on the board in her curly script: *Jesus wept.*

It's perfect because it's simple, she said. It's simple and beautiful and heartbreaking. You don't need to say how he cried or why he cried, the exact shape of his tears or the way his face contorted in pain. The act of weeping is enough.

Tegan's father wept.

She didn't think it was beautiful at all.

It was raw and terrifying and ugly and real. She hated it. It scared her, all the way to her bones.

So Tegan wept too.

FIFTEEN

Zelda doesn't come back.

Three days pass. I curl up in bed with Snickerdoodle and think about Zelda's pink cheeks as she handed me the prize. I remember her trying to look like it was no big deal and I remember the Pop Rocks in my heart. I remember thirteen freckles that looked like stars and *I'd pick you*. Ms. Chiu said memories are messy but that can't always be true. Because I remember everything about that moment. It's not a messy kitchen drawer; it's lake water so clear you can see every pebble, every tiny fish.

I remember it like it's the most important piece of the puzzle yet.

I sleep and eat and play mini-golf and read the Bible and pretend I'm not worried about Zelda.

I'm worried about Zelda.

What kind of meeting takes this long?

On the fourth day I drag Snickerdoodle to the parking lot and try to woo Trash Cat the Elder with bacon. He likes the bacon more than the sausage and dares to creep a little closer than before, but once he's a few feet away he sits down and won't budge.

I don't know why I'm so determined to win over this cat. Maybe I'm just that desperate for company. Or maybe he reminds me of myself a little bit. His fur is matted, his stubby tail hooked at the end like it was broken once and never properly healed. The tip of one ear is torn and there's a thick, puckered scar parallel to his snout.

No one loved this cat.

No one picked this cat first.

"I'm sorry," I say.

His ear twitches, the one that's torn. He sits on his stomach, limbs curled under him so he looks like a loaf of bread. There's a piece of bacon on the concrete between us, closer to me than to him. His whiskers twitch as he smells the grease in the air. He keeps his eyes half closed and acts like his proximity is a coincidence, like he just happens to be sunbathing in the middle of the Marybelle's parking lot, but every now and then his gaze skitters to the bacon and I can see the want in his eyes.

"I love you," I tell him because I want him to hear those words, even if he's not real, even if I'm not much of a cat person. His ear twitches again and his eyes squeeze shut but he doesn't come any closer.

I march back to my room and scream into my pillow.

I'm stuck.

I'm afraid.

Another three days pass, and still no Zelda. I don't even glimpse Kelvin.

I'm alone.

On the eighth day I stomp into the office. It's empty. The heater blares, the little flappy plastic thingies wriggling as hot air pours out, but I still can't feel its effects. Even in heaven, one piece of me will always be broken.

I lean over the counter. There are pens and cat-shaped sticky notes scattered all over the desk. Trash Cat Baby is propped up against the computer. I poke his little belly.

"Where's your mom?"

He doesn't answer.

Has she just abandoned me again or is she getting in trouble with Barb? Maybe Kelvin thinks her calculations suck so badly they called off the investigation early and shoved her straight into angel detention.

It should feel good to know I've maybe won. So why doesn't it?

And why am I still stuck in the Marybelle?

I press the bell but no one comes so I pick up a sticky note and a clicky pen. I write along the belly of the paper cat: *Where are you?* and stick it to the blank computer screen. I let my fingers linger against the paper for a moment before I turn away.

Because I need answers.

Luckily I know who to ask.

I head to the far side of the room and slip through the unmarked door. This time I don't take a seat on the edge of the couch. I walk all the way to the end of the waiting room and stand in front of the poster.

It's a good day to be happy!

The ocean in the image is calm, a deeper blue than the sky, all endless ripples and reflected clouds. Maybe Dad had me cremated and sprinkled my ashes in the ocean. That's not a bad way to go. That little pile of dust would travel a long way on the waves.

I squint and move closer. There are three seagulls in the sky. I didn't notice them before. One hovers just above the apostrophe and another touches its outstretched wing to the little dangly tip of the "y" in "day." The final one is a fuzzy gray blur in the middle of an "o." They're not really called seagulls, my dad liked to say. They're just gulls.

"Tegan?"

I turn around, expecting Ms. Chiu, but it's Barb standing in the doorway. We stare at each other, two cowgirls facing off at high noon. My hand twitches at my side.

"Are you here to tell me about Zelda?" I ask.

"Ms. Chiu will be with you shortly," says Barb, like I didn't even speak. Today her pantsuit is orange, her shirt a crisp white with a frilly collar. "I wanted to borrow you briefly first. Do you mind?"

Yes.

"No."

She smiles brightly. "Excellent. Come with me."

My feet take some convincing to move but I shuffle past her into the sterile gray office.

"Sit," says Barb.

I look at the chair like it's quicksand. "Where's Zelda?"

"You don't have to worry about Zelda," she says, sitting in Ms. Chiu's seat. "She's busy planning your final excursion. For the investigation."

Reluctantly, I sit. "It's not over?"

"Zelda has thirty days, remember?"

I nod, feeling a weird mix of relief and frustration. Honestly, this investigation sucks balls. It's like, *Hey, Tegan, either you stick this pin in your eye or you stick it in Zelda's, okay?* What kind of choice is that?

I glance around the bare office. It should be Red Robin.

"I thought we could have a chat," says Barb, folding one

leg over the other. Her heels are violet and so pointy her toes must be squished (do angels have toes?). "It's nothing for you to worry about. It's just that it's getting close to the end of the investigation—only eight days to go—and I thought, *Why not check in with Tegan? See how she's doing.*"

Nervously, I pick at a thread in my jeans. "I'm fine."

"Have you learned anything useful?"

"Heaps."

"Such as?"

"Stuff."

"Specifically?"

I pick the thread so furiously it rips off. "I've learned I got jealous easily. If my friend paid too much attention to someone else, or if the girl I liked liked someone else."

Barb nods. "And why do you think Zelda would show you that?"

I frown at the little black thread. Before the fair I'd have said because she hates me. Or because she wants to torture me. But I can still feel the ghost of her hand in mine and I can still hear her saying, *I'd pick you.* That's not someone who hates me, right?

"Because she's trying to show me why the Marybelle made me happy," I answer. "Where's Ms. Chiu? I booked in for my third session. Can I see her now?"

Barb raps her nails against the desk. "Are you finding the investigation difficult?" she asks, once again ignoring my questions. "Some of those memories must be painful to relive."

Is this a counseling session? Part of the investigation? I glance around, half expecting to find Kelvin watching me, pen poised over his clipboard. I wonder what his notes about me say now. He can't still think I'm not trying. I worked out why Evan choosing Clem hurt so much. I didn't look away.

"I'm fine," I grit out. "I'm trying really hard."

She nods, uncrosses her legs and crosses them again, the other leg on top this time. "Are you? Are you trying?"

I don't want to swallow because she's close enough to see my throat bob and then she'll know I'm nervous and she'll think I'm lying.

I nod. "Definitely. Zelda's doing a really good job. And Kelvin's been watching. He can tell you. I've figured out both clues so far."

Barb stares at me for a long time. I refuse to look away or even blink. Suddenly she lifts her hand and snaps her fingers.

A moving image materializes in midair, just like before. This time, the floating video shows the inside of a Dollar Tree (green, green everywhere). There's music playing over the speakers, low and crackly, and one fluorescent light is on the brink. The view is trained on the candy aisle.

"You're eleven years old," says Barb, "and eager to impress a girl." She gestures as four girls appear on-screen.

One of them is me. Eleven-year-old me. Her hair is long, past her shoulders. She hates long hair but her mom says it makes her look pretty. She wears rainbow sneakers (laces undone), jeans, and a stripy long-sleeved T-shirt (cuffs tugged over her fingers like she's scared to touch the world and leave a mark).

The girl who leads the group is short and sharp-eyed and sucks on a lollipop.

"Her name is Sadie and you really want to be her friend," says Barb.

I don't take my eyes off the screen. It's strange seeing myself like this. Somehow it's weirder than when Zelda zaps us into the past. This feels less real, less like it's me I'm watching. That little version of me on the floating screen looks like an actress playing a part. Which I realize she kind of is. An actress desperately performing whichever version of herself she thinks Sadie will like most.

"You have to prove you really want to be one of us," says Sadie. She stops. The other two girls—I don't remember their names—stand on either side of her like tiny army generals. Sadie, I remember, was the queen of St. Anne's middle school. Everyone wanted to be her friend. "Are you going to do it? Do you want to be our friend?"

"Why are you showing me this?" I can't take my eyes off the screen but I can tell from the sound of rustling fabric that Barb has stood up. She doesn't answer.

"Do I have to?" asks eleven-year-old me. She glances at the chocolate bars, all bright and shiny and only a dollar. She has a dollar in her pocket. She could just buy one.

"You want to be our friend, don't you?" says Sadie. "Then you have to steal one."

Eleven-year-old me glances above their heads, looking for a camera or a mirror. There's nothing.

"I don't think she wants to be our friend," says one of the others. She has a short black bob and bangs; I think maybe her name was Breanna. Bree. Bianca. Something beginning with "B."

"I do. I swear." Eleven-year-old me reaches out, wincing when her clumsy fingers nudge the nearest candy, rustling the wrapper. It's so loud. She expects a cop to come running into the shop to arrest her. There's a hitch in her breath. But she snatches up the candy—a pack of Reese's Peanut Butter Cups—and quickly, all fingers and thumbs, shoves it into her back pocket. She is breathing so loudly, almost hyperventilating.

Barb snaps her fingers again and the video vanishes. I blink and shake my head like I'm coming out of a trance.

"What do Sadie and her friends say when you reach the parking lot outside?" asks Barb. She's leaning against the far wall, arms folded.

I push out the words as evenly as possible. "They say they don't like peanut butter. They say I need to go back in and steal something better."

"And what do you say in return?"

I knit my hands together to stop them from shaking. "I refuse. Because I'm too scared. So they tell me I can't be their friend. But they laugh when they say it, and that's when I realize they were leading me on. They were never going to be my friends; they just wanted to make me steal something. No matter what I took, it wouldn't have been 'the right thing.' They were just messing with me."

Barb nods and I want to ask her what grade I get for passing her test. Will she etch out a smiley face on my forehead for being a good girl?

"What a horrible experience," she says.

I shrug. "I got over it."

"They made you steal. Stealing is a sin."

I think of Zelda's black boots. I think of Trash Cat Baby. I think of my heart.

"I'm sorry," I say, and I mean it. I am. I can almost taste the stolen candy and it makes me feel sick. Sometimes that memory pops into my head out of nowhere and I feel an overwhelming rush of shame and guilt. It rises up in me now, an unstoppable wave.

Suddenly, Kelvin appears beside me.

Before I even have time to scream, he presses his palm to my forehead, and the most excruciating pain I've ever experienced shoots through me. It's worse than dying. I got hit by a car and it didn't hurt like this. This feels like being turned inside out and dipped in a vat of acid while a thousand pins are poked into my brain all at once.

Maybe it lasts a second, or maybe it lasts five hours.

When he pulls away, I slump forward, clutching my head in both hands. "What the hell was that?"

Kelvin pulls a small bottle out of his front shirt pocket and squeezes a glob of liquid into his palms. He pockets the bottle and rubs his hands together, making slick, squelching noises. The stench of disinfectant stings my nostrils.

"That will be all, Kelvin," says Barb.

His bug eyes bore into me for a moment, and then he vanishes, his disinfectant smell lingering in the empty air.

Barb walks toward me. I think I see pity or sadness on her face, or maybe I just can't see straight because of the tears in my eyes.

"What you just experienced is a small taste of purgatory," she says softly. She reaches out and smooths back my hair.

"Why? Why would you…?" My mouth is so dry I can't get the words out. There's a burning in the center of my chest. Instinctively I reach up to rub at the skin there but I know that won't do anything; the damage is inside. "What did he do to me?"

She keeps stroking my hair, like a mother would. Or I don't know. My mother never did that. Maybe it's just what I think a mother should do.

"I'm worried about you," Barb explains. "I want you to take this investigation seriously. Less hot dogs and Ferris wheel rides and *holding hands* and more introspection. There's a difference between identifying a source of pain and letting that pain go. All Kelvin has seen you do is name your pain, then continue to hoard it. If you wish to be happy, you must let your pain go. Don't you want to be happy, Tegan? Don't you want to prove your soul is clean enough to let the happiness in?" She sighs, shaking her head. "I want you to push the negativity out and let happiness in. I don't want to send you to purgatory." She sniffs the air, displeasure twisting her features. "It leaves behind quite a stench, doesn't it?"

She sits back down and recrosses her legs. There's not a single crease on her suit. She snaps her fingers yet again and the floating movie screen reappears. It's the Dollar Tree again. Green, green everywhere. Music. Fluorescent lights. *You have to prove you really want to be one of us. Are you going to do it? Do you want to be our friend?* The rustle of a candy wrapper.

I watch the familiar memory play out, but the hot flush of shame doesn't come.

I don't feel anything. There's a gaping hole of nothingness in my chest.

And then I understand: Kelvin took everything. He took the anger, the shame, the guilt, the fear. He took it all and now I feel *nothing.*

Ms. Chiu, I feel empty.

"Perhaps your focus will improve from here on out," says Barb. "I'm rooting for you," she adds with a wink. "Any questions?"

I shake my head. If I open my mouth I'll scream. I'll scream so loud the heavens will break and the universe will end and it won't matter who's happy and who isn't.

Ms. Chiu, I feel terrified.

Barb smiles. "Wonderful," she says, and vanishes.

SIXTEEN

I break out of that office like there's a ghost on my tail, not even bothering to wait for Ms. Chiu. I don't care if it means I forfeit a session with her.

Because what the hell was that? My brain has pins and needles, my heart is inside out, and my lungs are ash. What did Kelvin do to me?

I stumble into the motel office on unsteady legs, prodding at the memory Kelvin stripped clean. But every time I get close, the giant black hole of *nothingness* where my feelings should be leaves me gasping for breath. I lose my balance, cursing as I bash my elbow against the display case.

"No swearing in heaven," says a familiar voice from behind the computer screen.

Zelda.

"Where have you been?" I cry, racing to the counter. The relief is a salve. All I can think is: *I'm not alone anymore.* Zelda's back. She didn't leave me. She'll do her wiggle-dance, call me her snickerdoodle, wink with both eyes, and I'll forget about Kelvin and purgatory and black holes. At least for a minute.

"Kelvin will mark you down for swearing," she says in a

weird, emotionless monotone. She looks tired, her eyes bruised and her mouth tight. "He'll cut out your tongue and use it as a paperweight."

Should I hug her? Can I hug her? "Do you know what he just *did* to me?" I thrust my arm over the counter to hold my sleeve under her nose—the sharp stench of hand sanitizer clings to the fabric, proof that what happened in Ms. Chiu's office wasn't a bad dream. Zelda looks down at the sleeve and back at me, no change in her expression. "Barb ambushed me and showed me a memory and was like, 'You sinned!' and then Kelvin vacuumed my brain and Barb was like, 'Focus on the investigation or we'll torture you like this for two thousand years!'"

Zelda's eye twitches. "They did what?" she asks, slowly, carefully.

"Barb showed me what it was like in purgatory," I say, drawing my arm back. "As motivation or something. Did they do the same to you? Is that why you were gone so long?"

She stares at me, almost unblinking. Unease makes my skin crawl.

"No. They didn't try to motivate me," she says. "I guess you're just special." She smiles, but it's a stilted twist of her lips and it looks sad, too sad to be called a smile.

"Zelda, what happened? Where did you go?" I tug the ends of my cuffs until they cover my fingers. "I was worried."

The shutters go down on her face, her expression blank again. "Why would you care?"

"Why would I—?"

I look around, confused. Trash Cat Baby isn't at his perch. The once-messy desk is clean now too. No more sticky notes. The pins and needles in my brain grow sharper. This isn't right. Something isn't right.

"Why would you care?" she asks again.

I open my mouth but I don't know what to say. Of course I care. I missed her. I was worried. Even though I need her to lose, I don't *want* her to lose. I wish we could both win.

"Because we're friends," I say. The neediness in my voice makes my cheeks burn. "Friends" doesn't feel like the right word, but I don't know what else to say. She held my hand, she won me Snickerdoodle, she said, *I'd pick you.* We're *something.*

But the blankness in Zelda's eyes as she stares at me lifts the hairs on the back of my neck. "I'm not your friend," she says.

I jerk back. For a second I wonder if I'm still in that office with Barb and Kelvin and this is...an illusion? Another test? Another warning?

Zelda steps out from behind the counter. I look down at her feet. The shoes she stole from my dad are gone and she's wearing the Mary Janes again. She looks the same as when I first met her, right down to the unimpressed expression.

"I'm just an angel," she says, coldly. "You're just my job."

I take a step back. And another. My confusion turns to hurt, then to anger.

Funny how that's always the way. At least anger is familiar.

And it's a comfort too. Anger is a feeling that burns so bright it incinerates every other emotion, so you no longer have to think about the hurt, the confusion, the tangle of thoughts and feelings that makes things complicated. Anger is simple.

"Screw you." I flip her my middle finger. She does the same but with her wing. And yeah, it's impressive but I can't tell her that. "Why are you being such a butt-face?" I snap instead. "Carol came and took you away and then I didn't see you for a week. I was worried."

She rolls her eyes. "Don't be dramatic."

"Dramatic? Kelvin is hankering to scrape my soul clean for two thousand years, but sure, take a week off even though the clock is running out on this challenge."

For a second I spy a flash of something in her eyes—regret, sadness, pity, I don't know. All I know is there's a feeling there, something behind the blank mask. Something real. But it's only a flash and when it's gone it's hard to trust it was truly there.

"I'm doing my job," she says. "I'm good at my job."

"So your job is to hate me?"

Her jaw twitches. "I don't hate you."

I can't help but laugh. "Are you sure? Because your behavior suggests otherwise. Except when it doesn't. In fact, your behavior changes so much I don't know what to think. Why don't you make a calendar and write down which days we're friends and which days we're enemies? Because honestly I'm not sure how to keep track otherwise."

"Excellent idea," she says, whipping out a pen and a sticky note from her back pocket. When she's done scribbling, she holds out the little cat sticky note for me to take. On it she's drawn an arrow. At one end it says *beginning of time* and at the other it says *end of time* and in the middle she's written: *The expanse of time during which Tegan Masters makes me want to fire myself into the sun.*

"That's so much effort." I stare at the note, stunned. "That's so much effort to say *I don't like you.*"

"Just—" she starts. She huffs and stomps her foot. "Just let me do my job. I *have* to do my job."

She vanishes and I'm alone again, shaking with anger. I don't understand what happened. It's like a whole other puzzle I'm expected to solve: on the one hand there's Zelda at the fair grinning and laughing and saying *I'd pick you,* and on the other hand she's sneering, *I'm not your friend,* and I'm supposed to connect the dots and work out how one turned into the other.

Does it matter? All it boils down to is I'm alone again. I'm dead and alone and no one ever picks me.

I shove open the office door and race out. It's late. Dark. How long was I with Barb? I run up to my room and turn on *Snorks* at full volume and sit on the edge of the bed. My brain won't stop whirring, creeping ever closer to full-on anxiety-monster rampage.

A is for air conditioner.

B is for Bible.

C is for cephalopod.

D is for door.

E is for empty cup.

F is for fridge. (Why can't it be freckles?)

Glass, heater, ice tray, jeans...K? Kelvin? Kelvin with his hand pressed to my forehead as pain shoots through my body and—no. There is no K. I'm not okay.

Snickerdoodle stares at me from the floor. His eyes bore into my soul. Does he think it looks different? Can he see the missing piece, the piece Kelvin took?

I shake my head. *Keep it together, Tegan.*

I used to do this thing when I was alive. I'd be like, *If I toss this scrunched-up ball of paper and it lands in the trash can then I'll pass my math test this afternoon.* Or, *If I don't step on the cracks then I won't wake up in the middle of the night to raised voices in the next room.*

I do it now: if I sit still for five minutes then I will wake up and realize that my argument with Zelda was just a dream. She'll come back—the real Zelda, the one who makes my heart feel too big and too small at the same time. She'll call me a butt-face and zap us into a memory of that time I went to Trundle Manor for school. We'll race around the rooms together and she'll point at all the taxidermied animals and say, *That's you.* I'll dare her to eat one of the pickled organs and she will and it will be gross but I'll laugh and I won't feel like I'm slowly rotting from the inside out. Kelvin will give me a pass and Barb will give me a new heaven and I won't have to lose a single piece of myself to be happy.

I count, starting at one hundred and moving backward. Five minutes. That's all. I just have to last five minutes.

I don't last one.

I stand up. I can't sit here, and I can't hold it all in anymore. All the good and the bad and the hidden and scary, I'm suddenly feeling it all at once.

I race back outside. The full moon is hidden behind clouds and there are hardly any stars, but I count the ones I can see. Seven. No, eight. There's a small one so low in the sky I almost missed it. But it's not even real. All these stars, this entire place, isn't real.

I jog down to the pool. There are several beach umbrellas along its edge, all of them closed and tied up. I pick one up. Or I try to but the base is heavy so I end up dragging it. It screeches as the metal base scrapes along the concrete. It's a bitch hauling it through the parking lot, but I drag that umbrella all the way up to the invisible barrier stopping me from leaving the Marybelle. And then I try my absolute hardest to smash my way out.

Because I am done.

This investigation sucks.

Being dead sucks.

Heaven sucks.

I don't want to be alone. I don't want anyone's sticky fingers rooting through my brain and my heart and my soul, tearing out pieces of me, one by one. I don't want any of this.

Barb wants me to let go of my pain? Well, here I go.

I sing the *Snorks* theme song loudly as I bash the tip of the umbrella against the invisible barrier over and over again. The barrier doesn't crack; the umbrella just hits nothing and stops. It doesn't even leave a mark.

I scream and drop the umbrella. It falls like a redwood, collapsing off to the side with a bang as I scream again and beat my fists against the nothingness.

I want to leave. People leave all the time—they walk out and leave people behind. But I can't. I can't leave.

How can I let the pain go if there's nowhere for it to go *to*?

I bash so hard against the nothingness that I trip on my own feet and fall on my ass. It stings, bringing tears to my eyes. I lie there, looking up at cloud cover so thick the moon is only a hazy glow. Right above me, there's a crack in the clouds, and one tiny star peeks out.

I reach out my arm, stretch it as far as it will go, but I can't touch the star. I'm in heaven—shouldn't I be closer? Shouldn't I be close enough to reach out and touch the stars?

Not if they're not real, I remind myself. I lower my arm and cross them both over my chest like I'm lying in a coffin.

I close my eyes and wish for sleep.

✦ ✦ ✦

I wake up in the parking lot, lying on my back, hands still folded corpselike across my chest. Sleep might be fake now that I'm dead but I'm glad my pathetic human brain can still succumb to the urge. I blink my eyes again and again; they're crusty and sore. I rub them and sit up, looking around. It's late morning. Maybe afternoon. The emptiness of the place weighs extra heavy today.

Two glowing eyes watch me from under the Cow.

"Here, kitty," I call in a soft voice. Trash Cat the Elder tenses, edging back farther under the car. I wish I had food on me. I wish he knew he could trust me. I wish I'd tried harder to be nice to him when I was alive.

"I'm not going to hurt you. I'm your friend, okay?"

He doesn't move.

I tap the ground in front of me, rocking forward. "Please." My voice is barely above a whisper. "Please."

I rock forward a little more and he bolts. The disappointment tastes sour in my mouth. At some point a girl needs to ask herself, *Am I the common denominator here? Is it a coincidence that no one wants to stick with me or am I just inherently that big of a butt-face?*

I feel a presence, someone walking up behind me. I pick out the *swoosh swoosh* of a skirt and then I smell it: rose perfume.

Ms. Chiu.

I turn around. She smiles down at me, gathering her skirt as she sits next to me.

"You didn't show up yesterday," she says. "If you don't call ahead to reschedule, you forfeit the session."

I shiver when I remember *why* I missed it. The agony of Kelvin tearing away a piece of my soul keeps coming back to me, like a horror movie villain who just won't die.

"It's fine. I don't need to talk to you anymore. I'm all better." I hug my legs close, tugging the elastic band on my sock. "And if

I wasted a session yesterday, I'll have to keep the final two in my back pocket for emergencies."

Ms. Chiu opens her eyes and slowly, deliberately turns to look at the beach umbrella, felled like a tree in the middle of the lot.

"I can explain that," I say.

"A mutual friend thought this might be a bit of an emergency," she says with a small smile. "And that perhaps you were too stubborn to make the appointment yourself. So here I am."

Friend?

I grit my teeth. "She's not my friend."

I want to be angry but mostly I'm embarrassed. Because this means Zelda saw everything. The screaming, the umbrella, the fall, the sleeping like a corpse in the lot, the whole shebang. She saw it all. Worse, she didn't come and check on me herself. She sent Ms. Chiu.

"She's not supposed to be your friend, Tegan. She's an angel. She's only here to make your heaven run smoothly. And that's just one small part of her duties."

I lean back, my palms flat against the concrete. What's a polite way to tell Ms. Chiu the reason I didn't schedule a makeup appointment with her today is because I don't want to talk and I *really* don't want to be subjected to her crappy takes on life, the universe, and everything? Would *Shut up, butt-face* work in this scenario?

"That said," she continues, a thoughtful tilt to her head, "I'd say that, yes, she's your friend. Against her better judgment, despite…everything she's up against, she thinks of you rather fondly."

I snort. "Well, she's got a funny way of showing it." Or she's just a liar. She said she'd pick me. But she didn't.

Ms. Chiu sighs, shifting her grip on her knees. "The question you need to ask yourself, Tegan, is who are you really angry at?"

I laugh. "Seriously?" I guess we're having session number four after all.

She nods. "You're angry. You're angry all the time."

"Maybe I'm angry at the angel who ambushed me yesterday and let Kelvin cut out pieces of my soul. Or at Zelda for using the investigation to rub my nose in what makes me sad. What about Lou? She was stealing Clem from me. And what about Clem? For being so easy to steal. And Evan. For only agreeing to go out with me so she could get closer to Clem. What about my dad for dragging us to the Marybelle?" My voice breaks. I take a big, wet breath. "What about my mom?"

"What about her?"

I shake my head because there's no way I'm going *there*. But I can't stop thinking about that time, a month before the Marybelle, when I went downstairs for a glass of water in the middle of the night and found Mom at the kitchen table, looking at Dallas real estate listings on her laptop. One-bedroom apartments. "Helping Aunt Lily find a new place?" I asked, and Mom almost jumped out of her skin. She snapped the laptop shut and turned around to face me. "Yeah," she said, and she smiled, but I remember thinking she looked sad. Sad, I assumed, because her baby sister was moving far away, following husband number four to Dallas, where he had a new job. *Would you miss me that much?* I remember thinking. *If I ever left?*

"Does it matter?" I ask.

Ms. Chiu glances at the umbrella. "I think it matters to you."

I laugh. "No, it doesn't. It was just…a mistake."

"What was?"

I throw my hands around. "All of it. Trying to make Clem choose me, falling for Evan, the Marybelle, me. I was a mistake, did you know that? Of course you did. But I wasn't supposed to know. I only found out because Aunt Lily got drunk at Quinn's baby shower and told me. She said that's why my parents got married. Well, Granny Scott is why they got married—she had rules about things like that, or I guess you guys have rules about things like that and Granny Scott was a stickler for following your rules.

"Aunt Lily said it was ironic. 'I'm the one who actually *wants* a baby,' she said. 'But somehow, Edie, who never wanted one, ends up with two.'" I wipe away angry tears. "Don't you think it's okay to be angry about all that?"

"I think anger has a purpose," Ms. Chiu replies, drawing out her words with care. "But it's like fire. It's not something you can easily control. It can turn on you at any moment. This is why we want you to let your pain go." She reaches for my hand, gripping tightly. "It's not just to make room for happiness. When you keep all your pain and anger and resentment locked inside you, it has nowhere to go, nothing to burn but *you*."

I look down at her fingers. The green ink smudge is still there.

If my anger has nowhere to go, no one to burn but me, well, that's fine. I'm already dead.

"Shut up, butt-face," I say.

Ms. Chiu laughs and squeezes my hand. "Okay," she says. "Okay."

SEVENTEEN

Three days later, I'm sitting by the pool hugging Snickerdoodle when Zelda finally reappears. "This will hurt," she says, and flicks my forehead. When the world stops spinning we're standing in the parking lot outside my old high school, me and Zelda but no Snickerdoodle. It's overcast with a harsh wind, trash dancing across the gravel between cars. Sitting on the curb in front of me is fourteen-year-old me.

She's not alone.

"I can touch my toes," says Quinn. Six-almost-seven-year-old Quinn. She's dressed in her ballet clothes so it's Wednesday—after-school band practice for me, ballet practice for her, and then we wait for Mom to pick us up.

Zelda is right. This hurts.

Quinn.

I will never forget her face. I will never stop missing her. It will never not ache to think of her. Kelvin can scrub all he likes but he will never clean Quinn from my soul—she *is* my soul.

My baby sister.

I stumble forward a step and call out her name, a broken

sound. She doesn't look at me. Of course she doesn't. She will never look at me again.

"Can you touch your toes?" she asks. She bends in front of fourteen-year-old me, fingers brushing the tops of her pale pink sneakers, ponytail dragging across the asphalt.

Without standing up, the other me leans forward and clutches the tips of her Cons. They're new. Not a hole in them, the rubber tread pristine. She watches a gap in the trees, waiting for Mom's car to appear.

"That's cheating," says Quinn. She pops up, face flushed from dangling upside down.

"You asked if I could touch my toes. This is me touching my toes."

Quinn pirouettes. She wobbles and for a moment other me's eyes flick toward her, ready to reach out and grab her if she falls.

"I can touch my toes," says Zelda.

I glance at her, weary.

I don't know what I expect when I look at her. To find her sneering at me? Wearing a whole new outfit? To find subtle differences in her face, enough to make me wonder if I ever really knew her?

But she looks the same. She looks *exactly* the same as the angel who sat in that Ferris wheel with me and held my hand and gave me Snickerdoodle and said, *I'd pick you.*

Even if she looks the same, though, something has changed. I just don't know what.

Did Kelvin mess around in her head too? Did he scrub her soul clean of me?

I hug myself tightly and turn back to Quinn, because she's the one who matters right now, she's always the one who matters. I look her over, hungry for every detail—the tear in her leggings, the smear of dirt on her cheek, the way she can't kick her legs straight when she tries to cartwheel. Quinn is the one who matters, not Zelda.

Focus.

I wasn't sure about Quinn at first, when I was eight and she was a baby. I wanted to send her back for a refund. Mostly because I didn't want to share Mom's affection. I mean, what's half of almost nothing? I didn't know why the other moms left smiley faces on their kids' lunch boxes and wiped gunk off their faces with a spit-wet hankie or why they threw around *I love you* like those weren't the rarest, most precious words in the word. I didn't have any of that, but what I did have I wanted to keep all to myself.

I didn't have to share in the end. Turned out Mom had as little interest in Quinn as she did in me. Maybe less. Which I should have guessed, what with drunk Aunt Lily spilling her wine and Mom's secret all over the baby shower. "You can't save a marriage with a baby," she slurred before Granny Scott started force-feeding her black coffee. Mom didn't speak to Aunt Lily for six months after that. But they made up. And Aunt Lily was right. About a lot of things.

"When's Mom coming?" asks Quinn. She cartwheels again, ponytail swinging.

Fourteen-year-old me swallows roughly and looks down at her feet.

I do the same—the Cons are so much more worn and dirty on my feet than on the other me. Look at the difference two years make.

"I don't know," says the other me. She taps her pristine shoes against the gravel, checking her phone for the hundredth time. It starts to spit with rain.

"Do you remember this?" asks Zelda.

I don't look at her. Which is a mistake because instead of looking at Zelda I look at the break in the tree line where fourteen-year-old me is desperately hoping a car will appear, and it turns out that's where Kelvin is hanging out.

Crap.

How much will it hurt if he scrubs this memory clean? What will it be like to remember this moment and feel nothing?

"There were a lot of times I sat in a parking lot," I say.

It's true. If I added up the time spent waiting for Mom to pick us up and compared it to the pitiful sum total of time I got to spend alive on Earth, the result might make me cry.

I swallow the rising bile in my throat and focus on Quinn. Maybe she's the clue. I was jealous of Lou and I was jealous of Clem and in the beginning I was jealous of Quinn too. She's dancing, but fourteen-year-old me is ignoring her—she can't stop looking at the break in the tree line. She can't stop hoping.

Somehow I don't think this is about Quinn.

"Mom's not coming," I say.

Zelda nods. "She's not."

Because this isn't one of the times Mom was late. This time, she didn't come at all.

I think of a text:

Mom, you're supposed to pick us up. Where are you?

The last one I ever sent to her. Seems fitting.

I clench my jaw.

I do have happy memories with Mom. I remember the time me, Mom, and Aunt Lily stayed with Granny Scott and Mom laughed until she cried when Aunt Lily fell on her butt trying to escape the chickens. I remember how sometimes she'd come home from a late shift at the hospital and I'd get up and make her a milky coffee, the kind she liked with a dash of chocolate syrup in it. She'd look at me as I handed her the drink, she'd really look at me, and she'd smile and say, *Thanks, Teegs.*

But happy doesn't stand out the way sad does. I can agree with Barb on that one; sad leaves a stain.

"Third and final trip," says Zelda. She curls her wings around her shoulders like she's cold, like she's hugging herself. "This one doesn't have a neat arc. It's kind of a mess. And this isn't the start. But you know that."

The rain is coming down steadier now and I feel it hitting me but I don't get wet. The rain was cold, I remember, but I can't feel that cold anymore.

Quinn loved the rain. She liked how it made her hair frizz and she liked dancing in it and she liked catching raindrops on her tongue.

"This is the story of a family," says Zelda. "A mom and a dad and two daughters."

I try to memorize Quinn's smile. I want it imprinted on the backs of my eyelids so that every time I close my eyes I'll see her smile instead of unanswered *Where are you?* texts, real estate listings, Aunt Lily picking at the buttons on a tiny hand-knitted cardigan (pink) and drunkenly telling me I was a mistake. "A happy accident," corrected Dad. Aunt Lily snorted. Mom said nothing.

Ms. Chiu, can I be angry about that?

I look at Kelvin, still watching me in the distance, pen hovering over his clipboard. It makes my skin crawl.

It makes me think about Sadie.

Because now, every time I remember stealing the candy for her I feel nothing. Not the shame, the guilt, the anger. That terrifies me for a lot of reasons but most of all because I needed those feelings. I needed them to remind me why friends like Sadie weren't worth it.

What happens if Kelvin takes away the anger I feel in *this* moment? Fourteen-year-old me is seething with anger right now. She's angry at her mom for forgetting her and she's angry at herself for being forgettable. She needs that anger. *I* need it.

I need it to remember not to give away my heart to someone who can't remember to pick me up from school once a week.

"I get it." I glance at Zelda. "I've found your clue. I don't need to see any more."

She brushes nonexistent fluff off her jeans. "Oh yeah? What is it?"

The words are hard to push out, dry and ashy in my mouth. "It's Mom. It's . . . She didn't care about us. Not enough." I laugh, the chuckle dry and ashy too. "But once again your calculations suck because I stopped caring about that a long time ago."

"Maybe," says Zelda, but she's distracted, focused on something over my shoulder. She taps her blank watch. "Look. Here comes Ms. Chiu."

I turn in time to see a swirl of fall-colored clothes and a dark ponytail half hidden under a Met Museum umbrella.

This is the day I met her.

"You girls waiting for someone?" she calls.

Fourteen-year-old me looks like Trash Cat the Elder with his hackles up. "No," she mumbles, scowling at her shoes.

"Our mom is late," says Quinn.

Ms. Chiu looks worried but other me can't see it because she's refusing to look at the unfamiliar teacher. I know how this ends, though. It doesn't take Ms. Chiu long to win other me over, to get other me to accept the offer of a lift in her car. The rain helps a lot. But it's Ms. Chiu's voice and her kind eyes and her blue wren earrings that do most of the work. I really liked those earrings. They were my favorite.

"Listen. If this trip is about how Mom didn't give two hoots about us then let's just go back to the Marybelle now." I fold my arms tightly across my chest. "I know that already. I've known that a long time. I didn't even need drunk Aunt Lily to tell me I was a mistake—I'd figured that out by myself. You've got, what? Four days to go on this investigation? Don't waste time on this."

Zelda hums but doesn't say anything.

"Are you saying that's not what this is about?" I can't help another glance at the tree line. Kelvin's like a spider on the wall—you have to keep an eye on him in case he disappears when you're not looking because who knows where he'll pop up next?

He's already vanished.

Great.

Has he scuttled back to tell Barb I'm still hoarding my pain? How do I make them see that I'm holding on to it because I need it? I need it to remember.

"It has to be that." I run my fingers through my hair. "We're in a parking lot getting rained on because Mom forgot to pick us up for the hundredth time. And it fits with the others—I was worried Clem would abandon me. Evan *did* abandon me. And now Mom. I get it. You're not subtle. But none of that adds up to why you think the Marybelle was my happiest memory. It makes me hate the Marybelle even more."

Zelda taps her nose. "Spoilers," she says. But there's no humor in the sound.

I hate her. I have to—I don't want to forget what happens when I give her my heart. It doesn't end well. It never ends well.

"I don't even care," I say. I try to sound confident, like it's all one big joke to me. "You can screw up this investigation as badly as you like. Fine by me. Because then I win. And you lose."

She doesn't react. Not a twitch, not a blink, not a *Screw you, Snickerdoodle.*

Nothing.

With a shaky breath I turn away and watch Ms. Chiu lead Quinn to her car. A red hatchback, small and old and rusted. Quinn tells Ms. Chiu she's going to be a ballerina when she grows up, or maybe an astronaut. "You can be both," says Ms. Chiu. Fourteen-year-old me drags her feet and her bag, making Ms. Chiu wait for her. She's still hoping her mom will come. She hasn't run the numbers, she hasn't worked out that the good times are too few and the bad times are too many, that the chances are this doesn't end well. She's gambling on a happy ending when the odds are not in her favor.

It never ends well.

I hate that other me. She's naive and she doesn't pay enough attention to Quinn and in two years' time she's going to die.

"I want to sit in the front," says Quinn, but fourteen-year-old me herds her toward the backseat.

"Quinn." I say her name again, like it's a prayer. My feet itch to chase after her. The laws of physics can suck it because I need to hold her and hug her and never let her go.

I never got to say goodbye. How shitty is that? I just left and didn't say goodbye. What do you do when so much is left unsaid? Where do those words go?

Will Kelvin take them too?

He can't do that. They don't belong to him.

Car doors slam: one, two, three. I can't see Quinn anymore, not really. Just the shadow of her through the darkened windows.

The engine starts.

Ms. Chiu, don't leave. Don't take my baby sister with you.

"How am I supposed to know what makes me happy," I say, watching the red hatchback drive away, "if you keep showing me things that makes me sad?"

Zelda hums and lifts her gaze to the sky. "I don't like the rain," she says, and I don't know if she's ignoring me or if this is just another way I don't understand how her mind works. "But I like how it makes the air smell," she says. Her blank mask almost cracks. For a second. A flicker of her lips, just the corners. Almost a smile. Almost. She turns to me, squinting against the glare. I stare back at her and try not to remember the feel of her hand in mine. I fail.

"Have you seen enough?" she asks.

Too much, I think.

I've seen too much.

EIGHTEEN

When Zelda taps my forehead, I don't even flinch. One second I'm watching Ms. Chiu's car drive away, praying for Quinn to *turn around, look back out the window, one last time, turn around and smile,* and the next I'm standing in the middle of my bedroom.

I want to touch everything. I want to jump in my bed and pull the covers over my head. I want to breathe in the lived-in smell—the shoes, the fresh laundry, the candles, the cotton balls damp with nail polish remover in the trash can—and never breathe out again.

I want to stay.

I glance up at Zelda. "You didn't take me back to the Marybelle."

"I didn't." Her gaze flits around the room like a gnat. It lands for a moment on the unmade bed. It's a twin. Quinn had to squeeze in to fit next to me on the nights she'd crawl into that bed. My back would be flush against the wall, the chill seeping through my T-shirt. The walls are thin, not enough insulation. That's what makes this old house so cold.

Not that I can feel the cold anymore.

I run my fingers along the edge of the desk, lingering on the familiar bumps and grooves. "But I found the clue. Mom didn't give a shit about me, about any of us. The end."

Zelda shakes her head. "You always look at the wrong thing. You always miss what's important."

The second she stops speaking, I hear raised voices.

They're downstairs.

The annoying thing about thin walls, besides the cold, is the easy way sound carries. If Dad farts in the living room, Mom hears it in the bathroom. When it's people talking—or arguing—you can hear it but you can't make out the actual words. It's just: mumble, mumble, mumble. Door banging. Footsteps. More mumbling. Louder mumbling. Another door banging. Mumble, mumble, mumble. Footsteps. Silence.

I glare at my bed as if that's going to stop me from hearing the angry mumbles; there's a stain on my bedspread, purple marker from when Quinn was drawing and got so enthusiastic she drew right off the edge of the paper. I was mad at the time. I yelled and she cried. Mom told me to say sorry, and I did but I didn't mean it—Mom never said sorry when she made me cry so why should I have to?

The raised voices grow louder.

I look up and find Zelda watching me. Her blank mask is firmly in place, no cracks.

"You're really going all out with the whole make-Tegan-sad thing, aren't you?" I say. "Did you collude with Barb and Kelvin? They want me to let it go. Like I'm Elsa."

The old Zelda would have laughed. She'd have burst into song. She'd have bopped my nose and said, *Spoilers.*

This Zelda crooks a finger and says, "Follow me."

She leads me out the door. I drag my feet, glancing over my

shoulder at my messy room, at the closed door next to it. There's a cross-stitched name plaque on it, covered with cats and stars. It reads, QUINN'S ROOM. Granny Scott made it. It's crooked.

"Move your butt, butt-face," Zelda calls from the top of the stairs.

In our second session, Ms. Chiu said you can't miss something you never had. But now I'm learning you can miss something you didn't know you had. Because I miss Zelda, and I didn't know how much having her on my side meant until she went and decided to be my enemy again. Maybe missing things is just an essential part of being human. It's like you need water and food and shelter, and you need things to miss.

Maybe that's another thing Kelvin wants to scrub out of me.

I pause at the top of the stairs. Zelda is already at the bottom, and sitting on the last step is a girl. Me.

I descend slowly, edging past the other me, holding my breath—I don't know why. She's curled up as small as she can make herself, pressed against the wall, frowning into her lap. She's eleven or twelve. She flinches at every word coming from the kitchen.

"This way," says Zelda. She stomps into the living room and the mumbles become clearer. I can make out everything that's being said, but I really wish I couldn't. I glance back at younger me.

"That's a bullshit reason and you know it, Peter."

"Edie, *please*. Keep your voice down."

"You don't care if they hear—it's *you*, you don't want to hear what I have to say."

I step around the corner.

Mom and Dad are in the kitchen. Mom's making a coffee.

The machine whirls and grinds and beeps angrily as she pushes every button extra hard. She slams her cup down, throws a spoon into the sink. Dad has his back to me, hands in his hair, tugging.

"I'm listening, of course I'm listening," he says.

"Then what don't you get?" she snaps.

The funny thing about seeing Mom after so long is that it's not funny at all. It's a hole-in-my-heart kind of pain that takes me by surprise because I thought I was over it. I thought I was too angry to be sad.

I was wrong.

She turns to face Dad. She's not that old, late thirties, but she looks tired, worn out. There's a stain on the sleeve of her college sweater, yellow paint from when she helped renovate the spare room at Aunt Lily's house because Lily was pregnant and it was going to be a nursery. But Aunt Lily lost the baby and then she lost husband number two. I used to see Mom pick at the paint stain with a frown, and I'd think: *Why do you keep wearing that sweater if it reminds you of bad things?*

Maybe she was trying to remind herself to stay angry too.

"We already paid the school fees for the year," says Dad. "If we pull her out now, it's a waste. And we don't have that kind of money to lose."

"It's not about money. Don't make this about money." She hits the coffee machine with the heel of her palm to make it go faster. It doesn't work.

"You're right. It's not about money, it's about commitment. When you commit to something you need to stick it out."

Mom's back grows rigid. "People make mistakes, Peter. They can change their minds."

I guess this is about St. Anne's. Me needing to transfer out, to get away from Sadie. I glance back at the stairs but from here I can only glimpse a pair of legs, jiggling nervously.

I take a step closer to the kitchen, toward Mom. Because the funny thing that isn't funny at all is that I've missed her. Not like Quinn. Not like Clem or Dad. I've always missed her; even when she was standing right in front of me she was never really there.

Ms. Chiu, I think you can miss something you never had.

"She can't just run away every time things don't go her way," Dad is saying. "We'll talk to the girl's parents. Figure this out. She doesn't have to leave the damn school."

Mom scoffs. "Did you see her crying? She hates it there. We shouldn't have sent her in the first place."

"Well, that wasn't my idea, was it?"

Mom laughs, harsh and bitter. "Oh, so this is *my* fault? Of course it is."

"They're really going for it, huh?" says Zelda.

I curl my hands into fists and say nothing.

Mom shoves the milk back in the fridge and slams the door. They keep arguing. The topics shift. Something about Aunt Lily. Something about Mom working too many hours. Something about space: Mom says she doesn't have enough. You crowd me, she says. You all want something from me all the time. Like leeches. I can't breathe when I'm here, she says.

My heart lurches. I can't breathe either, Mom.

I jump in fright as younger me suddenly stalks past, making a beeline for the kitchen, her face a storm. Mom and Dad stop arguing; Dad smiles.

"Hey, kiddo."

The other me heads for the fridge without answering. She

pretends like she wasn't just listening, like she hasn't heard every version of this argument before, like it wasn't her fault they're fighting this time. *Mistake.* The word swirls around in her head. *Mistake.*

She opens the fridge and bends to look inside. She's thinking, *At least Mom is on my side this time.*

Behind her back, Mom gives Dad a look. She wants to keep arguing but Dad's just smiling, acting like everything is peachy. He's not going to argue in front of the other me. Which is ridiculous—doesn't he know she's heard every fart, every door slam, every *mumble mumble mumble*?

Mom marches toward the stairs with her coffee. Dad tries to grab hold of her but she yanks her arm out of his grip, spilling coffee over the side of her cup. She doesn't stop to clean it up. She doesn't even look down at the dark stain on the kitchen tiles. She keeps walking, sneakers squeaking against the tiles.

She is good at walking away.

Why do I still want to chase after her?

"Looking for a snack, kiddo?" says Dad. The other me ignores him. She's fixing a peanut butter sandwich. She's mad at him because of what she overheard; she thinks he's not on her side. He always says, *We're Team Masters. We stick together. Nothing's more important than family.* She thinks that must be a lie. She doesn't understand they weren't arguing about her, not really.

"Peanut butter," says Dad. "Good choice."

He shoots her his everything-will-be-all-right smile, then he leaves. He walks upstairs after Mom and in less than a minute the *mumble, mumble, loud mumble, door slam, mumble, mumble, mumble* starts up again. Other me tosses the knife into the sink, next to Mom's spoon—the clatter is loud but she doesn't flinch. She's used to the noise.

I look away, the tightness in my throat making it hard to swallow.

Zelda has plonked herself on the couch and is flipping through TV channels on the remote.

I hug myself. "You're bad at this challenge," I say.

She shrugs. "Maybe. Or maybe you are. For example: Do you know why I brought you here?" She flicks to a quiz show and stops. The crowd on the TV applauds. "Do you?"

"Do you know Trundle Manor?" I counter. I approach the back of the couch. I'm looking down at Zelda, at the tips of her pearlescent wings, the messy part in her hair, the golden-toned skin at the back of her neck. I'm not looking at the other me.

She doesn't answer me. She answers the quiz host when he asks: *How many bones does a shark have?*

"None!" she calls out. "Trick question. A shark skeleton is made of cartilage."

Mumble, mumble, loud mumble, door slam, mumble, mumble, mumble.

"I went there once with my friends. It was fun."

"Helium!"

"We could go there. They have taxidermied animals and pickled organs and so much weird stuff. You'll love it. I'm sure there's a clue there. It was probably a defining moment. Maybe."

"Alabama!" calls Zelda.

I startle as younger me drops her plate into the sink and stalks out of the kitchen, into the backyard. Upstairs the voices continue. *Mumble, mumble, mumble.*

"That's our cue," says Zelda. She stands, flinging the remote back onto the couch cushions and making her way through the living room.

I follow her on autopilot. I don't understand this. I found the clue. I just want to leave. *Mumble, mumble, loud mumble.* She opens the back door and leads me onto the covered porch. In summer, it's Mom and Aunt Lily's favorite place to sit, drink wine, and talk about the old days. Or bitch about Dad. Or both.

Zelda doesn't linger. She leads me into the yard, where younger me sits on a folding chair, her feet propped up on the edge of the trampoline while Quinn bounces up and down.

I exhale slowly, some of the tightness in my chest releasing. There she is.

Younger me takes a bite of her sandwich. "Do a flip."

Quinn does a jumping jack in the air.

"That's not a flip."

"I'm going to be an Olympic gymnast," says Quinn.

"Not if you can't flip."

The voices inside the house grow louder. A door slams and I flinch. The other me flinches too.

The back door flings open and Mom steps out. She falters when she realizes other me and Quinn are in the backyard but she doesn't retreat. She sits on the back step, coffee in one hand and an unlit cigarette in the other. She gave up smoking when I was seven but she still liked to hold a cigarette in her hand because she said it calmed her.

"Mom! Mom!" cries Quinn. "I'm going to be an Olympic gymnast." She does three jumping jacks in a row.

"Very good," says Mom, not quite looking at Quinn. She rolls the cigarette between her thumb and pointer finger.

The front door opens and closes in the distance. A minute later, a car starts up. I recognize the deep rumble of the Cow. Other me tries to make eye contact with Mom. Other me wants to say sorry, she wants to ask if her mom still thinks she's a mistake, she wants to say thank you for being on her side this time. She says nothing.

"I can spin too," says Quinn. She pirouettes in the air, almost a full circle, but she can't stick the landing; she falls onto her knees, laughing, bouncing.

Mom tucks the cigarette into her pocket and drains the last of her coffee. She sets down the empty cup on the porch and stands, striding down the yard toward the trampoline with a scary kind of purpose. There's a stool at one end, near where other me has her feet resting on the bar. Mom climbs up the stool and onto the trampoline.

"Mommy's going to be an Olympic gymnast too," crows Quinn.

Other me watches in shock as Mom climbs to her feet, wobbly as a newborn foal. When she's finally upright she starts to bounce, arms outstretched, face unsure. Quinn laughs, delighted to be playing with her mother. She bounces harder, higher. They both do. And then Mom is laughing too, in a way other me has never heard before. Strands of hair fall out of her ponytail and whip around her face. She looks wild and happy and free as she bounces higher and higher. Other me smiles.

No. I shake my head.

No, no, *no.*

This is why Kelvin can't take my anger. If he takes it away, I'll forget. I'll forget that I'm supposed to hate my mom and I'll love her again. Nothing hurts more than loving her.

I turn to Zelda and she's watching me, always watching me. She doesn't look away when our eyes meet. Her mask is in place but I swear I see something in her eyes, something real, something that cares.

I turn back. Mom and Quinn hold hands, bouncing in a circle as they sing "Ring Around the Rosie." They fall onto their backs at the end, and Mom laughs so much there are tears in her eyes.

I hold a hand to my mouth.

This is the thing that hurts: There were good times. More than I'm ready to admit. There were hikes and ice hockey and baking and weekends at Granny Scott's. It's just easier to make a demon out of Mom so I can say, *See? It doesn't matter that she didn't love me, she wasn't a good person.* But that's a lie.

Maybe she did love me. Maybe I loved her. Maybe it's complicated. Messy. No clear arc.

"Okay," I say to Zelda. "So you're *not* trying to show me that Mom didn't give a damn about us."

Mom pulls other me onto the trampoline so she can join in. She's awkward at first, unsure of what's happening and unsteady on her feet. But then Quinn bounces and laughs and Mom laughs and other me laughs too as she kicks off her shoes and they fall to the ground; one rolls under the trampoline.

"I told you," says Zelda. "I told you." She watches as younger me bounces in a circle with Quinn and Mom, her face blank but her eyes a storm of *something*.

I can't look at Zelda but I can't look at other me having fun, either. Because she's so happy. Her head is thrown back and she's laughing and she's happy but it's not going to last. It never lasts. She needs to learn that holding tight to her anger and pain helps her remember that.

Is that what I'm supposed to learn? That the Marybelle was good because it was the ultimate pain and it taught me to never give up that feeling in case love slips through the gaps?

I can't do this.

I turn to the yard next door, Mrs. Nowak's yard, and see her cat playing in the grass. Her name was Tootsie. She didn't like to be cuddled but she'd slink between your legs in figure eights and meow until you scratched under her chin. I point. "Look. A cat."

Zelda doesn't look. I see her swallow. I see her twitch, like she was about to turn but then remembered she wasn't supposed to and only just stopped herself in time. She hardens her expression. "We're not here for the cat," she says, and taps my forehead.

NINETEEN

We're on the front steps of my house, a miserable gray sky above us, and in front of us is a small yard with overgrown grass and a maple tree. Quinn's bike rests on its side in the middle of the yard. Every now and then there's a strong gust of wind and the back wheel turns, creaking. Fallen maple leaves rustle like ghosts.

"We could have walked through the house to get here," I say. "You didn't need to do your—" I waggle my fingers in her face.

"It's not the same day." Zelda looks around with a serious face like she's revving herself up to take a hard test. "It's another day."

"When?"

She doesn't answer. She sits on the top step, cupping her knees. After a moment I sit too. I wait and wait but nothing happens. I can't get Mom's laughter out of my head. I hate that instead of anger it makes me feel...God, I don't know, hope, and maybe shame too. Why didn't she laugh like that more often? Was it my fault?

I feel like I'm losing control.

A pair of birds chatter to each other, and it reminds me of sitting on the front porch with Dad once when I was little, watching two birds screech as they fled Mrs. Nowak's cat. "Listen to them," Dad laughed. "They're telling Tootsie to get lost."

I remember turning to him with awe and asking how he knew that, how he understood what the birds were saying. He tapped the side of his nose and smiled. "I just do," he said. So kid me figured understanding birds was something you could do when you were an adult.

"I'm sorry," says Zelda. Something in the tone of her voice unsettles me and I can't look at her. I scan the tree instead, searching for a glimpse of the birds making all that noise. It makes me think of the aviary, and I really wish I was back there. Here's an idea, Barb: We get to choose which memories become our heaven. We can jump from one memory to another whenever we feel like it, and we never have to set foot in the bad ones. You can have that idea for free.

"I'm sorry I can't explain to you why things have to be this way," says Zelda, "and I'm sorry you hate your heaven. I'm sorry you're not happy. I'm sorry you're dead."

The birds keep twittering and I don't understand a word they're saying. Maybe because I'm still not grown-up and now I never will be.

I'll never understand birds.

"But most of all," says Zelda, and I finally work up the courage to face her. She squints against the sun, nose scrunched up, hands wrapped around her ankles so her knees are bunched up against her chest. "Most of all, I'm sorry about this." Zelda nods toward the road, to where a familiar brown station wagon has just rounded the corner. It jolts over the curb as it turns into the driveway and my heart jolts too. The sun's glare on the front windshield makes it impossible to tell who's inside but I can guess.

"Why?" I croak. "Why would you do this?"

Zelda looks at me, her eyes glassy with unshed tears. "Because I have to."

A car door slams before the engine has even shut off. I turn as footsteps approach us, fast. Someone is running.

The girl who runs past us—a blur of flannel and jeans and sneakers so worn that one sole flaps with every step—is fifteen. She has never seen the ocean, despite having just spent a long weekend six blocks from the Wildwood shoreline at the Mary-belle Motor Lodge. But she is no longer worried about that. She isn't searching for the ocean anymore. She is searching for her mother.

"Tegan!" Dad calls from the car. He's wrestling with the seat belt tangled around his arm as he tries to climb out of the driver's-side door.

Quinn calls for her sister too. She's in the backseat; Trash Monkey dangles from her grip, stained with dirt and burrito and pool scum. The weekend at the Marybelle hasn't been kind to Trash Monkey. It hasn't been kind to any of them.

The front door hangs open. Inside the house, footsteps move from room to room, pounding. The broken sole slaps against the hardwood floors. Later, other me will glue it back on, but right now she doesn't care.

I feel Zelda's eyes on me but I don't have the brain space to acknowledge her. I watch Dad help Quinn out of the car. She's asking him what's wrong with Tegan. "Nothing's wrong, princess," he tells her. "Everything's fine. Your sister's just excited to be home."

I choke on a cry. I want to scream: *That's a lie! Everything is wrong.* But I can't get the words out and he won't hear me anyway. I wonder: Is that what you told her? When I died? When I left the house that morning and never came home? Did you say everything was fine then too?

I reach out as they pass, fingertips brushing Trash Monkey's soft fur.

The front door swings shut behind them and the only sound I can hear is their muted footsteps inside the house; the birds suddenly have nothing to say.

Zelda fidgets but doesn't get up. Shouldn't we follow them inside? Shouldn't she drag me through the house, chasing fifteen-year-old me from room to room? We could be there when she ends up in her parents' bedroom, when she sees that the wardrobe has been emptied on one side, when she realizes her mother took everything with her to Dallas, when she realizes her mother never had any intention of coming back. We could see her break down and cry, and then I'll have to admit that, yes, there is one memory worse than the Marybelle.

But Zelda doesn't move. I listen to the footsteps and the *mumble, mumble, loud mumble, door slam*. Eventually the birds start chattering again. What are you saying, birds? Why can't I know your secrets? Did you see what happened when my mother left? Did she tell you why she was leaving us?

I wipe my eyes. "You said this wasn't about Mom but…"

Zelda startles at the sound of my voice. We turn to look at each other at the same time. The tears sparkle in her eyes.

"What do you think?" she asks.

I think Kelvin is warming my seat in purgatory because the only thing I know for certain is that maybe my mom kind of loved me and maybe we laughed together sometimes but she still left us, she still walked away and didn't say goodbye. And if I don't feel angry about that, if I don't hold on to that anger with everything I've got, I'll remember the sad truth: that I wasn't enough to make her stay.

The door behind us swings open and the other Tegan rushes by us. She gets as far as the end of the driveway before she stops. Her body is tightly wound, a coiled spring on a mousetrap. She groans, long and low, and then she slumps to the ground, head in her hands. She cries silently, the kind of crying that's all wet, quiet gasping. Her shoulders shake but the only sound I can make out from where we sit is the chatter of the birds.

"You must think I'm oblivious," I say. I feel rather than see Zelda turn to look at me. "I didn't figure out she'd left us, not until this moment." I glance at her but can't hold her gaze for long. It was obvious, wasn't it? The laptop. The one-bedroom apartments in Dallas. The way she'd sometimes look at me with a furrowed brow and I could see what she was thinking, clear as a bell: *What if I'd made a different choice?*

"A week before Aunt Lily moved, I overheard her talking to Mom on the back porch. She was saying, 'What have you got to lose? You only live once.' If I'd realized what she meant, maybe I could have answered: *Us. You'll lose us.*" I turn to Zelda. The tears are falling now, and it's beautiful and tragic. What do they call that? Bittersweet? "Do you think it would have made a difference?" I ask. "If I'd told her what she was going to lose?"

Zelda takes a deep breath and smiles, just a little.

"No," she says, and I really, really love her for saying it. "No, it wouldn't have made a difference."

I nod. At least I know that. I wish I'd listened to my dad when he said you could tell a lot about a person by the shoes they wore. My mother always wore running shoes. She was always ready to run.

"I'm sorry," says Zelda. "I'm sorry she left you."

"She didn't leave us." I laugh—what else can I do? "She was never here to begin with."

Whenever I talked to her, she'd get this look in her eyes, like: *I'm not listening to your words. I'm listening for the end of your words so I can walk away.* She never said, *I love you,* she said, *I'm tired, Tegan, can't this wait?* She forgot to pick us up from school. She missed ballet recitals and end-of-year concerts and parent-teacher interviews. She was never happy, even when she was bouncing up and down on a trampoline, laughing.

My mother didn't leave us. She was never here. And the funny thing, the funny thing that is not funny at all, is that as soon as I admit this, I forgive her for it.

I forgive her.

I forgive her for the choices she made and I forgive her for the choices that were made for her. I forgive her for bending under the weight of Granny Scott's rules. I forgive her because Dad had wanted to be a father more than anything, and because everybody thinks if you're a woman you're supposed to want to be a mother more than anything. I forgive her for being unable to stop being her own person—to stop having her own hopes and wants and needs—when she became my mom.

I hate her.

I love her.

I wished she'd loved me more.

I forgive her.

But if I can't blame my mom for leaving anymore, the only person I have left to blame is myself, for not being enough to make her want to stay. To make her say, *I pick you.*

I take a deep, trembling breath.

"So that makes *three* people who didn't love me as much as I loved them." I cut a look at Zelda. "But how does that make the Marybelle my heaven?"

She shakes her head.

"Well done, though." I clap. "You chose the perfect combination of memories to stick the knife into my heart and say, *Look, Tegan, you weren't imagining it: Everyone walked away from you eventually. Including your own mother, and you can't even hold it against her.*"

Zelda's gaze doesn't falter. Her eyes burn into mine and I feel like Icarus again.

"You're so close," she says. "You're almost there."

I laugh and look away. I'm not close, I'm a mess. Everything in my head is a mess.

Bitterness wells up inside me. "When I finally told Clem my mom had left, she said some people are not built to want things like a family. I understand now how that can be true. And I think it's okay. But Mom could at least have loved us, even if she didn't want to be a family. She's my mom. She's supposed to love me, even if I was a mistake."

"It's complicated," says Zelda.

"It sucks," I say.

I flinch as the door behind us opens. I don't turn around, but I recognize the sound of my father's footsteps, as familiar to me as my own heartbeat. I grip my knees tightly as he moves past us, down the driveway to sit beside his crying daughter.

"Hey, now," he coos.

"Did you know?" other me asks.

I feel the phantom touch of his skin against mine as he slides his arm around her shoulders. I remember how it stung where his skin touched mine, and I remember thinking: *Am I allergic to my father now?*

Why hasn't Zelda shown me a memory focused on him?

"I'm sorry, Teegs," he says, a mumble I can barely hear over the twittering birds. "She's gone."

I curl in on myself. Zelda's wing brushes my shoulder and I don't know if it's an accident but I know it doesn't sting.

"He made me watch him fall apart," I say. "Four days stuck in that place, watching him fall apart, worried out of my mind. But I still had hope. I hoped we'd go home and Mom would be waiting for us. I hoped she'd fix whatever was wrong with Dad. I hoped one day we'd be the happy family Dad always said we were. That's what the Marybelle represents: crushed hope. Not happiness."

I turn to Zelda, but she can't look at me and that almost makes me laugh.

Because, absurdly enough, I still hope. I hope for a Ferris wheel and a hand in mine and a smile and a promise: *I'd pick you.* I hope that somewhere in Dallas my mom cried when she found out I was dead. I hope I mattered. I'm scared I didn't.

All of that anger in me and it's for nothing—I can't get rid of my hope.

"We're still a team," says Dad to the other me. "I'm still here."

Ms. Chiu, why does that hurt to hear most of all?

TWENTY

Zelda taps my forehead and the front yard disintegrates like a scattered jigsaw puzzle, then re-forms piece by piece as the Marybelle. Snickerdoodle has fallen into the pool. He floats facedown like a drowning victim. He's from the ocean, I reassure myself. He knows how to swim.

I startle at a light touch against my forearm.

"I'm sorry." Zelda looks at me like I'm Trash Cat the Elder hiding under the car, afraid of everything. Maybe I am. I have battle scars too.

"I'm sorry," she says again, and I wish she wouldn't say those words.

That's what Dad kept saying about Mom. When I made a bonfire with all the belongings she'd left behind—*I'm sorry, Tegan.* When I flipped that desk and he had to pick me up from school—*I'm sorry.* When I asked him why he dragged us to Jersey to watch him fall apart instead of telling us the truth—*I'm sorry, baby. I didn't mean to scare you.*

"You're not sorry," I say, backing away from Zelda. "You just want to win the investigation."

She shakes her head. "I want you to be happy."

"If you wanted me to be happy you'd have said sorry back when I told you this wasn't my heaven. *Oh, this is the wrong memory? Sorry, Tegan Masters. Let me fix that for you.*" I kick the nearest pool lounge. One leg collapses with a crash. "You don't care about my happiness. You just want me to forget that you made the wrong choice and don't know how to deal with the consequences."

Her wings slump and she ducks her head. "You don't know what you're talking about," she mutters.

"And if you told me? If you filled in the blanks? But you're not going to do that, are you? Because spoilers, right?"

She won't look at me. I feel a surge of anger, familiar and welcome. I know what to do with anger. I kick the other leg on the pool lounge. It doesn't collapse but the whole thing shudders and it feels good. It feels good to break things that aren't me.

"Well, you're not going to win," I say. "My mom left us, and instead of telling us the truth, instead of dealing with it like an adult, my dad dragged me and Quinn to the shittiest motel in America and fell apart in front of our eyes. 'Everything is fine, Tegan,' he said. But I watched him cry and I watched him sleep all day and I watched him call a disconnected phone over and over again and I couldn't leave his side even for a second because I was terrified of what he'd do if I wasn't there to stop him. How is any of that happiness? How does anything you've shown me prove that the Marybelle was my happiest memory?"

She mutters something I can't hear over the pounding of my own dead heartbeat. I take a step closer. "Say that again," I demand.

For a moment she doesn't move and I figure she's going to ignore me. But then she lifts her head and her eyes are steel. "It's complicated," she repeats, slow and clear.

Everything is fine.

Today is a good day to be happy.

If you see the positive in the world, the world will see the positive in you.

I'm sorry.

Spoilers.

She's gone.

It's complicated.

I want to cut these words out of the dictionary. I want to fire them into the sun.

"It's complicated?" I choke back a laugh.

"What do you think happiness is?" she asks.

"The opposite of this!" I kick the lounge again. I want to burn this whole place to the ground. I want to watch it disintegrate and I want it to be my doing.

"Exactly!" she yells, and I see a fire in her I haven't seen since Carol stole her away from me at the fair. "Stop looking at the wrong thing and start looking at what is staring you right in the face!"

"I *am* looking. You think I'm not? They're going to drag me to purgatory and rip half my soul clean out of me, and you don't think I'm motivated to try?" I start picking up things and throwing them, whatever I can grab, whatever I can lift. I throw them into the pool. A table. The lounge. An empty pizza box. My shoes. I drag the other umbrella in too. Water splashes all over me—I feel the moisture but not the cold. I hate it here. I hate it. "But I looked and I saw and I feel worse than when I started."

Zelda watches me, arms folded, jaw locked. She doesn't say a word, she doesn't try to stop me.

"Are you going to send Ms. Chiu to do your dirty work

again?" I yell. I've run out of things to throw. "Are you going to tell her Tegan's lost her mind and she's trashing heaven? How does *anyone* stay sane in this place? Or do they just send the dissenters to purgatory to have their souls scrubbed and scoured until they're too numb to feel anything?"

Zelda vanishes.

"Good! Leave!" I yell at the empty space. I yell so hard my voice cracks. "Everybody leaves! Why should you be any different?"

I march into the restaurant and start tipping over chairs and tables. A chair lands on my foot and pain shoots up my leg but I don't care. I'm dead. It's not real. I tip over the trestle table and the silver domes tumble to the ground, food spilling everywhere. The crash is so loud. Surely every dead person in all of heaven heard it. Maybe it was so loud that people on Earth heard a thunderous rumble and looked to the sky. Maybe my mom looked, wherever she is. Maybe Dad looked and Quinn got scared and he said, *Don't worry, baby, everything is fine.*

I march back outside, headed for the golf course.

I take a club to the giant mushroom and beat the crap out of it. I attack the windmill, the dinosaur, the kiosk.

"Are you done?"

I swing around.

Kelvin leans against the giant toad, clipboard hugged to his chest. "I haven't seen a hissy fit this big since a certain fallen angel tried to start a revolution."

"What are you doing here?" I spit.

He raps his nails against the clipboard. "My job."

I flinch. Is he here to suck out more of my feelings? "I'm not—" My tongue is thick and I stumble over my words. "I mean, Barb told me I needed to let my pain out. So I did." I motion at the broken kiosk. There's a dent in the poster dad's forehead that wasn't there before. "It's catharsis. It's not…I'm fine."

Kelvin hums and makes a note on his clipboard. I picture it, the words he's writing. *Pathological reluctance. Not trying hard enough. Fail. Too emotional. Too stained.*

I lower the club. "Be honest," I say. "Is there a chance I can win this challenge? Or have you already made up your mind?"

He meets my eye. "Actually, Tegan, I'm inclined to fail you both."

The blood drains from my face. "What? That's not…Those aren't the rules."

"It's clear to me Zelda made a mistake. But I think Admissions made a mistake too." He taps his pen against his clipboard. "And when Barb reads my report she's going to agree with me. You aren't at all convinced by Zelda's calculations and it's not because you aren't trying—they just suck. But you suck too. You're impulsive, bitter, hysterical, and utterly contaminated with *feelings.* You need a seriously good clean."

"That's not—I was fast-tracked for a reason. I can do this."

He ignores me. My grip around the golf club tightens.

"I'm going to level with you," he says, almost sounding bored. "I hate the fast-track system. Yes, I know purgatory needs a break sometimes, but this isn't the answer. You're human. There's no such thing as a human clean enough to enter heaven without being scrubbed first. You humans are such a miserable lot. You don't even want to be happy; you *enjoy* being miserable. We have to *force* you to accept happiness. Isn't that pathetic?" He brushes his greasy bangs out of his eyes with the end of his pen. I stumble back, shock weakening my limbs. "So don't fight the inevitable, okay? It's only going to make it hurt more." He smirks. "Ciao." In the blink of an eye he's gone.

The only thing keeping me upright is the golf club. I lean against it, trying to catch my breath. I feel his clammy hand against my forehead, the pain, the emptiness left behind.

"No. No, no, *no*." What have I done?

I can't win.

Two thousand years of agony. I'll lose everything. I'll lose me.

I drag the golf club behind me as I race back to the pool and fish Snickerdoodle out of the water. He's soaked to the core, but I hug him tight, hardly noticing the pool water that saturates my sweater. I head for the office, golf club and sodden plushie in tow.

What have I done?

I look around. There's no Trash Cat Baby. The bell's still there, the sticky tape as yellowed and peeling as ever. *Please ring for attention!* The heater hums loudly, the ribbons wriggling, pumping out hot air I can't feel.

No one is behind the desk.

"Zelda?"

No response.

I press the bell, holding it down until my finger hurts.

No one comes.

Shit. Shit, shit, shit.

I drop the club; it hits the floor with a clatter. Did they hear that on Earth too? I squeeze Snickerdoodle closer; water drips from his tentacles, splattering all over my feet. I don't know what to do.

What do I do?

I kick the base of the counter. It's hollow and the sound reverberates. I kick it again and again and again. My toes are bare and it hurts but I need to do something. *Anything.*

What do I do?

I look up. The manager's door is ajar. Like someone was in a hurry and forgot to close it behind them. I frown, running my hand through Snickerdoodle's damp fur.

"What do you think, Snickerdoodle?"

I could go to Barb. Tell her Kelvin's a human-hating Lucifer wannabe and he's not following the rules. Filing a complaint didn't go so well the first time but I don't want to go to purgatory. I don't want to lose a single piece of myself—I'm incomplete, still struggling to fit all the puzzle pieces of myself together. How am I supposed to complete that puzzle if they *take* pieces away?

I breathe deep and step forward, leaving a trail of water behind me. I push the door open, slowly. It creaks (shut up, creepy door). On the other side is a familiar endless corridor.

My stomach flutters. Is this how I felt when I stole that candy bar? I can't remember. Kelvin took that feeling from me.

Without another thought I rush through the door. I have to find Barb. I have to.

I move quickly. The corridor is never-ending and I don't know which door is Barb's. I should have counted them when I was here last time.

"Do you know, Snickerdoodle?"

He doesn't answer so I keep walking. Every now and then I pause outside a door to press my ear to the wood and listen. Silence. Maybe I should open one. I could pop my head through—just enough so they can't tell I'm wingless—and be like, *Oh hey, have you seen Barb? I need to tell her Kelvin is a dickcheese.*

My step falters as I consider that maybe breaking out of heaven, no matter the reason, is bad. I bet there's a super-long list of rules—thou shalt not do a bunch of stuff—and breaking into this endless corridor is probably high on the list of thou-shalt-nots. I might have spent only eight months and six days in Catholic school but I know angels are sticklers for rules and if you break them your ass is toast. Just ask Lucifer. Just ask Granny Scott.

Oh. Oh no. What if they decide that breaking out of heaven means not even purgatory can save me so they send me to hell instead?

Okay this was a bad idea.

I turn around and run back the way I came. I can call Barb from the office—they heard me last time, right? The telephone appeared when I complained out loud. Damn it! Why didn't I think of that earlier? I run and run but the corridor never ends. What happened to my door? I run until I don't have a single breath left in me, and then I keel over, gasping. What the hell? How do I get out of here?

Heart pounding, I reach out and open the door closest to me. I peer through it and see an empty waiting room. Or a ballroom? It's ginormous, a sea of gold and red and thick cream carpet and wood paneling. There are chairs, ye olde ones with velvet and gold trim, a glittering chandelier, and doors, like twelve of them. The far wall is decorated with a large mural of a summery sky, cursive gold lettering in the center exclaiming: *Today is a good day to be happy!*

I swallow down bile as my hand tightens around the door-knob. Whatever this place is, it isn't the Marybelle.

I'm about to close the door again when I hear voices to my right, somewhere farther up the corridor. I whip my head around, searching the distant shadows.

Is that a flash of white up ahead?

Someone is moving toward me, several someones.

I freeze, terrified. What should I do? Run? Hide? Beg their forgiveness? If I get caught and they're like, *Naughty Tegan,* I can hardly complain about Kelvin wanting to fail me. They'll just say he's right, I'm not ready for heaven, I need two thousand years of torture first.

The voices get louder. The flash of white is definitely a figure, three figures to be precise, headed my way. There's no way they won't see me.

I throw myself into the golden room and shut the door, squeezing Snickerdoodle so hard he pees a bunch of pool water all over the carpet. Hopefully no one comes in after me and is like, *Hmmm, why is this carpet wet and why does the water smell like two-star algae-infested pool water from New Jersey?*

I'll hide in here until they pass and then I'll keep searching. One of these doors has to lead back to the Marybelle.

I can't hear the voices anymore—the soundproofing in this place is way better than in my house. You could argue about getting a divorce all day long here and no one would hear you. I decide to wait five minutes, then see if the coast is clear.

I turn in a slow circle. There are five doors on my left and five on my right, and there's a door on either side of the mural on the opposite wall. Every door looks the same.

Almost the same.

One of the doors, the one to the left of the mural, is sparkling. I step closer. The glimmers of light are refracting off the chandelier, but they're only shining on this one spot. It's mesmerizing.

"Start looking at what is staring you right in the face," I whisper.

I jump when I hear voices again. They sound like they're just outside the door I came through. Like, right outside. My heart beats so hard it bounces out of my chest and into my throat as the doorknob slowly turns.

I lunge for the door with the light. I wrench it open and throw myself through, slamming it shut behind me. I can't get caught. I can't get thrown into hell.

I stumble forward, Snickerdoodle still tucked under my arm, as the world spins. Something wet soaks through my socks. I look down. Dirt. Grass.

I look up and the world slowly comes into focus.

Trees, birds, bees, flowers, grass, mud, cloudy sky.

It's a garden.

I'm standing in a garden.

TWENTY ONE

The ground is littered with red-and-gold leaves, their brightness muted by an overcast sky. Birds play in the boughs of the giant maple directly in front of me, sending more leaves floating to the ground. It makes me want to run, kick up those leaves, feel their soft crunch under my feet.

A ring of trees around the boundary casts long shadows over the small oblong garden. It's not much of a garden, really. Just the maple in the middle, its leaves blanketing the grass, and a few flowers (yellow, purple, white) scattered around the edges.

"Don't eat any apples, okay?" I tell Snickerdoodle.

It's nice to breathe air without smoke and trash and sea salt mixed in. It's crisp, the kind of air that leaves a trail of ice all the way down your lungs—or, it would if I could feel the cold, which I can't, even here.

It's beautiful. I could happily stay in this garden until the coast is clear inside the room and—

Crap.

When I glance over my shoulder I see more trees, more red-and-gold leaves, more grass, more overcast sky, but I do not see a door. My fingers flex around Snickerdoodle's middle.

I guess there really is no way back from this.

My human brain remembers anxiety and it knows that right now—trapped in an unknown garden in heaven, a garden I snuck into without permission, while my every move is being watched by a greasy-haired snitch who wants to send me to purgatory—is the perfect time to freak out. So it does all the classics: rapid heartbeat, hot flush, racing thoughts (*Purgatory! Pain! Hell! Kelvin!*).

Surely the one perk of being dead should be zero anxiety.

"Come on," I say, hugging Snickerdoodle tightly. "Let's keep moving. Maybe we'll find another door."

Since my shoes are back in the Marybelle pool, I get to experience the pleasure of walking through a carpet of crisp autumn leaves in just my socks. The crunch is deeply satisfying.

Ahead I see a dirt path. A path usually leads somewhere, right? That's its whole function. So this one might lead me to the door out of here. I hurry toward it.

The grass is overgrown on either side of the muddy, narrow trail and wet stalks slap at my legs as I pick my way downhill. The sky grows dark as the trees close around me until up ahead I see a rotted wooden fence with a wire gate hanging open.

Through the gate are open fields that stretch for miles, dotted with patches of trees huddled together. In the distance there's a lake, and beyond the lake I see a hill with a concrete path twisting around it, all the way to the top.

"Let's head that way."

I trudge through the field. My socks and jeans are soaked but the *whoosh whoosh whoosh* sound as I move through the long grass is soothing—it sounds like rolling waves.

I reach the lake. It's bigger than it looked from afar, bordered by a concrete path with benches at intervals. Ducks play in the water, and two white swans glide in lazy circles. There are two things I know about swans: One, they mate for life. And two, they can break your arm with their necks.

"I appreciate your duality," I say as one swan glides by me. I give it a thumbs-up. The swan ignores me.

I keep walking. My anxiety about being lost has moved to the back of my mind, eased a bit by the gentle lapping of the lake water and the patches of sunlight breaking through the clouds. I just need to find a way out before anyone notices I'm gone.

The path leads to the base of the grassy hill, where it winds counterclockwise to the top. There's another path too, a dirt path that's been worn into the side of the hill from many feet trampling down the grass. It leads off to the right, a steady upward climb instead of round and round, and I decide to take it.

A desire line. That's what this path is called.

One time when Mom took me and Quinn walking in Frick Park, Mom pointed to a muddy trail at a crossroads that was just like this one—created by people who didn't want to take the official path, who thought they knew a better way to go or wanted to follow their heart.

"We should go that way," she said. But I didn't want to get my Cons muddy, and Quinn had already skipped ahead, so we stuck with the main trail.

I should have known then, I guess. That Mom was someone who would always want to take the desire line over the path someone else had set for her.

I follow the dirt path up the hill. At the top is a plateau with a bench. I can see for miles, see the whole park and an unfamiliar city beyond.

Sitting on the bench is a man.

Snickerdoodle tumbles from my grip and I quickly bend to sweep him up again. When I straighten, the man is looking at me.

"You're not Zelda," he says.

He's got an accent. British. Like a pickpocket in *Oliver!* He's as old as Mrs. Nowak, with papery skin and wrinkles and sunspots and gray hair, and he's wearing a suit and dress shoes that would have made my dad whistle in appreciation. *Now there's a man who knows how to dress his feet,* he'd have said.

"I'm not Zelda," I agree.

The man gives me a look, taking in the whole of me, but he's wearing a goofy smile, so I don't think he's angry I crashed his garden.

"You're not an angel, either," he says. His voice has that crackly tone old voices sometimes have. He flexes his hand where it rests on the bench, fingers brushing the stems of a bouquet lying beside him: daisies (yellow and white) wrapped in paper (brown) and string (brown). "The lack of wings gives you away," he adds.

"I'm not an angel," I say. "I'm dead."

"Ah. Me too. Me too."

A black bird flies overhead, squawking obnoxiously. We both tilt our heads to watch its flight path.

"What's your name?" He toys with the bouquet string. "American, aren't you?"

I nod. "Tegan."

"Pretty name. And who's this little one?" He points at Snickerdoodle.

"A very wet and fed-up octopus. Snickerdoodle."

"Pleased to meet the both of you. I'm Robbie, and this is my bench. Well, our bench. Mine and Mary's."

"Mary?"

His smile turns soft. "Love of my life."

I hug Snickerdoodle tight and think of swans and how nice it must be to be "forever" about someone. But if there's one thing I've learned it's that forever is not always the right thing, that some people are "for now" and some people are "never" and some people are "should have let go a long time ago but I said forever so I'm sticking to it no matter how miserable it makes me."

We can't all be swans.

But I wish I had been. I would have liked someone to feel forever about me.

"Is this your heaven?" I ask.

He nods. "Weather's a bit chilly but Zelda did an excellent job." He knocks his fist against the bench two times. "She's a trick, that Zelda."

I'm struck with a pang of guilt at the sound of her name. She was doing her job and I lashed out. I was a dickcheese.

"She's a delight," I say, and he chuckles.

But Zelda's not the only one I've been rude to. I just wandered into this guy's heaven, which is like stomping through his brain in my muddy socks. "I'm not supposed to be here. Sorry."

He shakes his head. "No, no, I don't mind," he says. "The company's nice. Haven't seen another human, dead or otherwise, in a long time."

I look down at myself—disheveled, red-eyed, muddy. I feel pretty inadequate to be someone's first human interaction in years. Especially since he's all dressed up and carrying a bouquet of flowers. His shoes are extra shiny.

"You have a nice heaven," I tell him. I want to be polite but also it's true. Zelda did a really good job.

"Sunday afternoon, October eighteenth, 1964," he says. "A pretty young lady named Gladys had just broken my heart down by the lake and I came up here to lick my wounds. So here's me crying my eyes out when this steely-looking redhead sits beside me and hands me her handkerchief. 'I like a man who isn't afraid to cry,' she says.

"Mary MacInally. I asked if she would do me the honor of accompanying me on a stroll through the heath and she said yes. We walked all afternoon and we fed those swans and we laughed and we fell in love. We were married three months later."

Robbie looks off into the distance and I wonder what he's seeing. Is he seeing her? Mary MacInally? Is he happy? Is he sad? Maybe both: His heaven is the day he met his soul mate, but she's not here. Which sucks. This place is beautiful but it sucks.

"Did you know swans mate for life?" I ask.

He turns back to me. "I did not know that."

"It's true. And they can break your arm with their necks."

He grins. "Did you know all white swans belong to the queen?"

I shake my head. "They look like they belong to themselves."

He laughs. "I think you're right. Our dog, Weasel, he used to yap at those swans back there every time we walked him through the heath. They were his number one enemies. I was enemy number two—he didn't like sharing Mary with me. 'I was here first,' I'd tell him, but there's no point talking sense to a dog. I didn't mind, really. I could understand why he wouldn't want to share her."

He squints at me. I hate to think what he's seeing. I must look like a wild girl. Raised by wolves. He watches me in silence for a long time. I wish I had more swan facts to share.

"Can I ask you something?" I say instead. "You're old so you must be pretty smart."

He chuckles. "Ask away."

"Imagine you learned three things about yourself. The first thing was that you got jealous when your friend made another friend because you were scared she'd lose interest in you and you'd be alone. The second thing was that you really wanted a cute girl to fall in love with you, to pick you out of all the options she had, but she didn't. And the third thing was that your mom might have had good reasons for leaving you, but that doesn't make it hurt any less."

He frowns at me, fingers toying with the flower petals.

"What would you think it meant?" I ask. "If someone showed you those things about yourself, what would you think they were trying to tell you?"

His frown deepens. "I'm not sure," he says, "but it would make me feel sad. It would remind me of Gladys telling me Frank the accountant had caught her eye. It feels rotten to be the one left behind. I was lucky my Mary came along and said, 'You'll do for me. You'll be my person.'"

I look down at my mud-stained socks, toes wriggling. That does sound nice. I really would like to be someone's person.

"I'm sorry I can't answer your question," he says after a while. "And I'm sorry to meet you like this, Tegan. You're too young." He offers me the daisies. I almost reach out to grab them but then I remember myself.

"I can't. They're Mary's."

He laughs softly. "No, they're for a girl named Gladys who didn't want them. And Mary didn't like daisies. She liked bluebells. I bought her a bunch every Sunday for the forty-one years we were married.

"She left before me, you see. Left me and Weasel behind to miss her together." He shifts to one side and gestures to a line of text carved crudely into the bench's backrest: *For Mary, Beloved companion to Robbie and Weasel.* "I carved this myself, as you can see, and Zelda kindly let me keep it this way. But back in the land of the living, if you were to walk up to this bench now, you'd see the real deal, a big brass plaque. I paid for it to be done after Mary passed on. Now no one will ever forget that this spot right here is where I met the love of my life."

When he looks back at me he's smiling. "So take the daisies," he says. "I think you'll appreciate them more than Gladys would have."

I reach out and take the bouquet. It's lighter than it looks and smells like springtime. "Thank you." My throat feels thick. My human brain has not forgotten how to feel sad.

"Those are pretty," says a voice next to me.

I almost drop the flowers.

Barb.

Barb in a pink suit.

Barb in a pink suit standing right next to me.

A cocktail of shock, fear, and dread burns through me, or maybe it's the fires of hell already licking at my feet.

"I can explain," I blurt.

"Hello, Robbie," says Barb with a nod to the old man.

"You're new," he says, blinking with curiosity. "So many visitors today. Aren't I a lucky man?"

Barb laughs politely, then turns to me. "Are you ready to leave?"

I can't get my mouth to form words so I just nod. Barb gestures for me to move first.

"Visit again if you can," calls Robbie. I wave over my shoulder with the hand holding the bouquet; the daisies swish side to side. Barb leads me away with a firm hand pressed to the center of my back.

We take the main path down the hill. Clearly Barb doesn't believe in desire lines.

"In my defense, I was having a bad day," I say. "Kelvin is sabotaging me and—"

"I'm not mad, Tegan," she says. I sneak a look, and it's true, she really doesn't look furious. She's not about to throw lightning bolts at me. "I just hope you learned something."

"Learned? What do you...?" I stop walking as the pieces fall into place. Because heaven is a lot of things—sucky being top of the list—but it's not easy to break into. I face her. "You let me come here, didn't you? This is another one of your tests. Like the purgatory thing."

She smiles. "I might have unlocked a few doors."

Manipulative son of a— "Why?" I snap. Is there an angel in heaven I can trust *not* to have an agenda? "Why would you do this?"

Barb continues walking, motioning for me to follow "As you know, I've been keeping a close eye on your case," she says. "Last time we met I showed you what you had to lose. This time, I thought I'd show you what you had to gain." We reach the bottom of the hill and Barb leads us around the lake in the opposite direction to the route I walked last time. "This is what your heaven *could* be, Tegan." She waves her hand in a sweeping arc, indicating the trees, the grass, the swans. "Other people find their happiness in heaven. Like Robbie. Don't you want to be happy, Tegan?"

Happy?

Is Robbie happy?

I look back over my shoulder but I can't see him anymore. We're too far away. He's up there, though. Alone. Sitting on a bench, a handful of carved words reminding him of who should be sitting beside him. Is that happiness? Or is that sucking all the good stuff out of a memory and leaving you to wallow in the husk?

In a weird way it reminds me of the investigation. All the memories Zelda showed me were of the people I didn't have. I guess heaven does that too. It says, *Here's a place to remind you of the loved ones who are no longer with you.*

It makes me think about purgatory too. If I let Kelvin root through my soul and yank out all the bad things, isn't that just taking more away from me? Instead of giving?

Why does heaven keep wanting to take things away from me?

"I sympathize with you, Tegan," says Barb. "I've read your file. I know why the Marybelle hurts you so much. And it troubles me greatly to think that, should this investigation work out in your favor, you might be too scarred from your experiences thus far to accept happiness in any heaven. But surely now you can see what's possible."

I frown. "Are you saying you agree with me? That the Marybelle was the wrong choice? You think Zelda made the mistake?"

Barb's step falters but she doesn't stop. "That's not for me to say," she hedges. "If it was clear-cut we wouldn't be undertaking this investigation. But the protocols *are* clear and we must follow them to the letter to determine who made the mistake. And deal with the offending party accordingly."

My scalp prickles with unease. I feel like I'm missing something. Something big.

Barb smiles. "I'm sure you understand."

Ahead of us there's a door in the middle of the path, and we're moving right toward it. Maybe it will take us back to the Marybelle, back to Zelda. Zelda, who is so desperately trying to prove she was right, that she didn't make a mistake.

Is she just being stubborn or is her motivation as great as mine?

"What kind of trouble will Zelda be in if she loses?" I ask.

Barb pauses when we reach the door. "I'm afraid she was already on probation," she says, shaking her head sadly. "Zelda is very talented, but her attitude has ruffled a few too many feathers. Recently she has come to think of herself as…above her duties, and that's not a trait an angel should possess. I had been hoping she could turn a corner, but this kind of error, if indeed she made an error, cannot be ignored.

"And then, to see that she wasn't even taking the investigation seriously, that she was making a mockery of the system." Her eyes shift to Snickerdoodle in my arms. I hug him close. "Fortunately, she does seem to be taking her duties seriously now, and I'm pleased to see that. Nevertheless, if she cannot convince you, she will have to be demoted."

Demoted?

I swallow. My stomach churns and I don't know why. Or maybe I do. Because if Zelda is demoted, does she go away for good? Do I get a different angel? If I get to stay in heaven but without Zelda, well, that just feels wrong. It feels like sitting alone on a bench made for two people.

Barb reaches for the doorknob.

"What does 'demoted' mean?" I ask. The unease is a knot of worry in the center of my chest now.

She pauses, hand resting on the golden knob. "It means her services will no longer be required."

"And that means?"

"It means *she* will no longer be required."

I freeze. The world spins but not because Barb has transported us anywhere. My feet are firmly rooted to the path and we're still in Robbie's heaven. It's me that's spinning, it's my thoughts racing a million miles per hour.

"Just so we're clear," I say. I can barely push out the words. "You mean you take away her angel badge and she has to find another job?"

Barb chuckles, her eyes crinkling into sweet half-moons. She places a hand on my shoulder and squeezes. "Her job will be terminated, Tegan," she says. "And so will she."

(PLEASE REACH FOR ME)

Tegan sat on the carpet, her back pressed against the cabinets in the kitchenette, her thighs numb from sitting on the floor too long. She drummed an impatient beat against her knee and watched her father. He was a lump under the covers of his bed, sleeping.

They hadn't left the motel for three days, had barely left the room. Anytime she asked what was wrong he would conjure up a smile—a pathetic, watery smile that fooled no one—and tell her everything was fine.

Everything was not fine.

Yesterday she had stolen his phone again. She'd sat on the edge of the bathtub, the shower running to cover the noise, and called her mother.

We're sorry, you have reached a number that has been disconnected or is no longer in service.

She'd called home but no answer—her mother was supposed to be home by now. So Tegan had called Aunt Lily. No answer. She'd sent a text.

It's Tegan. What's happening? What's wrong with my dad? Where's my mom?

Five seconds and then: *ping.*

Message not delivered.

She'd stared hard at the screen: confused, worried, disbelieving, and then angry. So angry.

Fingers stabbing at the screen furiously, she'd sent another message.

You blocked him? You blocked my dad?

Five seconds and then: *ping.*

Message not delivered.

Now, she sat surrounded by trash from three days of takeout that no one had bothered to clean up and watched her father. She was too scared to leave him and she was too scared to sit and watch him fade away.

For days, she had been making sure she could see the rise and fall of his breathing. Sometimes she sat outside, legs dangling between the railings, letting the cold air seep into her bones. Sometimes, she walked around the motel. But mostly she sat and watched and worried and kept her promise not to leave him.

But was he going to leave her? He was fading away in front of her eyes and it terrified her. After all, he was the one who closed the shop to pick them up from school when their mother forgot. He was the one sitting front and center at every ballet recital and every band performance. He was the one who hugged and laughed and soothed and said, *We're a family. We stick together to the end, no matter what.* She couldn't lose him.

Quinn murmured to Trash Monkey as she made him dance along the outer edge of Tegan's suitcase. Her hair was knotted and greasy; she hadn't washed or combed it for days. Tegan didn't have the energy to fight her about it.

She felt restless.

She picked at the loose sole of her shoe. "Dad?" Her voice was rough from disuse.

He didn't shift. She waited.

"Dad?"

He rolled onto his side but said nothing.

"I'm going for a walk," she told him. She was afraid of leaving but she was afraid to stay too. What if they never left? What if they were stuck in this motel forever and the world forgot about them? What if she sat here and watched him disappear? "I'm going to walk to the beach," she said.

He rolled onto his back, the sheets twisting around him. "Not right now, Tegan. Please."

"Why not?"

He didn't answer. She was tired of the silence. It was worse than his smiles and his *everything will be all right*. Her fear had curdled into anger.

"I'm going for a walk," she said again. This time she stood, shaky on her legs.

Quinn was dangling Trash Monkey over Tegan's open suitcase, threatening to make him walk the plank. But she stopped playing to look up at them.

"No," he said.

"Why?"

He didn't answer.

"Why not?" she persisted.

He shifted onto his side again, trying to hide from her. She wouldn't let him. She would poke and poke and poke until the truth came out. She needed him to be honest, she needed him not to leave her.

"Why not?"

"This is a family vacation," he said. "We stick together."

Tegan clenched her hands into fists.

"We aren't a family!" Her shout echoed. "Mom's not here. Her plane landed yesterday—she's home now. Why aren't we? Why did you drag us to this shitty motel in the middle of the night? Why won't you let us leave?" Her anger carried her across the room, toward her father. "Why won't you tell us what's going on?"

"Don't you shout at me!" He sat up. His thin hair was sleep-mussed, pillow creases marring his unshaven face. He smelled sour from not showering enough. "Don't you shout at me." He wore no smile, no mask. Just red-faced anger.

Good. Tegan wanted that. She wanted something real. "Why not?"

"Because I'm your father." He spat his words. "And I said so."

Quinn looked at them, one after the other, her mouth open in surprise. Trash Monkey dangled from her grip, awaiting his fate.

"You said nothing." The words felt like fire in Tegan's mouth, burning her throat raw. She hoped they burned down this entire room. "You never say anything."

His eyes widened.

"I know everything isn't okay," said Tegan. "I know you and Mom have been fighting again. I know you've been trying to call her this whole time and I know she's not answering. I know Aunt Lily blocked you. We're in the worst motel in Jersey and we shouldn't be here and you keep saying everything is fine but it isn't. You're breaking apart in front of me and telling me not to notice and I'm terrified. Don't tell me everything is fine."

She was begging him. Every word she said was a prayer. *Please hear me.*

"It's my job," he said quietly, focused on his lap. "I'm your father. It's my job to shield you from the bad things."

Tegan laughed. She gestured at the room, at his phone, at Quinn, at herself. "Then you're not very good at it, are you?"

Her father shrank back as though the words were fists. He and Tegan stared at each other, and Tegan didn't know how to pull herself back from this ledge. She wanted to jump. She wanted to sink. She wanted to run.

"Please tell us the truth," she said.

He frowned, lips moving, forming silent words. He didn't seem to know where to look.

"Please," said Tegan. She reached out her hand. She wanted him to reach for her too. She prayed: *Please reach for me.*

A bang startled them both. Quinn screamed and dropped Trash Monkey. Tegan spun around, searching for whatever had caused the bang. It was the clunky old heater attached to the wall. The light had gone out and it was no longer pumping lukewarm air into the room. Broken.

She looked back at her dad. His eyes cleared, as though he was waking up from a long dream. A nightmare.

"Damn it," he cursed, throwing back the musty sheets, climbing out of bed. He pushed past Tegan and moved toward the heater. He held his hand in front of the vents. "Damn it."

"Dad," said Tegan.

He wouldn't look at her, but he smiled at Quinn. "It's broken but we can fix it. Everything is fine." He patted down his jeans, finding the room key in his front pocket. He was a mess—his clothes rumpled, his eyes bloodshot, his skin pale. "Hold tight," he said. "I'll go see the guy in the front office."

He could use the phone. Why didn't he just call the office?

He said family stayed together and now he was leaving. He was walking away from her.

"Dad," said Tegan. "Don't walk away. Don't leave."

He turned his back on her. Tegan breathed hard as she watched her father grab his coat and disappear out the door.

He did not look at her.

He did not reach for her.

He walked away.

TWENTY TWO

Terminated?

The word crashes through my head like a car running a stop sign. I hurry through the magic door and into the motel office, chasing Barb. "Excuse me. Hold on just one second."

Barb waits patiently as I screech to a halt in front of her. "Yes?" she asks.

"Is there a different meaning for 'terminated' that I don't know about? Because if terminated means 'forgiven for making one teeny tiny error,' then great! Forgive her." I flinch as the door I just raced out of vanishes with a *pop!* behind me.

Barb is statue-still in the middle of the office, head tilted to one side like a curious bird. "That is not the definition of 'terminated,'" she says. "The standard definition is 'brought to an end.'"

End.

The word is a punch.

End? Like, *death*?

Ms. Chiu, I am freaking out.

The daisies rustle as I gesture wildly. "That's barbaric! You're an *angel*. You can't...*kill* Zelda."

Barb smiles benignly at me. "The rules are simple. The only

way Zelda can avoid demotion is by proving her calculations were correct. You *must* be convinced by her."

I shake my head. "No."

"Yes."

"You're mistaken."

"I'm the Manager. These are my rules."

"Then you suck!" I stomp my foot, leaving behind a muddy sock-print. "Kelvin's the one who should be demoted. He wants me to fail. He's going to fail both me and Zelda because he's a dickcheese."

"Kelvin is an upstanding angel, chosen for this task because of his integrity and—"

"Okay, fine. I love the Marybelle. I'll sleep in the parking lot and eat mushrooms and bathe in the tampon-infested pool for the rest of eternity if it saves Zelda. There. She has my approval."

She chuckles. "Tegan, your concern is admirable, but I will not allow you to forsake your eternal happiness out of misplaced obligation. Surely you've worked out by now that we can read the truth in your heart, that it cannot be faked. I'm sorry, but Kelvin will be the one to determine if Zelda has done enough to convince you. She has four days left. She might still succeed."

I glance around the office at the cracks in the walls, the crooked drawing of the water park, the peeling tape: *Please ring for attention!* I think about soggy pizza, John Denver, and a blanket fort.

I think about driving home to find the wardrobe empty, my mother's belongings gone.

A bitter laugh gurgles up my throat but morphs into a sob as it escapes my lips. Because there's no way. There's no way in hell *or* heaven I'll ever be truly convinced by Zelda's calculations.

Ms. Chiu, I can't breathe.

Barb pats my shoulder. "There, there," she says, like I'm three years old and crying because I dropped my ice cream and not because I *accidentally killed Zelda.* "You won't be on your own. You'll be provided with a replacement angel."

"I don't want another angel."

It's true. I'd take any version of Zelda—grumpy, snarky, shoveling mushrooms in her mouth, saying *Sorry,* saying *Spoilers,* calling me a butt-face. I want all the versions.

I pick her.

"Remember," says Barb, her hand still on my shoulder, squeezing tightly, "today is a good day to be happy."

Happy?

Happy? I could scream the word. Scream it so loud it tears the whole word into pieces.

I don't even know what it means. Is happiness a half-empty park bench? Two swans? A secondhand bouquet of daisies? A weekend in the worst motel in New Jersey?

Is it an angel who's scared of heights holding my hand on a Ferris wheel?

My fingers flex automatically, like they're reaching out to grasp the ghost of a memory. But there's nothing to grab hold of.

Barb removes her hand and smiles. I hate her. "See you soon, Tegan Masters."

"I hate you," I say, but I doubt she hears me because she has pulled a Zelda and zapped the hell out of Dodge in the blink of an eye.

I grip one of Snickerdoodle's tentacles like it's a lifeline. "What have I done?" I ask the empty office.

The office doesn't answer, which is good. Because if it told me, *You've sentenced Zelda to death,* I'd self-combust.

Snickerdoodle drips and the paper wrapped around the daisies rustles every time my fingers flex—still reaching for something that isn't there. How do I untangle this knot in my stomach? It's not just guilt. It's a kaleidoscope of emotions. It's complicated.

I can't let anything happen to Zelda. She's important. She's a puzzle piece. Without her, nothing makes sense.

I look up.

Through a small gap in the posters stuck to the office window I see the pool.

And I see Zelda.

She's lying back on a lounge, legs crossed one over the other, arms folded, pouting at her lap. My vision blurs—too many damn tears. Go away. You're no help. Crying never helps.

On autopilot, I move until my face is pressed against the glass, right where the little gap lets me see Zelda.

She checks her watch. She unfolds her legs and folds them again. She looks at the pool, lips moving as she talks to Tammy. What is she asking? *Do you know where Tegan is, Tammy?*

She looks up at the rooms, eyes searching until they settle on one door, somewhere near the middle. Her shoulders heave up and down with a sigh, then she looks back at her lap, bottom lip tugged between her teeth.

My heart twists. It's a goddamn pretzel. I squeeze my eyes shut trying to block out the worry but of course it doesn't work. I rest my head against the glass and breathe.

I thought it was bad when Zelda came back from her meeting with Barb and she'd built up all those fences around herself so I couldn't reach her anymore. She was standing right in front of me and I missed her so much.

How will it feel to miss her when she's gone? Truly gone. Not hidden but demoted, terminated, dead. I try to picture a universe without Zelda and I can't breathe.

Ms. Chiu, I don't want to lose her.

I bury my nose in the top of Snickerdoodle's damp head. Not even the fading chlorine stench can overpower the cloying scent of daisies, so sickly-sweet in the small space. It's too much.

I look up through the gap again.

Zelda rolls her head back to look up at the sky. She reaches to the side, somewhere I can't see, and when she draws back her hand she's clutching Trash Cat Baby. The clouds above part for a moment and a slant of sunshine illuminates her, making her wings shine. She squeezes Trash Cat Baby to her chest and smiles. A small smile. A smile that is shy, tentative, real.

Ms. Chiu, I'm scared.

✦ ✦ ✦

"You can save Zelda, right?" I drop into the chair opposite Ms. Chiu. No hi, hello, how's being a shapeshifting-immortal-therapy-bot treating you. "You can waggle your fingers and *shazam!* she won't be demoted? That's a thing you can do, right?"

I was holding on to my last counseling session for an emergency. This is an emergency.

"Hello, Tegan," says Ms. Chiu with a polite smile. She crosses her legs. "How are you today?"

I scoot my chair closer with little bunny-hops. "I found out Zelda's going to be demoted and then I found out what demoted means and then I found out it's all my fault and there are only three days left in the investigation so I'm pretty terrible actually. How are you?"

She smiles and the office suddenly transforms into Red Robin, a basket of fries already on the table between us. She pushes it toward me. "I am reliably informed these are both delicious and a suitable cure for when you are feeling sad. So I hope you don't mind the scenery change."

I help myself to a handful of fries. The grease and salt really do make me feel slightly less jittery. But the fries don't solve my problem.

I fix Ms. Chiu with a look. "Can you save her?"

There's a reason the shapeshifting-immortal-therapy-bot looks like Ms. Chiu. Ms. Chiu finds rain-soaked kids in parking lots and drives them home. She lets them cry in the front seat of her car and doesn't tell them *Today is a good day to be happy.* She lets them sleep in class if they need to because they were awake half the night listening to their parents argue. She hears out their mumbled excuses for not handing in an essay and instead of detention she asks, "Is there anything I can do to help you?"

Yes. You can save Zelda.

"No," says Ms. Chiu. "There's nothing I can do to stop Zelda's demotion."

I drop my head to the table, gluing my cheek to the tacky laminate. It's gross. It's what I deserve. There's a tightness in my chest I can hardly breathe around.

Terminated?

And it's all my fault.

The scariest thing is that when I brush aside the guilt and shame, I'm left with one simple fact: I like Zelda. I don't want her to go because *I like her.*

She makes me laugh. She confuses me in the best way. She keeps me on my toes, like a never-ending turn on *Dance Dance Revolution.* She surprises me. She makes my heart feel too big for my chest. She makes me feel sort of okay about being dead. She makes me feel like hope isn't such a sucky emotion after all.

She can't leave.

"How can you be okay with this?" I lift my head to glare at Ms. Chiu, peeling my skin away from the sticky table. It hurts. I feel like human Velcro. "You're an angel. Your motto is 'guide and protect.' Probably. Zelda makes one tiny mistake and you're like, *Welp! Guess I'll have to kill her!* That sucks. That really sucks."

I am once again trying not to cry. Being dead involves a lot more crying than you'd think. Or maybe it doesn't usually. Maybe there really is something wrong with my soul. Because the goal is happiness and happiness shouldn't involve this much crying. And it definitely shouldn't involve me tearing my hair out trying to figure out how to save the one person worth a damn in this whole ridiculous place.

Ms. Chiu looks at me with pity. I drop my head to the table again because I can't deal with that. I don't deserve pity. I killed Zelda. I suck the most.

"We're not human, Tegan," she says. "It's not death in the way you perceive it."

"But she'll be gone. She'll cease to exist. How is that any different?"

I can't believe that's even possible. Zelda is…She is the most high-definition person who ever existed. The world is black and white and gray and she is Technicolor. If you erased her from the universe, you'd tear a hole in the fabric of space and time and all of existence would be sucked into the vacuum and *poof!* end of the fucking world.

"What scares you most about being dead?" asks Ms. Chiu.

I scoff. "What's even the point of that question? I'm already dead. And talking about my messed-up feelings doesn't save Zelda so don't change the subject."

"I think you are afraid of being forgotten," she continues, like I never said a word. "Your whole life you've felt unseen. It makes you angry, angry at yourself for being too easy to overlook. So what you crave most of all is to matter, to be seen, to be the center of someone's universe. To be so important to that person that without you they feel incomplete, as if there's a hole in their heart."

I groan. Why did I ever think she was better than Mr. What's-his-face? This is worse, this is way worse.

"You crave it because there are so many holes in *your* heart," she says, reaching for a fry. "When your mother left, when Clem paid more attention to Lou, when Evan didn't reciprocate your feelings. They mattered so much to you that realizing they did not return your love in the way you wished left holes in your heart."

I glance up at her. She's turned toward the window. Sun warming her face, eyes closed, chewing on a fry.

"You think the holes are vital. Without them, you think love doesn't matter. It's why you loathe the idea of purgatory so much, is it not? You don't want to lose the pain, the anger, the loss, all the little holes carved into your heart, because without them how will you ever know you loved?"

Her brow furrows and I sit up. I feel like I'm watching a car accident in slow motion. My own accident. I can't look away and I can't stop it. All I can do is watch myself die.

"So you're afraid," she says. "You died and you are certain you must have left a hole in someone's heart—your father, Quinn, Clem. But what kind of hole? How deep? How lasting? What if the hole is mended? What if one day Quinn tries to picture your face but it's suddenly too blurry to remember? What if years from now she is able to go days, weeks, months without missing you? What if you never meant enough to anyone to be missed forever? This is what scares you the most about being dead, because you think your value is determined by the size of the hole you left behind."

I grip the edge of the table so tightly my knuckles are white. I remember another time when I did the same thing, stiff fingers gripping handlebars. Then bang. Then sirens. Then darkness. Then nothing.

"It's not your fault." Ms. Chiu opens her eyes, her gaze finding mine immediately. I struggle not to flinch. "It is hard to be truly happy when all you can see is what isn't there," she says.

I shake my head. "Shut up."

She smiles. "Do you disagree?"

"Seriously. Shut up." I try to sound angry, to snap, to spit fire, but the anger seeps out of me, slipping through the holes in my heart, and I just sound tired and small and scared. "You're a terrible counselor. You can't save Zelda and you say stuff like that. Shut up."

Unfazed, Ms. Chiu plucks another fry out of the basket and chews on it thoughtfully. "I can't wiggle my fingers and save Zelda. I am sorry about that." She frowns at the residue of grease on her fingertips. "But I can advise you. Even if I am terrible at my job, I can at least recommend that you ask yourself one thing. Ask: If I was looking for something important, why search the spaces where there's nothing? Why not look at what I have?"

She pushes the basket of fries toward me.

"That's where you'll find happiness," she says. "In what you have."

What did I have?

I had a battered pair of shoes. I had a best friend. I had a kind teacher. I had a sister I worshipped and a dad who let me ride the rocket ship long after I'd outgrown it.

Is that enough?

I look at my fingers, splayed on the sticky table. I lift my hands, slowly peeling the skin free. My palms are slightly red from being Velcroed to the table but if I squeeze my eyes shut tightly enough, if I still my mind, I can almost feel the ghost of another hand in mine. Is that what Ms. Chiu means? Should I not think about how right now my hand is empty? Should I focus on how once upon a time my fingers were linked in a hand that was the perfect fit?

If I did that, maybe I'd see I have one more thing.

Zelda.

The angel who has been begging me to see past the holes in my heart for almost a month. Showing me all the times I was focused on *want* and never *have*. She told me I only saw the vase and not the two faces. She said it, I didn't hear it, but she said it: *Stop looking at the negative space and look at what's right in front of your eyes, butt-face.*

I try it.

Better late than never.

I picture Zelda sprawled on the pool lounge, clutching Trash Cat Baby to her chest, sunshine making her wings glow, a smile curving her lips. I think I would like to be someone who makes her smile. That's better than being a hole in her heart, right?

I could fill the holes in my own heart with that kind of warmth and maybe that would be nice.

I take a deep breath and reach for the fries, locking eyes with Ms. Chiu. "Okay." I nod.

Maybe Ms. Chiu can't save Zelda, but I can. I can try.

Because if Kelvin can change the rules, so can I.

Because if he says we can both lose, surely we can both win.

Because what I have, despite the odds, is hope. I still have hope.

"I can do that," I say, and Ms. Chiu smiles.

TWENTY THREE

The next morning Zelda finds me fishing my shoes out of the pool with a broom I stole from the janitor's cupboard.

"You're up bright and early," she says.

A silvery-pink blush low in the sky signals the rising sun, and if I'd actually gone to sleep last night, she'd be right. But there are only two days left in the challenge so I'm stressed and I'm scared and I can't even bring myself to look at her.

Terminated.

"I had to take care of this," I say with a quivering voice. I wave at the pool lounge, the table, the umbrella, the pizza box (brown pulpy mush), everything I fished out of the pool. I hook the shoes and drag them up onto the concrete, dropping them in a soggy pile at my feet. You can tell a lot about a person by their shoes and mine are weeping. "I know it all resets after a few days but I…" I glance at her. She narrows her eyes. I quickly look away.

Did she know the whole time? Barb kept her back after announcing the challenge to "hash out some details" so she *had* to have known she'd be demoted if she lost. But she never said a word about it.

Instead, she won me Snickerdoodle.

I drop the broom and grab the daisies. Last night I put them in a vase (green) and filled it with water from the bathroom tap. I thrust them at her now. "I'm sorry. These are for you."

She balks at my offering like it's a bouquet of turds. "What? No? Why are you—? Shut up."

I shake the vase. Water sloshes over the sides. "Take the flowers."

"I'm allergic."

"No, you're not."

"I could be."

"Please? I was a jerk to you. It's not your fault Mom left, and I shouldn't have taken it out on you. So take the damn flowers."

She grabs the vase and sniffs. "These smell amazing. You're annoying." She stomps her foot. "Shoot. You don't have to be sorry. It was my fault; I made you confront something awful." She thrusts the flowers back at me. "Sorry."

"I don't need—"

"Take the flowers, butt-face."

I accept the vase but it doesn't make me feel any less guilty. "You have nothing to be sorry for."

"I do. We both do."

"Okay, but…" I pluck out a flower and, before I can talk myself out of it, slip it behind her ear.

"What are you…?"

"We're both sorry so we should both have flowers," I say.

Zelda ghosts her fingers over the petals, cheeks pink. "Thank you," she whispers. I look at her pretty blush and think: *I could lose you. I don't want to lose you.*

Ms. Chiu, please make them stop taking everything away from me.

I turn around before Zelda can see my feelings splashed all over my face. "I made us lunch because I thought we could go on another excursion, only we might get hungry and we don't want to take any more detours, right?" I hold out a lumpy bundle of brown paper. It's the paper I saved from the daisies. "It's only cold burritos but I peeled off the mushrooms from my pizza last night and unrolled your burrito and stuffed them inside and I added ketchup so hopefully it's gross and you like it."

Zelda narrows her eyes at the lumpy package. "You *want* to go on another excursion?" She gestures at my soggy shoes. "Even after what happened last time?"

I shrug, feigning nonchalance. Since she never said, *Oh hey, Tegan? FYI, if I lose this investigation Barb is going to smite me so maybe take it seriously,* then I figure she doesn't want me to know. But that doesn't mean I can't save her anyway. "I mean, this investigation sucks, right?" I say. "So why can't we both win? You can prove your calculations were legit and I'll prove I don't need purgatory and no one has to lose. Except for Kelvin. Someone needs to push that greasy jerkasaurus off a cloud."

She narrows her eyes. "You'd accept the Marybelle as your happiest memory?"

"I mean, not right now." I hold her gaze—she says she can tell when I'm lying and I'm *not* lying. "But I'm finally willing to be convinced."

She scans my face like she's speed-reading the longest, twistiest book of all time. "Fine," she says.

"Fine?"

"Fine." She taps my forehead.

When the world stops spinning we're standing outside the

school gym. It's nighttime and I'm wearing the fanciest, floofiest full-length yellow ball gown.

"Um, Zelda?"

I look up and gasp. Zelda is also in a ginormous floofy ball gown. Hers is lilac with a leopard-print sash, and she's wearing the black boots she stole from my dad. I stare at her, stomach full of butterflies. I have forgotten all the words I ever knew.

"You don't like it?" Zelda looks down at herself.

"It's…" I wade through the sludgy depths of my brain, trying to recall at least one word: "Perfect."

She spins. The skirt flares and I notice crystals in her wings that sparkle in the lights. "Am I pretty?" she asks.

"No." *Yes.*

"I am."

"You look like a butt-face."

She grins. "I do, don't I?"

I can't deal with Zelda looking like *that* so I look around instead. There are kids everywhere, all dressed up and climbing out of their parents' cars. Homecoming? Maybe the start of my sophomore year?

"I'm not going to lie," says Zelda. "I'd already planned this trip. After last time, I felt bad and, well, I thought we needed one more chance. So. Ta-da!"

I'm hit by a wave of emotions.

Homesickness.

Guilt.

Confusion.

Anxiety.

Hope.

Determination. I *will* save her.

"I'm ready." I hold out my arm for her to take.

She looks at it like it's another turd bouquet, but then a smile spreads across her face and she links her arm through mine.

"Show me what you got, butt-face," I say.

Arm in arm, we climb the stairs to the foyer. We look like a couple of rejects from a school production of *Cinderella* but who cares?

"What's the story this time?" I ask. "We did Clem, Evan, Mom. Now what?"

"Think of this as an epilogue," says Zelda. We reach the top step. "To everywhere we've been, every story."

I was right about the dance. There's a HOMECOMING sign as we enter the foyer, a photo booth, and a station where teachers mark off attendees' names. Through a set of double doors, the gym is all lit up and decorated with streamers and balloons, and music blares.

"You and your friends are over there," says Zelda, nodding at the back right corner of the gym. "You're having an excellent time playing Slap Butt Foot Stomp Tag."

I snort.

I can't see much because its dark and there are too many people blocking my view, but I remember it. Paul invented the game. It's like freeze tag but you stomp on the person's foot to freeze them and they can only be released when someone slaps their butt.

I gaze at that far corner anyway, hoping for a glimpse of my friends even though seeing them hurts.

"Do we go find them?"

"Nah." Zelda tugs me down the steps. "We dance," she says.

I love dancing. In my bedroom with the door closed. In the kitchen with Quinn, singing "Hot Potato, Hot Potato." With Clem, bouncing from couch to couch in her living room when her dads aren't home. With Lou in the T.J.Maxx changing room when our favorite song comes on. With Paul in the back of his mom's car while we wait for her to pick up the pizzas. At Game Zone, winning the top score on *Dance Dance Revolution*. But not here. Not actual dancing in front of people my age. I know no one can see me, but dancing in public makes my limbs stiff and unwieldy. If that's what it takes to save Zelda, though, I'll be the dancing queen.

We weave between my classmates and end up in the middle of the dance floor. Zelda flings her arms in the air and waves them around. She jumps up and down and flutters her wings. Her dancing is awful, and it's adorable, and I hate how much I love it. I glance around, looking for Kelvin, but I don't see him. "I'm not going to question your methods," I shout over the music. "But maybe you should just tell me why you brought me to this dance?"

"Spoilers!" shouts Zelda.

I shuffle side to side, swaying my arms as I look around. There's a mantra in my head: *Happiness is in what I have.*

So what did I have here?

My memories are hazy, but I think Clem tried extra hard to make me laugh and forget that Evan was here with a date, the kick drum guy from band. That's why we played Slap Butt Foot Stomp Tag. Lou and Paul drank beer Paul's cousin had smuggled in, and Lou threw up in the rosebushes. The Marybelle hadn't happened yet, was still months away. I think I was happy. But not big happy. More of a bubble-under-the-surface kind of happy, constant and warm but never all-consuming. Is that what I'm supposed to see? That happiness can hide under the surface? Is that the epilogue to all Zelda's stories so far?

Isn't an epilogue an ending?

"Are you sure we shouldn't find me and my friends?" I ask.

Zelda grabs my arm. "Photo booth," she says.

She leads me back to the foyer, where there's a massive line waiting to use the booth. Zelda cuts in and pulls me inside; of course, no one notices.

"You'd make a fortune at Disneyland," I say.

The booth is a tight fit.

"Sometimes wings are inconvenient," mutters Zelda, struggling to squeeze into the tiny space with me and her wings and our ball gowns. We're basically sitting on top of each other. *Thirteen freckles*, my mind helpfully supplies. And a whole galaxy of stars in her eyes. Which is corny, I know, but when am I going to be corny if not at homecoming?

"Say cheese," says Zelda.

I quickly look at the camera when I realize I've been staring at Zelda.

We smile and pose, accidentally knocking our heads together on the first couple of tries, but we get the hang of it in the end.

"Am I going to show up on these?" I stumble out of the booth like a baby deer.

Zelda steps out after me with a dancer's grace. "You're not a vampire."

"Vampires are real?"

"Spoilers."

"You should tell me one spoiler. I'm dead. I need treats."

I grab the slim photo card as it shoots into the tray. In three out of five shots my eyes are closed but in one photo, the final one, we both look pretty awesome. She's giving me bunny ears and I'm grinning so hard there are galaxies in my eyes too.

We look good together. We look like puzzle pieces that fit.

I turn to her. She's so close. "Why are we here?"

"In an existential sense?" She grins but her eyes are dull, like they're not in on the joke. It makes my heart throb.

"Be serious. Why this memory? How is it connected to the Marybelle? I *really* want us both to win."

Zelda holds up her hand, fingers curled into a fist. She lifts her thumb. "I have never worn a ball gown," she says. She lifts her index finger. "I have never been to a school dance." Another finger pops up. "I have never given someone bunny ears while having a photo taken." Another. "I have never thrown my hands in the air like I just don't care." The final finger, her pinkie. "I have never slow danced." She waggles all her fingers at me. "I have now done four out of those five things. Can you help me with the final one?"

She holds out her hand.

I look at it. Her fingers are trembling.

I don't remember anything special about this memory, but I do remember another moment, sitting on a Ferris wheel with a hand squeezing mine. I remember how it felt. It felt like having.

I can't say no.

I slip my hand in hers. She leads us back to the dance floor, where, shyly, she rests her other hand featherlight on my shoulder and places mine on her waist. Her breath ghosts across my cheek as we shuffle side to side. I've never slow danced either. It's awkward. And wonderful.

We don't stop. Fast and slow songs pass us by, a homecoming king and queen are crowned, people start sneaking away to after-parties, and we don't stop dancing.

The whole time we dance, I think, *How can I look for happiness in this memory when the happiest thing is happening to me right now and I'm already dead?*

"I wanted to be a guardian angel," says Zelda suddenly. I lift my eyes to meet hers but she's looking over my shoulder. "I liked my job, designing heavens, but after a while it felt like a bad joke, only ever getting to see the memories and never the real thing.

"Guardian angels get to go to Earth. They're in charge of fate. Of making sure the right things happen at the right times. It's a hard job, but I'd finally *be* there. I could eat mushrooms and cheese and beans for real. I could go to a cat café. I could go to a school dance and wear a ball gown and maybe even slow dance. I'd hang out with you weird little humans all day and it would be fun."

She keeps her gaze fixed over my shoulder. The disco lights (pink, green, and purple) sparkle across her face.

"So I applied for a transfer, and when it was denied, I acted up a little. Took a few unauthorized visits to Earth. Kelvin snitched on me and I got in trouble—he hates me, always has. We trained together and he was jealous that I got better grades. Also, one time I superglued his office furniture to the ceiling. And I dyed his hair green while he was sleeping. And I once filled his cubicle with scorpions. Okay, so maybe he has good reason to hate me. But the point is, he snitched and I almost fell. So Barb hauled me in and said I clearly wasn't ready to be a guardian, but if I focused on doing my job and stayed out of trouble, in a few thousand years *maybe* I could reapply. Yours was the first heaven I designed after…all of that. It was a punch in the gut when you said I got it wrong. I thought, *Well, gee, I'm not good enough to be a guardian angel and apparently I'm bad at this boring job I don't even want.*"

She glances at me nervously, then looks away again. We're hardly moving now, mostly just holding on to each other. I don't know about her, but I'm terrified of letting go.

"I was angry and I took it out on you." Her fingers flex, pressing into the skin of my shoulder for a moment. "I'm sorry."

I shake my head. "I was angry too. I'm sorry too."

"We're both sorry," she says. "We have the flowers to prove it." She smiles, the big gummy smile I love. Suddenly she dips me and it feels like I'm falling.

But I don't fall. Zelda holds me tight and pulls me upright again. If I still had blood running through my veins, it would all rush to my head.

The music stops suddenly but Zelda doesn't let go.

I look around and see that they're packing up. Most people have left; only a few teachers, the janitor, and fifteen-year-old me remain.

There's a familiar tightening in my chest when I look at her, sitting on the steps in her sparkly cocktail dress (*ugh* green). She fiddles with her phone, pretending to be busy so it doesn't look like she cares that she hasn't been picked up yet.

Maybe I wasn't so happy in this memory after all.

Zelda tugs me closer and keeps dancing. The only things still working are the lights, sparkling across her golden skin. "Maybe being a guardian angel would have sucked," she says. She glances at the other me. "Watching a sixteen-year-old get hit by someone running a stop sign would definitely suck. But they can't fix things—they can only nudge. Human nature has to take care of the rest. And sometimes they have to let people make the wrong choice. Like texting on their phone instead of watching the road."

"That does suck."

"It really does." She frowns, lost in her thoughts.

I tug on her sleeve until she looks up at me. "At least you'd get to go all the places you've always wanted to go to," I say.

She grins and I melt a little inside. "First I'd go to a cat café," she says. "Then, there's a church in the Czech Republic made entirely out of human bones, so I'd go there. And there's a giant prawn in Australia and a giant banana. A penguin too. In Italy there's a kind of cheese that has maggots in it so of course I would need to eat that. And I would visit a ghost town and an aquarium and the gates to hell—the ones in Turkmenistan, not the *real* gates to hell, I can't tell you where those are because that's a spoiler. It rhymes with 'underwear' but that's all I'm saying. And I would cuddle a panda." She shrugs. "I have a list," she says, and I picture a bulletin board covered in cat sticky notes with her excited scrawl: *Giant prawn? Maggot cheese???*

I bury my laughter in her shoulder.

"What? Why are you laughing?"

"Nothing. You're weird."

"So?"

I shake my head. "Weird is good."

She huffs. "I know that."

A door bangs open and I hear hurried footsteps as Dad arrives. Under his coat he's wearing pajamas—the Gritty pj's I bought for Father's Day—and his hair sticks up like it always does after he's been sleeping. He has to get up in a few hours to drive to Indianapolis. He really needed an early night.

"I'm sorry, sweetie." He almost drops the car keys. "Your mother…She lost track of time. She went to Lily's and…" He smiles at the teacher who stayed behind to keep an eye on me. Fifteen-year-old me has her back to us so I can't see her face, but I know she desperately wants to throw herself into her father's arms and cry. "Lucky you called me, hey?"

They leave, Dad apologizing profusely to everyone, an arm wrapped around his daughter's shoulders. She leans into him as much as she can get away with.

"Is this about Dad?" I ask. I watch his back until it vanishes out the doors.

"Do you want it to be?" Zelda asks.

Maybe. I don't know. When I think about Dad it's hard to remember anything other than the Marybelle. Everything is measured by its relation to that weekend. Before the Marybelle, after the Marybelle. Maybe that's unfair. I should let myself remember Gritty pj's and bed-hair more often. Because when I do I feel the tiniest spark of warmth in the center of my chest and it's nice, it's really nice.

I look up at Zelda. She's already looking at me, eyes alive in a way they haven't been for so long. The tiny spark of warmth grows.

The lights are suddenly switched off, plunging us into darkness. Instead of pulling away I hold Zelda tighter.

"If you could choose," she whispers, close enough for her lips to brush against my ear, "if you could pick any memory at all, what would be your heaven?"

I scrunch my eyes shut and let my forehead rest against her shoulder.

"It's complicated," I say. I can't say the truth. Because it's this moment. It's this moment right now.

TWENTY FOUR

Zelda taps my forehead and the world spins. I brace myself to land in a new place, somewhere pulled from the deepest, darkest recesses of my mind. But as soon as the world comes into focus, I smell chlorine and I see green, green, and green.

We're back at the Marybelle.

For a split second I think: *This is the weekend, it's the moment. Focus, Tegan, find the clue (Dad rescued me from the dance and I had to rescue him from the Marybelle—is that it? Is that the clue?). We can both win.*

But then my foot connects with Snickerdoodle, discarded on the concrete, and my heart deflates like someone stuck a pin in it.

This is heaven.

"That's it?" I gasp. I'm not even wearing the ball gown anymore. "Only one stop?"

Zelda waggles her fingers and all the broken, sopping-wet things I fished out of the pool are set to rights. "Only one stop," she says.

"But where's part two, part three?" I demand. "You always take me to more than one memory. I collect the clues and we argue and eat snacks and eventually I work out what you're trying to show me."

Zelda shrugs. "That was it."

"But I didn't figure out the clue! It was something to do with Dad but I don't— The investigation ends in *two days*."

Doesn't she know? Doesn't she care? If she doesn't convince me about the Marybelle we both lose.

"Was it not about Dad? Was it something else?" I ask.

Smiling, Zelda pulls the flower out from behind her ear. The petals are bruised and the stem is crushed and I can't help thinking Robbie must be so disappointed in me that I couldn't keep his beautiful flowers safe. "Thank you for the dance, Tegan Masters," she says, slotting the flower behind my ear.

I grab her wrist before she can pull away. If I hold on tight I can't lose her, right? "What was the clue? What did I miss?"

"You didn't miss anything," she says. Her smile widens. "And now neither have I."

"What are you—?"

Poof! she's gone and I'm left holding nothing but air.

The flower slips from my ear and lands at my feet.

◆ ◆ ◆

On the last day of the investigation, there's a weight on my chest I can't shift. I don't sleep, I can't. I spend all night trying to remember everything that happened at the Marybelle.

I remember Dad kicking the door.

I remember counting the cracks in the bathroom tiles.

I remember *We're sorry, you have reached a number that has been disconnected or is no longer in service.*

I remember an old sneaker, mud-stained and lying on its side in the middle of the green.

I remember Dad crying in the bathroom.

I remember the heater breaking.

I remember soggy pizza, John Denver, and a blanket fort.

What does any of that have to do with Zelda's calculations?

The angel herself finally reappears late morning, stretched out on a pool lounge wearing sunglasses with mirrored lenses and a plastic orange frame. I bet they cost five bucks at a gas station. I bet she stole them. The reassurance I feel seeing her again is matched only by my fear of losing her.

"I've had a revelation," I say, marching up to her.

"You're in the right place for it." Zelda waves her hand and a bowl of chili fries appears on the table next to her.

"You can do that?" Have I been eating sweaty pizza for *nothing*?

Lazily, she waggles her fingers at me. "Angel magic."

"How come you've never— Doesn't matter. Let's talk about my revelation." I plop down on the edge of the adjacent lounge, my desperation reflected in her glasses. "Why don't we go to the actual moment?"

Zelda doesn't react.

"I know you showed me on the magic movie screen thingy," I say, "but if you physically took me back there and pointed at the exact moment and said, *Ta-da! That's it! That's your happiest moment! Behold it and weep, butt-face!* I might see it differently this time. We've only got a couple of hours left but if we—"

Zelda mimes zipping her lips and eats the key.

"Excuse me?"

"Zip it. Eat a chili fry. Relax," she says.

"Sorry. Are you saying you're *not* going to take me to my happiest moment? Because I think that's an excellent plan."

Zelda sighs loudly and reaches for a fry. "You won't believe me."

"But I want to!" I throw up both hands in frustration. "I've been to therapy *five times*."

"I showed you the moment. You know exactly what it is. And you didn't believe me."

"But I wasn't paying attention. Not really. I'll try this time."

"You can try all you like but you have to *feel* it. Right here." She pats her chest above her heart.

I grab a fry and munch on it anxiously. I know I have to feel it. I know I can't fake it because Kelvin will read my heart like a book. Trust me, I know.

"But what if—"

"You ever heard that saying…" she interrupts. There's a smear of chili at the corner of her mouth and I itch to rub it away. *Can't see the forest for the trees?* It's like that but in reverse. It's like looking at a single leaf through a microscope and then being expected to describe a forest. You can't see the forest. You can only see the leaf. And *you*, Tegan, you can barely even see the leaf—you're not the best at looking at things head-on, are you?"

God, I wish I could see her eyes behind those ridiculous sunglasses.

"But I dragged you kicking and screaming, and I showed you the forest, Tegan," she says. "Every branch, every length of bark, every cute rabbit hopping through the grass, every mushroom. Now it's up to you to weave it all together and see how that one leaf fits with everything else." She shrugs. "Because on its own, it's just another leaf."

But I've been trying.

I keep trying.

All I see are three stories about not having what I want and one tiny epilogue where I had it all, but that was dead me, not fifteen-year-old me. Fifteen-year-old me needed to be saved by her half-asleep dad in Gritty pj's.

"Maybe it's like love," says Zelda. "It's a web of feelings and moments, isn't it? It's their smile and their laughter and their silly habits. It's a thousand and one moments that add up to love. I couldn't introduce you to someone for the first time and say, *Hey, Tegan, you love this person.* You have to live through the falling-in-love part to understand the love itself."

Love?

I was wrong. There are fourteen freckles. A small one was hiding on her bottom lip, right above the smear of chili.

"I hope you can see it," she says.

I curl my fingers into a fist and think about swans. Two swans floating in a pond. And I think of a man sitting on a park bench waiting for a fiery redhead who will never come. My heart feels hollow but I swear, Ms. Chiu, I swear I'm trying to see past the gaps.

Zelda, however, is not.

I sit back as realization hits. "You're giving up, aren't you?"

She taps her nose. "Here's a lesson for you. Why waste precious time fighting a losing battle when you could eat chili fries and sunbathe instead? Kelvin was never going to rule in my favor. And Barb has always been on his side." She snorts. "She showed you purgatory and she let you sneak out to see Robbie to 'motivate' you, aka to keep you more focused on avoiding purgatory and less focused on giving the Marybelle a chance. The odds, Tegan, were never in my favor."

I'm angry at her. I'm scared and consumed by guilt and I'm so angry.

"Smile," she says. "You have dimples when you smile." She pokes my cheek and makes squeaky noises like she's corkscrewing her finger into the depths of my dimple. "Did you know children smile up to four hundred times a day but adults only smile up to twenty?" she asks.

"Because being an adult sucks."

"That is a universal truth," she says.

I give in and grab hold of her hand. "Let's try one more time," I say, I beg. "Take me to the moment. I swear it will work. Was it Quinn? Sleeping in my lap? Was it because we were finally going home and I was relieved? Was it the blanket fort?"

She removes the glasses. Despite the wry smile on her lips, her eyes are sad. "I'm guessing Barb finally told you what happens when I lose, huh? And that's why you're Ms. Eager-to-Help all of a sudden?"

I sit back heavily, arms folded. I can't look at her. I'm too busy self-combusting with guilt.

"You didn't know," she says.

"Shut up."

"It's not your fault."

"Shut up."

"I don't blame you."

My laughter is wet. I quickly wipe my eyes. "Bullshit. You blamed me heaps."

She grins. "Well, yeah. At first I wanted to spit in your mushrooms. But I got over it." She shrugs. "You grew on me. And I knew you didn't mean it. How could you know I already had a billion strikes against me because I'd kicked up a fuss about not being made a guardian angel?"

"I'm still a massive dickcheese."

She waggles her head side to side. "Yeah. You are a bit. But so am I. We make quite the pair."

I'm still too guilt-ridden to look at her but my eyes find hers anyway because I can't seem to help myself. Maybe it's like when you can't stop pushing your tongue against a sore tooth, or maybe it's penance, or maybe she's just that beautiful.

"You're really giving up?" I ask.

"Do you know why you were happy here?"

I shake my head.

Zelda smiles. "Then I'm not giving up—I still know I was right. We just ran out of time."

I cover my face.

"Are you crying?" Zelda sits up. "Over me?"

"Shut up. I'm not crying." I am definitely crying.

Zelda's eyes are suspiciously wet too, but at least she's smiling. "Hey, on the plus side, this investigation ticked so many things off my bucket list. I went out with a bang. You gave me that."

I remember the slow dance and the Ferris wheel and the hot dog and the penguins and I can't help smiling. Is that irony? That we both got the things we wanted but only when our lives were over?

Ms. Chiu is right: Happiness is in what you have. So maybe I can give Zelda one last thing.

"Wait." I stand up and point my finger at her. "Wait. Right. Here."

I march away before I can second-guess myself. There will be time for regret and guilt and crying later—I'll need ten thousand years in purgatory for this moment alone.

It doesn't take me long to gather what I need from the office. There's not a great selection but there's enough. I dump what I've collected on the pool lounge next to Zelda. She gives the pile a wide-eyed look, then stares up at me.

"Wait," I tell her, and march off again.

I grab Snickerdoodle from my room and drop by the office again for Trash Cat Baby, who has thankfully reappeared on the countertop. I deliver the plushies plus a table and four chairs from the restaurant to the pool, and then I get to work.

Zelda watches me in silence, but I can tell she's itching to ask what I'm doing.

What I'm doing is drawing cats.

Lots and lots of cats.

I stick the cat sticky notes around us and I cut out the drawings and stick them around too. Kelvin appears and scowls at me. I smile at him and he makes a note on his clipboard. *Poof!* He vanishes, taking my hope with him. Because I've lost. We've both lost. Zelda will be demoted and I'll be sent to purgatory, where I'll spend thousands of years losing over and over again. But right now, right here, I can smile because Zelda likes my dimples and we've got chili fries and cats. Lots and lots of cats. So why not be happy, even if it's sad too?

I'll be the band playing while the *Titanic* sinks.

When I'm done with my drawings, I march into the breakfast room and dish up two plates of mushrooms slathered in ketchup. I deliver the plates to the table outside, one in front of me and one in front of Zelda. I go back for coffee even though I don't drink it. I set down two mugs of black, bitter sludge between us and I sit.

"This," I tell her, "is a cat café."

She looks around, stunned.

"I couldn't get real cats, obviously," I explain. "I used stickers and I drew some on printer paper and cut them out. I'm not good at drawing so some of them look a little melted. Sorry."

There's a cat drawing right by her feet. It's the ugliest one I drew so I made sure it was front and center because Zelda likes weird things, broken things, gross things.

"I call her Dragon Cat the Ugly because her tail looks like a dragon's and her fangs are bigger than her head and she's the most melted of them all."

Zelda picks up Dragon Cat the Ugly and cradles her in her arms. "She's hideous," she coos. She's smiling so widely, all teeth and gums. I love it.

Zelda leans over the table and pokes my cheek. "Look at those dimples. I'm going to give them names."

I swat her hand away like it's a fly, but I also want to be liquid amber and trap her hand in mine forever. "Stop it," I say.

"The one on the right will be called Diana. The one on the left will be called Maggot Cheese."

"I hate you."

"No, you don't."

"I don't," I agree. "Not even a little bit."

I don't hate her.

But "like" isn't right either. It isn't big enough.

Zelda said love is a web of feelings, a thousand and one moments combined. It sneaks up on you, one smile at a time.

Maybe love snuck up on me.

I swallow over the knot of feelings gathering in my throat and reach for my mug. I hold it out for a toast with Zelda. She grabs her mug and clinks it against mine.

"To ugly cats and mushrooms and beans that make you fart," I say.

Zelda takes a swig of coffee. "That's disgusting," she says, and takes another swig. "I love it."

Me and Zelda eat sweaty mushrooms and drink disgusting coffee and I point out every cat around us and what their names are and she cradles Dragon Cat the Ugly the whole time.

"Why?" she asks when I've run out of cats to name. "Why do this?"

I shrug, shoving the last of the mushrooms into my mouth in one go so I don't have to speak for a while. But Zelda watches me chew and I know she's waiting for an answer.

"Because I knew it would make you happy," I say.

Because if angels also get a heaven, maybe Zelda's will be a shitty fake cat café in the worst motel in New Jersey. And every time she hugs Dragon Cat the Ugly, she'll remember me, and I'll remember her, and it might feel like we still have something, like we still have *us*.

"Come with me," she says, and stands suddenly. Dragon Cat the Ugly crumples in her arms but she doesn't let her go.

I stand up too.

I expect a tap of her finger against my forehead but instead she turns on her heel and I have no choice but to follow her. She hurries along the walkway to the metal stairs.

"Where are we going?" I race to keep up with her.

She doesn't answer.

She leads me up the stairs to the rec room. In the back corner is a door I always figured was storage. There's no label on it and it's painted the same seafoam green as the walls so it's basically camouflaged. Zelda heads right for it and when she opens the door it's not storage.

Stairs. Steep, metal stairs. Zelda climbs them.

I am bursting with questions but I say nothing. I follow her, the stairs bouncing with every step we take. At the top there is a door that Zelda pushes against with her shoulder until it finally opens.

I throw up a hand to shade my eyes from the sudden blinding light. For a second my brain is like, *Oh my God! This is it, the real heaven! Any second now the pearly gates will appear in front of me and I'll be let into the real heaven. Because all of this was just one of Barb's tests and I passed, so Zelda isn't being demoted after all.*

But my eyes adjust and it's a regular old roof.

It's the roof of the Marybelle, a flat expanse of concrete with a few shed-looking things that probably house generators and stuff like that. There's a waist-high barrier around the edge and I can see the rooftops of buildings for miles. Zelda turns to face me as I linger in the doorway.

"How are we here?" I ask. "I never came up to the roof when I was alive so this should be out of bounds."

"Nothing a bit of angel magic can't fix. I'm very powerful. And sexy. And good at breaking rules." She grins. "Now look there." She points to the ground next to the doorjamb—there is a dirty plastic bag and inside it are three tiny plastic soccer balls for playing foosball.

I throw up both hands and groan. "Why are they *here*?"

She shrugs. "Because that's where they were before, and I created the motel exactly to spec. I'm good at my job."

Zelda looks pleased with herself, hugging a very crumpled Dragon Cat the Ugly to her belly, wind swirling her hair. She looks like a superhero. I take a photo of her in my mind and tuck it away—*Don't get lost in the fourth drawer down*, I tell it. *And don't you dare take it away from me, Kelvin.*

"Thank you," I say with prayer hands. "For solving the most

important mystery of all." I toe the little soccer balls, and the plastic bag rustles. "Was that my one spoiler?"

She huffs and walks away, disappearing down the side where I can't see. "I didn't bring you here for that."

I worry about letting the door close in case it locks us out, but then I think maybe we should hide up here like the foosballs, away from Barb and Upper Management, so Zelda can never be demoted.

"Hurry up," calls Zelda. "The light is good."

I let the door swing shut and follow the sound of her voice. On the other side of the roof there is a maze of metal vent things and chimney things and shed things, so I can't see Zelda until I climb over the last obstacle, some kind of huge metal pipe, and reach a small flat section of roof with a view over Wildwood. I stop in my tracks to take it all in. Six blocks of shops and offices and houses (gray, white, brown), the Ferris wheel (red) and parking lots (gray) and the boardwalk (sandy brown) and the sky (cloudy gray) and the beach (pale yellow) and—

Blue.

I see blue.

I see the ocean.

I grip the concrete barrier. I can't take my eyes off that beautiful stretch of blue.

My heart clenches for a moment, as though it has finally realized it can stop beating, then starts again with a clunk, like an old car backfiring. I let out a rush of breath.

I feel different. I feel as though everything inside me has just shifted to make room for something new.

I am sixteen, dead, and I have seen the ocean. It was here the whole time.

I look away. I surprise myself by how easy it is to look away from that blue and face Zelda instead.

"How? I don't have a memory of this so…how?"

She smiles. "Magic."

"You really suck, you know that?" I'm crying. I know I'm crying. She's laughing at me but I'm crying. "You can't leave me. I like you. I want you to stay with me. It's not fair if you leave. I like you so much."

She smiles and grabs hold of my hand, turning to face the ocean. There are tears on her cheeks too, shining in the weak afternoon sun. "I'm not leaving yet," she says.

I should look at the ocean. I should sear that expanse of blue into my brain so I never forget it. I've wanted this for so long and now it's right there in front of me. But I can't look away from Zelda. Because the ocean is just a place. It doesn't mean anything without the person standing beside me. And the Marybelle is just a building. It could be hell, without Quinn and Dad, with only the echoes of my worst memories to keep me company. Or it could be heaven—it *is* heaven—with Zelda.

Ms. Chiu, I see it.

I might not know what made me happy on Earth but I know what makes me happy in heaven.

"I pick you," I say, and she kisses me. Just a featherlight brush of lip against lip. She leans back again and blinks.

"I always wanted to do that," she says, and does it once more. When she pulls away this time, she smiles. "I like it."

I like it too. But "like" is still not big enough and maybe not even "love" is big enough. The feeling of kissing Zelda is bigger and brighter than any single word could convey.

And I want to do it again.

A cough startles us both and we spin around at the same time.

Carol stands behind us on the roof, knitting. The scarf is so long now it pools on the ground at her feet.

She glances up, a quick look at me and a longer look at Zelda. She settles her gaze back on me and sighs.

"The Manager will see you now," she says.

(MOSTLY BLUE)

The temperature dropped quickly.

Tegan and Quinn climbed under the bedcovers, chasing warmth. Tegan was so cold. She hadn't felt warm since they got here, and now the heater was broken. The cold had reached her bones and it wouldn't let her go.

"Why are you and Daddy fighting?" asked Quinn. She hugged Trash Monkey to her chest, her fingers digging into the plush toy's fur. She and Tegan had the same fingers: stubby. Tegan liked them better on her sister.

"Because I'm tired and I want to go home," said Tegan.

Quinn blinked slowly, looking up at her older sister through messy clumps of hair. "To see Mom?"

"I guess so."

The door swung open and their father hurried inside, bringing a burst of wind with him.

"Too late for a repairman." He kicked off his shoes by the door. He was talking fast, barely a breath between words. "Manager says he'll get someone to come by tomorrow and take a look. He said we could swap rooms but I said Team Masters is made of sterner stuff than that."

Tegan watched him pull spare blankets out of the cupboard in a flurry, tossing them onto the bed without looking. It was the most animated she'd seen him all weekend.

"It'll be just like camping," he added.

"We've never been camping," whispered Quinn. She shifted closer to her sister, squishing against Tegan's side.

Their father held out a wool blanket like it was a net he was about to cast. "How about we build a blanket fort?" he said. He smiled, but there were cracks. Tegan could count them. "We used to do that all the time, remember? Movie night under the blanket fort with popcorn, Coke, and hot dogs. You both loved movie night."

His eyes landed on Tegan, pleading for her to play along. But she refused. She tried to cast a spell in her mind: *Tell me the truth.* She had read books where girls woke up with powers that could save the universe, and she had always hoped one day it would happen to her, that she would wake up and discover she had gained the power to cast spells. She would say: *If I toss this ball of paper into the trash can and it goes in first try, then my parents will stop fighting,* and for once, her wish would come true.

So she cast her spell and she held her father's gaze and she watched him lower the blanket.

Slowly, the smile faded from her father's face.

The pain she saw behind the mask was ugly and raw. It filled her heart with hurt. But she couldn't look away. Tegan looked at her father and she saw him.

She had never loved him more.

He always said she and Quinn were the best thing to ever happen to him, that they were a team, that they would always have each other. But how could she be sure? She wanted to look into his eyes and be sure.

"We'll go home tomorrow," he said, finally. The words looked like they hurt him to say but he said them anyway. "I think we're ready to go home, hey?"

Tegan breathed a sigh of relief.

She hoped he was telling the truth. She hoped her mother was waiting for them at home. She hoped everything was fine.

She hoped and hoped and hoped.

"Come on," said her father. "Blanket fort."

He built a fort and the three of them crawled inside, where they ate cold pizza and watched TV through the gap in the blankets. They played I Spy until every turn was "S" for *Snorks*. Tegan's father started singing John Denver off-key, and she and Quinn tackled him, hands slapped to his mouth to make him stop. He tickled them in retaliation and sang louder. They all sang. They even laughed a little. The TV light flickered throughout the fort, all the colors of the rainbow but mostly blue.

Quinn fell asleep with her head nestled on Tegan's lap. Tegan ran her hands through her sister's hair, not caring about the pizza grease on her fingers or the knots tangling the fine blond strands. The sound had been turned down on the TV but the light still flickered. It was warm inside the blanket fort. Tegan no longer shivered. The cold had vanished from her bones.

She looked at her father. He was fiddling with his phone but the screen was blank so Tegan guessed it was just out of habit.

"What's happening?" asked Tegan. "Why are we here?"

Her dad smiled but this time it was a sad smile. "Because I didn't know what else to do," he admitted. He looked up and met her eye. "Because we always talked about coming here on vacation. The four of us. As a family."

"I'm scared," she said.

"Me too," he said, and it was the first time he had ever admitted this to Tegan. It was real. It was honest. "But we're a team. Whatever happens, we're going to stick together. I'm here. I'm not leaving you. You're my whole world." She looked into his eyes and she saw.

He was telling the truth.

He was choosing her.

He reached for her hand as she started to cry. Tegan had always wanted to hear those words from her father. To hear them and know he meant them.

He held her. He kept her warm. He let her cry. He cried too. And Tegan knew her father meant every word.

TWENTY FIVE

Carol marches us down the endless hallway of gray doors.

At my side, Zelda wears a grim expression, and I have to wonder: Is it too late for us to run away?

My heart leaps into my throat when Carol stops at a random door and it swings open.

It's a conference room.

We're high up in a skyscraper. Outside the floor-to-ceiling windows is a sprawling, densely packed city I don't recognize. I wonder if it's even real. The room itself is unremarkable. Dark wood paneling on the walls, a long table with twelve chairs, a water cooler in one corner, three air vents pumping out heat. On the far wall at the head of the table is a poster of kittens in a basket. *It's a good day to be happy!* the poster reads.

I grit my teeth.

Carol marches in but I grab Zelda's arm to stop her from following. "We could run," I whisper.

She snorts. "Where?"

"You've got angel powers. Kathmandu. New York. Shanghai. A farm in Ohio. I don't care."

"I've got angel powers. But so do they."

"Fine. But you promised me one spoiler."

"I didn't promise anything."

"One spoiler. Tell me why I was happy."

"I can't tell you that because—"

"I have to feel it. The forest and the leaf. Love. Yeah, whatever. Sounds sus, but maybe if you tell me first, *then* I'll feel it. I promise I'll—"

"Hurry up," says Carol primly as she rounds the head of the table. "You'll keep Barb waiting."

"Shut up, Carol," snaps Zelda.

Carol gasps, almost dropping her knitting. "Well, I never!"

Zelda lifts her chin, defiant. "You know what? I'm seconds away from being demoted so I'm going to tell you what I've wanted to say for a long, *long* time. You"—she jabs her finger at Carol—"suck. You're a stick-in-the-mud. Your knitting sucks. You're a turdburger. And you look terrible in beige."

Carol splutters in outrage for a full minute and only snaps her mouth shut when Barb appears next to her, followed by Ms. Chiu, Kelvin, and three angels I don't know.

What's Ms. Chiu doing here?

"Apologies for the delay," says Barb, clutching a slim manila folder to her stomach. Her pantsuit is green because of course it is. "There was a last-minute discussion I hadn't anticipated." Her eyes flick briefly to Ms. Chiu.

I think I'm about to throw up.

Barb motions for everyone to sit. Carol shoots us both dirty looks, then turns away with a huff. I get the urge to be insolent and refuse to sit but Zelda tugs me down. *Behave,* say her eyes.

"You are of course familiar with the Counselor," says Barb, taking her seat at the head of the table.

Ms. Chiu sits opposite me. Her warm smile is a comfort, even when I know she's not the real Ms. Chiu, even when my mind still races with garbled, panicked half-thoughts. Why is she here? To counsel me into submission as they take Zelda away? As Kelvin drags me to purgatory?

"No fries today?" I ask her.

She rests her hands on the table and her smile grows a fraction. "I'm afraid not," she says. "Another time."

Carol seats herself at the lower end of the table, opposite Barb, knitting and scowling and huffing. The three angels I don't know take seats next to Ms. Chiu. This is starting to feel like a parent-teacher conference.

"You know Kelvin, of course."

Kelvin scowls at me from behind his greasy bangs. He doesn't take a seat, just stands in the corner like a creepy lampshade.

"And these are Gordon, Jeric, and Florence." Barb points to the unfamiliar angels. "They're representatives of Upper Management."

I look to Zelda for her reaction. She nervously pinches the skin at her throat, not meeting anyone's eye.

"These are unusual circumstances," says Gordon. His voice is gruff but he's got a face like a jolly garden gnome. The two angels beside him murmur in agreement. Jeric looks like a stock photo model and Florence definitely has a Tumblr account where she posts NSFW Destiel edits.

"It's hardly unexpected," says Florence, shooting knowing eyes at everyone else, "given the particular angel involved."

I hate her.

"How have you both been?" asks Barb. "Since I last saw you."

I fix a smile to my face. My customer service smile. My

this-dude-is-a-dickcheese smile. "Trying to save Zelda from being murdered in cold blood. How about you?"

Upper Management tuts and shakes their heads. Ms. Chiu shoots me a quelling look but I'm running out of fucks to give.

"I gather that means you're keen for us to get straight to business," says Barb, more diplomatically than I deserve. She opens the manila folder and there is a single sheet of blank paper inside. Kelvin already handed in his findings? That's not fair. I thought he'd need to press his clammy hand to my forehead to read my true feelings. I was planning to think super hard about how awesome Zelda is and how happy she makes me while he was doing it in case that made a difference.

Under the table, my legs jiggle so uncontrollably that Zelda's seat vibrates. She places a hand on my thigh to stop the shaking. But then she grips kind of hard so maybe it's just as much for her as it is for me. I place my hand over hers and squeeze.

"When we first met," Barb starts, "you were upset to be stuck in what you felt was your worst memory." She places a palm down on the blank paper and glides it across the table toward Gordon. "Your case was discussed with Upper Management, but we could not reach a consensus on the cause of your dissatisfaction." Gordon picks up the paper like it's a dead rat. His little gnome face scrunches as he reads. After a moment, he shakes his head and passes the paper to Jeric. "Some felt that Zelda's working out was correct and that Admissions had made a mistake in fast-tracking you," continues Barb. Jeric reads the paper, shakes his head, and passes it to Florence. "Others were firmly of the opinion that, given Zelda's past indiscretions, the fault surely lay in her calculations." All eyes flick to Zelda; her hand squeezes my thigh so hard I almost yelp. Florence shakes her head at the page and hands it to Ms. Chiu. Aside from Carol's constant *click clack* the room goes eerily silent. Ms. Chiu frowns at the blank page, laying it on the table in front of her.

Barb takes a deep breath. "We agreed that giving Zelda one month to demonstrate why the Marybelle was your happiest memory was the appropriate way to investigate who was at fault. You, Tegan, would also be assessed to determine your soul's readiness to accept happiness." Barb fixes me with her unreadable brown eyes. "That month is over."

"Sure is," I say with false cheer. "And I'm so glad you did because I have changed my mind. The Marybelle is amazing and I'll be happy to spend eternity there." Screw it. Why not lie through my teeth and see what happens?

Barb gives me an indulgent smile. "As you are well aware, Tegan, that's not how this works. Kelvin has submitted his findings and we know you're still unconvinced about the Marybelle. He was equally unconvinced by your emotional stability. This is not quite what I anticipated, but I have to say I agree with his findings: *both* Zelda and Admissions were at fault."

Surprise, surprise.

I meet her steely gaze head-on. "Then I withdraw my complaint."

"I'm afraid you can't do that."

"Well, I'm afraid you suck."

A deep line forms between Barb's brows as she stares me down, and it's probably the angriest I've ever seen her. Good. I'm angry too. And not at myself this time.

"Look," I snap. "Just because this is heaven doesn't mean it's perfect." Upper Management gasps. Carol tuts. I do not give a single fuck. "You guys definitely got a few things wrong, let me tell you. You're not perfect. You suck. Heaven sucks. And I'm not even talking about the Marybelle. All heavens suck. How can you expect us to live happily ever after when you take away what's important?"

Barb opens her mouth to interrupt, but I'm not stopping. I might as well go out in a blaze of glory. "What about Robbie? You've got him sitting on that bench with his dead wife's name carved into it, but she's not there. The whole point of that memory is her. It's not the park, it's not the bench, it's not the swans, it's *her*. She made him happy.

"And if I was ever happy at the Marybelle," I continue, "it had nothing to do with the food or the mini-golf or the pizza. It was Quinn and it was Dad. And now you're going to murder Zelda *and* insist my soul needs a two-thousand-year-long flea bath so I can 'enjoy' spending eternity alone?"

I turn to Ms. Chiu. Her head is tilted, eyes curious. "You said I'm supposed to look at what I have and not at what I don't. Well, I had Dad and Quinn, but you designed my heaven without them. And now you want to take Zelda away, even though she's the only thing that makes being dead bearable. She's funny and weird and annoying and beautiful and she makes me happy. She makes me the happiest."

Zelda grips my arm, her eyes wide. "Tegan? What are you—?"

"Have you asked anyone?" I go on. I can't seem to stop now that I've started. "Have you asked anyone if they're actually happy? Or maybe they don't know anymore, not after purgatory has turned them into simpering, obedient pod-people." I tug at my collar; it's getting way too hot in here. I glare at the heating vent.

"You all may have omnipotence, and you have magic powers, but you don't get it. Determining peak happiness with a math equation is ridiculous—happiness is a constantly shifting thing, it's not going to fit in a single answer. My happiest moment is also my worst. I'm a whole forest. I am the holes in my heart as much as I am the things that filled my heart. Trying to simplify that into a single moment is the worst idea ever."

The angels all look at me like I just blasphemed. Maybe I did. But one angel—the one who matters—tugs on my arm until I look at her. I half expect to find her mad at me for making a scene, but she's not. She smiles.

"You're funny and weird and annoying and beautiful too," she says, beaming. "And you suck at mini-golf."

"Well, you have terrible taste in food," I say. "And you steal things."

"You talk to a tampon."

"Shut up, butt-face."

I love her. I *everything* her.

Gordon leans into Jeric's side and whispers: "Are they...*you know*?"

"Isn't that against the rules?" whispers Florence.

Zelda snorts. "HR can suck my big bad attitude. And it's not against the rules. I checked." She holds my hand for everyone to see.

Florence turns red-faced, muttering and huffing. I'm flushed too. Is it because of Zelda's hand in mine (maybe that's what love is—a feeling of warmth bigger than all the bad things you collect in your soul)? Or is it the heat pumping through the vents? I can't feel changes in temperature anymore, but—

Oh.

Oh.

Ms. Chiu, I see it.

"The heater is broken," I say. I feel like I've been hit by a car all over again.

Carol snorts. "The heater is not broken. It's working perfectly fine. See?" She motions to the vents with her knitting. "Besides, it's an illusion. Everything here is an illusion."

I ignore her. My eyes shift to Ms. Chiu. "The heater is broken," I say again. Louder and more sure of myself this time because I see. Ms. Chiu, I see. "The one in my room. It's been broken the whole time I've been here, but I haven't felt cold once. I thought it was a weird heaven thing, but Robbie said his park was chilly, so it wasn't a heaven thing, it was a me thing." Upper Management lowers their heads and whispers to each other. I catch a few words: *Insolence. Troublemaker. Not right. Problem. Purgatory.* I ignore them because Ms. Chiu has a look on her face. A smile, a my-student-is-on-the-cusp-of-discovering-something-and-I'm-pleased-as-punch-about-it smile.

"The heater broke on our final night," I explain. Barb isn't smiling, but she looks curious. "Our room had been cold even with the heater blasting at full speed, but then it broke and the room got even colder. So Dad built a blanket fort and all three of us huddled in there together, and for the first time that whole weekend, I wasn't cold."

I want to turn and look at Zelda but I'm afraid I'll see hope in her eyes so I can't. I focus on Ms. Chiu instead. I focus on her growing smile. "Quinn was happy and sleeping in my lap because I made her safe. It was my bed she climbed into when she was scared, and it was me she showed off her ballet moves to. She never worried about Mom being late, because she had me.

"And Dad—" My voice cracks. Zelda squeezes my hand. "And Dad picked me," I say. "He was worried about Mom and he was in so much pain, but he said I was his whole world and he meant it. He said that he'd never walk away from me, no matter what. I didn't know why we were there, but I knew Dad was on my side. Always." Ms. Chiu's eyes sparkle. "I lost the memory of that moment because of everything that happened after—I couldn't see it in all the mess—but it was a good moment. The best."

Finally, I turn to Zelda. "I was happy. I knew I was someone's forever. You showed me all the people who didn't choose me so that I'd understand how much it meant to me when someone finally did." I squeeze her hand. "I'm sorry it took me so long to see it."

She looks down at our entwined hands. "That's okay," she says. "You can't help being a butt-face."

She smiles my favorite smile and it's everything.

Reluctantly, I turn back to the others. "That was it, right?" I say. "That was the moment?"

Ms. Chiu looks at Kelvin. I look too. Reluctantly, Kelvin nods. "She believes it," he says, scowling. Relief rushes through me. I did it. *I did it.*

Until Carol goes and ruins it.

"It's a pity," she says, "that it's too late. The challenge ended and you didn't work it out in time." *Click, clack, click* go her needles. She might as well have stabbed them through my heart.

We really were never supposed to win, were we?

"Zelda will be demoted, and you"—she cuts a sharp look at me—"are going to purgatory." Her gaze shifts to Zelda. The corner of her mouth lifts into a self-satisfied smirk. "Now who sucks?"

TWENTY SIX

"No." I shake my head furiously.

Barb holds up her hands, placating. "Tegan, I think—"

"No." I stand up. "I said no. I know what my happiest memory is now, but I still believe spending eternity in an empty copy of the Marybelle is wrong. Your whole idea of heaven is wrong. And I'm not saying that because I lack clarity or objectivity." I cut a hard look at Kelvin. "I've never seen things this clearly in my whole life.

"Tell me no one has ever said they're unhappy before," I challenge. "Can you tell me that? How many people have had to be scrubbed down to nothing before they can endure living in a shell of their former life?" Upper Management refuses to meet my eye and I know I'm right. Ms. Chiu frowns deeply.

"The investigation was pointless because heaven is wrong. Purgatory is wrong. Scrubbing away the bad stuff doesn't make people happy. Happiness can be small, it can be bittersweet, it can be knotted up in sadness, it can last forever or it can curdle over time, it can be two negatives equal a positive." I look at Barb, begging her to understand. "You said yourself happiness is complicated, so why do you want to make it simple?"

Barb's face is unreadable, and I turn away, frustrated. "You really don't get it, do you? But Zelda does. She let Robbie carve that message into his seat to honor Mary, and she won me a six-legged octopus because I needed cheering up. So if you want to keep running heaven like a frozen-in-time ghost town, and if you want to persecute any angel who thinks this might not be the best way, then you're all just dickcheeses."

There's a moment of silence, then the room erupts. Upper Management all talks at once, shaking their heads: *Insolence. Troublemaker. Not right. Problem. Purgatory.* Carol knits furiously. Kelvin flicks his bangs out of his eyes, his face a nasty scowl. Barb tries to make everyone listen, but the more she shouts for quiet, the louder they shout to be heard. Zelda covers her mouth, trying to quell the giggles.

Did I break heaven?

"If I may," says Ms. Chiu. The effect of her voice is instant—everyone zips their lips and tosses the key. She frowns at the blank sheet of paper for a long moment before looking up to meet my eyes.

"Tegan's argument, though worded somewhat crassly, has merit," she says.

Gordon splutters, "You can't be serious!"

Ms. Chiu glares at him until he shrinks down in his chair, red-faced and silent. "I am satisfied Zelda proved her calculations were accurate," she continues, "and that Tegan fully believes in the results, which were the requirements of the original challenge. The deadline was not quite met, but I'm sure we can allow a small extension considering the emotional toll both of them have suffered over the last month." She glares at Carol this time. "Therefore, Zelda should not be demoted."

I don't scream but it's a close thing. I grab Zelda's arm and tug as I dance up and down on the spot. This moment. This moment right here could be heaven.

"Really?" Zelda blinks. She's rocking with the force of my aggressive celebratory dance but she's also pretty much frozen in shock.

Ms. Chiu smiles. "Really."

Kelvin looks like I served him a plate of Marybelle mushrooms, but he can suck it. "It's not fair," he mutters.

"They did meet the terms of the challenge," agrees Barb, looking between me and Zelda. "And I concur. A small extension is permissible."

Carol tuts but doesn't have the guts to argue.

"I'm not going to be demoted?" Zelda looks around, wide-eyed. "I get to stay?"

I grab her hands and hold on.

"You're not going to be demoted," I say, and as Zelda breaks out into a smile, all teeth and gums and freckles, I change my mind. *This* moment is heaven.

"And I am satisfied Tegan doesn't require the assistance of purgatory," continues Ms. Chiu.

Kelvin gawps. "But—"

"She has shown remarkable clarity and objectivity under extraordinary emotional constraints," steamrolls Ms. Chiu. "She might have lost her bearings once or twice, but she always found her way back, learning more about herself along the way than even we could have predicted."

"This blows," mutters Kelvin, kicking the carpet.

Suck it, Kelvin.

"Finally, I think we should also consider Tegan's concerns about our current conception of heaven," continues Ms. Chiu. "I find her thoughts most interesting. I'm so glad I attended today's meeting."

Upper Management scowls like they swallowed lemons, but they nod and agree that yes, it's all very fascinating.

Barb frowns at her empty manila folder. "I guess we'll put this under review, but for now…" She looks up at me, expression cool and assessing. "Tegan, are you saying you are happy to stay at the Marybelle?"

I don't hesitate. "With Zelda, yes. But you'd better look at changing things stat. There's a nice old man on a park bench waiting for his wife to show up. Don't be a dickcheese and keep him waiting any longer."

Ms. Chiu barely manages to cover her laughter with her hand. She turns it into a cough. Carol sighs loudly.

"Meeting adjourned," says Barb, sweeping up the manila folder. Behind her, the kittens peek over the edge of their basket and I think, *Yes, it is a good day to be happy.*

◆ ◆ ◆

The meeting room vanishes and suddenly it's just me and Zelda and Ms. Chiu in the motel office. My poor dead brain tries to process everything that just happened. It fails miserably.

"I'm not leaving," says Zelda, stunned. She looks around the office. The ribbons on the heater dance as the hot air is pumped into the room and it warms me to my bones, or maybe that's Zelda's smile. "I'm not being demoted," she says. She does a jumping jack, then she rounds on me, pointing. "You're not going to purgatory! We're both staying! Suck it! You're stuck with me."

I try to look displeased but, as I recently realized, I'm not a great actress. "I don't need you. I've got Snickerdoodle and Tammy and Trash Cat the Elder."

"You *like* me," she singsongs. "You think I'm *awesome*." She dances around me. "You *like* me. You think I'm *sexy*."

Ms. Chiu clears her throat. Oops. I forgot she was there.

Zelda stops dancing and we both turn to face her. She's struggling to hide her amusement so I guess we're not in trouble.

I step forward, head tilted up to look her in the eye. "Thanks for backing me up in there." I guess it doesn't matter if she's the real Ms. Chiu or a shapeshifting-immortal-therapy-bot; she will always pick up a rain-soaked kid and drive them home. "You saved our bacon."

"No thanks required," says Ms. Chiu. "It was all down to you."

I shake my head. "No. It's never just me."

She smiles. "Of course."

I glance over my shoulder at Zelda. She's trying—and failing—to contain her excitement. She's an unlit firecracker waiting to go off.

I turn back to Ms. Chiu. "I'm sorry about calling you a dick-cheese and I'm sorry if I was too blunt about how much heaven sucks but it's true. I don't think this investigation was very fair and they definitely had it in for Zelda but I hope Barb really does look into it all."

"She will." Ms. Chiu speaks with such certainty that I believe her. "I don't normally attend departmental meetings. I've been on a short sabbatical, just a few millennia, so I was unaware there had been complaints. I'm afraid things have gotten a bit...off course in my absence. I was glad to hear your perspective. I will be paying closer attention moving forward." She pats my shoulder, giving it a little squeeze before letting go.

I'm happy and I'm relieved it's all over but I'm sad too. I think this might be me saying goodbye to Ms. Chiu. And I think this might be me saying goodbye to myself. Alive me. The me who I was and who I could have been if I'd ridden my bike a little slower or if I'd stayed back at band practice a little longer or if the nameless person behind the wheel of that SUV had seen the stop sign.

Ms. Chiu, I'm okay about being dead. It's just another piece of the puzzle.

Her smile is knowing as I turn my head away, wiping at my eyes. "I'm disappointed our five sessions have come to a close," she says, "but perhaps I'll see you again anyway."

I feel fourteen and soaked in rain, sitting in a parking lot waiting for a car to show up, knowing it won't. I see Ms. Chiu hurrying toward me, under her Met umbrella, her shoes (blue) splashing up water.

She leans in and waits until I look her in the eye. Deep brown and old and knowing and kind. "Everything will be fine," she says. I splutter a laugh. She smiles. "But if it's not, you've got Zelda."

I nod.

I do.

I have Zelda. And Snickerdoodle and Tammy and Trash Cat the Elder, and I have myself. One day I might have Quinn and Dad too.

Dad promised, after all. He said we'd always stick together. And I believed him.

She squeezes my shoulder once, then turns and walks away. I watch her, holding my tongue, trying not to ask her to come back. The unmarked door to the waiting room closes with a gentle click behind her. I'm happy and I'm relieved and I'm sad. I'm okay.

I turn back to Zelda. She's already dancing—flinging her arms, jumping up and down, flicking her hair, and fluttering her wings. "You *like* me. You think I'm *awesome*. And I'm not *dying*. Because I'm *sexy*."

"None of that makes sense."

"You *like* me." She pokes my dimple. "Hello, Maggot Cheese."

"Stop it. Just because Ms. Chiu is gone doesn't mean you can be a butt-face." I glance once more at the closed door. I hope I do see her again. I hope she takes me to Red Robin and we can just hang out and not do the heart-to-heart stuff. I hope it's on a Wednesday so I get to see the blue wren earrings. "I don't get why Ms. Chiu was in that meeting but I'm glad," I say.

Zelda snorts. "You know who she is, right?"

"A shapeshifting-immortal-therapy-bot?"

She laughs. "Think a little higher than that," she says. She taps the side of her nose. "Think all the way to the top."

All the way . . .

No.

No, no, no, *no*.

Suddenly I feel like I just gulped down a gallon of hot sauce. Zelda laughs at the look on my face.

"But I called her a dickcheese! I made her eat fries! I said she was a terrible counselor!"

Zelda's laughing so hard she can hardly stand up straight.

"No, you don't understand! What if she sends a plague of locusts to eat me alive?"

I have to wait for her laughter to subside. Zelda rests both hands on my shoulders. "She likes you. You're safe." She holds my gaze, mirth sparkling in her eyes. I can't look away.

I nod. "Okay."

And then I do what I've been wanting to do since the roof, since before then, since always. I kiss her. I cradle her face in my hands and press my lips to hers. She gasps. I kiss her deeper. I think: *There is no word in the entire universe big enough for this. For us. Not even "happiness." This is more. So much more.*

She shifts closer, and I feel the way her body thrums with joy and life and love as she links her arms around my neck and kisses me back.

We kiss and we kiss and we kiss and we only pull away when our lips grow numb.

"What now?" I whisper. She's still close. I don't want to let her go. I want to kiss every one of her fourteen freckles.

Zelda grins. I know it means trouble. "Celebratory round of mini-golf?"

TWENTY SEVEN

"You know this isn't allowed, right?" I say.

Zelda pockets the key—this time the chain is a scrawny orange street cat. She glances over her shoulder and winks. "But that's what makes it fun."

The door opens and I see a familiar garden. Red-and-gold leaves carpet the ground. The sun tries its hardest to peek out from behind the clouds while birds chase each other through the boughs of the giant maple.

Zelda runs, kicking up the leaves and yodeling with joy.

I hesitate in the doorway. "I didn't last long in Catholic school but even I know shit went down the last time a human did something forbidden in a garden!" I shout after her.

"Trust me. You're going to want to see this." Zelda twirls like she's Maria in *The Sound of Music*. I run to join her, kicking up leaves as I go.

We throw leaves at each other and wrestle on the ground and Zelda wins. She kisses me while she picks leaves out of my hair so I don't mind losing.

I point at her freckles and count each one out loud. She hates when I do it. I do it all the time. "Fourteen."

She flicks my nose. "We're late. Stop wasting time." She hauls me to my feet.

"Time is meaningless."

"No, time is complicated."

"You're complicated."

Hand in hand we follow the dirt path through the trees and to the gate, where we can see miles of parkland spread out before us.

"Swans!" I cry, and take off running. The long grass slaps against my calves as I run, soaking my jeans.

Zelda runs alongside me, waving her arms above her head, singing the theme song from *Snorks*.

We slow down at the bottom of the hill and walk, breathing hard, struggling to contain our laughter.

"Did you know a fifth of all swan couples are gay?" asks Zelda.

"That's my new favorite swan fact," I say. "Though I'm still partial to the fact that they can break your arm with a head-butt."

"That's also extremely cool."

We stand by the water and watch the swans circling, ducking their heads underwater every now and then to eat the weeds and little fishies. A handful of ducks dart around them. It's peaceful.

"We should get a pair of gay swans for the Marybelle pool. Kelvin would be *so* mad."

Zelda waggles her head as if debating the idea. "I'll talk to HR but I daresay the most I can do is add a second tampon to be friends with Tammy."

"That's a fair compromise."

We keep walking. Zelda insists we take the desire line up the hill, but halfway to the top she announces that we need to start a new path of our own, so we trudge through the grass, getting our jeans even wetter.

"Won't Barb know we're here?"

Zelda shrugs. "She's a little distracted right now. So I'm hoping she doesn't notice."

I don't have time to ask what she means because we've crested the hill and Zelda grabs my hand to make me stop.

Robbie sits on his bench, one hand resting on the end of a bouquet of daisies. He's staring straight ahead so he can't see what I can see.

A woman. Red hair, a skirt (blue), a jacket (blue), and a no-nonsense look on her face. She moves purposefully toward the bench. Robbie seems lost in thought, so he doesn't see her. I squeeze Zelda's hand in anticipation. She's not young, is the thing. She's old like Robbie. So she's not the Mary from the day they met. Does that mean she's the real deal?

The woman sits beside him and he jolts, pulled out of whatever daydream he was in. I see him blinking at her, confused. He looks at her for such a long time, unable to move and unable to speak. He raises his hand and cups her face. Maybe he's testing if she's real, or maybe he just can't sit next to her, even for a second, without touching her. I cling to Zelda's arm.

"You're crying," says Zelda.

"Shut up, butt-face." I am crying. I am very much crying.

We're too far away to hear what's being said, but I wouldn't want to hear it anyway. This is their moment. It's a privilege to watch it, but we're intruders here. This is Robbie and Mary's moment and it's been a long time coming.

"This is a test," whispers Zelda. "To see what happens when we put people in the memories."

"Is she real?"

"Real," says Zelda, and I cry a thousand times harder.

"Obviously not everyone gets the real deal," explains Zelda. "But we're looking at inserting illusions until real meetings can take place too. There are a few different tests happening right now. I thought you'd like to see this one."

"I think Robbie passed with flying colors." I can't help thinking about Quinn. That beautiful, weird, ridiculous kid I love with all my heart. And Dad too. Dad in his Gritty pj's, singing John Denver, his arm around my shoulders as we sit at the end of our driveway. Dad, who would always pick me.

I even think about Mom.

"They look happy," says Zelda.

I squeeze her arm again. "If you sneak in chili fries when we get back to the Marybelle I'll be happy too."

"Your Ms. Chiu wiped my record clean and I'd like to keep it that way so stop getting me into trouble."

"Like you need my help."

Robbie clings to Mary, weeping like a baby, and I have to look away because it's too much. I'm happy and I'm okay. I'm dead and that's all there is to say about that. I would have liked forty-one years with Quinn and Dad. With Clem and Paul and even Lou. I would have liked to grow up. I would have liked to wear out my shoes and buy another pair and wear them out too. And maybe I would have liked to see my mom again so I could tell her it's okay, I get why you walked away even if I can't help wishing you hadn't. I like Ms. Chiu—the real one and the fake one—but I think maybe it's okay to see the things you don't have so long as you're also looking at what you do have. And what you want. It's about balance. It's not ignoring the bad stuff and pretending everything is fine. Some things are fine and some things aren't. It's complicated.

Zelda turns to me, smiling. "Should we—"

"What do you two think you're doing here?"

Oops.

I know who it is even before I turn. The *click clack* of knitting needles gives her away.

Carol scowls. "You're not supposed to be here."

Zelda's eyes go wide, cute and innocent like Trash Cat Baby. "But look at them. Look how sweet they are. We couldn't miss this! And it was Tegan's idea!"

Carol clicks her tongue and turns away. "Come on, you two. Out!"

I glance once more over my shoulder at Robbie and Mary. They're still holding each other, the daisies crushed against Mary's back. Forever is much better with the people who matter.

Carol looks absurd in her beige skirt and beige blouse and beige heels, marching through the muddy grass, knitting the whole time. It's a wonder she doesn't trip on the end of the half-knitted scarf trailing behind her.

I lean into Zelda. "What's the deal with the knitting?" I whisper.

"It's space and time," she whispers back. "Carol might be a butt-face but her job is kind of important. If she drops a stitch we're in trouble."

I have a million and one questions about that but I decide they can wait—I'm in a good mood and asking twisty questions about the universe will only hurt my head. Besides, if I asked, Zelda would only wink at me and say *Spoilers*. Just because she lets me hold her hand and kiss her (a lot—there is a *lot* of kissing) doesn't mean I get full spoilers privileges. Yet. I'm working on it.

An angry Carol leads us down the hill and along the path by the lake. I wave goodbye to the swans and the ducks.

"Ask Carol if she can knit me a couple of swans," I whisper, but not quietly enough because Carol shoots a glare over her shoulder. Zelda and I collapse into each other laughing.

"And to think," says Carol, pausing outside the door in the middle of the path to wave us through, "they're considering making you an honorary angel."

I blink at Zelda and she blinks back. I have a million and one questions about *that* but they can also wait.

We walk through the door.

TWENTY EIGHT

I'm standing on the rooftop of the Marybelle Motor Lodge and I'm looking at the ocean with an angel by my side and I'm dead.

"You have fourteen freckles," I tell her.

She blushes and preens and tells me I'm ridiculous. "Shut up, butt-face," she says, "and look at the ocean." But I don't, because I'm looking exactly where I should be.

Ms. Chiu, I am happy.

CREDITS

Written by:
Shivaun Plozza

Literary Agency:
Katelyn Detweiler (Literary Agent)
Denise Page (Head of Operations)
Sam Farkas (Foreign and Subsidiary Rights Associate)
Jill Grinberg (Agency President)
Lisa Barelli (Contracts)

Editorial:
Alex Aceves (Associate Editor)
Rebecca Godan (Production Editor)

Design:
Kerry Martin (Creative Director)
Nicole Gureli (Designer)

Production:
Lisa Lee (Director of Production)
Judy Varon (Production Manager)

Sales:
Morgan Hillman (Sales Director)
Hannah Finne (Data Manager)

Marketing and Publicity:
Terry Borzumato Greenberg (VP of Marketing and Publicity)
Michelle Montague (Executive Director, Marketing)
Mary Joyce Perry (Digital Marketing Manager)
Alison Tarnofsky (Marketing Manager, Trade)
Elyse Vincenty (Marketing Manager, Trade)
Melissa See (Digital Marketing Coordinator)
Sara DiSalvo (Publicity Manager)
Anna Abell (Senior Publicist)
Tiffany Coelho (Marketing Coordinator, School & Library)
Kayla Phillips (Marketing & Publicity Assistant)

Contracts:
Julia Gallagher (VP, Business Affairs)
Erin Valerio (Contracts Manager, Business Affairs)

Freelance:
Kei-Ella Loewe (Jacket artist)
Barbara Perris (Copy editor)
Regina Castillo (Proofreader)

Assistant to Ms. Plozza:
Fenchurch (Cat)

With special thanks to:
Mum, Dad, Alexis Drevikovsky, Peta Twisk, Rosey Chang, Marie
Davies, Sarah Vincent, Cathy Hainstock, Jenna Guillaume, Will
Kostakis, Nicola Santilli, Jess Walton, Alison Evans, and Nina
LaCour.